THE URBANA FREE LIBRARY
W9-AHZ-017

JACKED UP

JACKED UP

ERICA SAGE

Sky Pony Press
New York

Sky Pony Press books may be purchased in bulk at special discounts for sales promotion, corporate gifts, fund-raising, or educational purposes. Special editions can also be created to specifications. For details, contact the Special Sales Department, Sky Pony Press, 307 West 36th Street, 11th Floor, New York, NY 10018 or info@skyhorsepublishing.com.

Sky Pony® is a registered trademark of Skyhorse Publishing, Inc.®, a Delaware corporation.

Visit our website at www.skyponypress.com.

www.EricaSageBooks.com

10 9 8 7 6 5 4 3 2 1

The Library of Congress has cataloged this book as follows:

Names: Sage, Erica.
Title: Jacked up / Erica Sage.
Description: New York : Skyhorse Publishing, [2018] | Summary: Sent to Jesus Camp by his nonreligious parents, Nick gains a new perspective on his sister's suicide and the secret he has been keeping about it, with the help of new friends and the ghost of Jack Kerouac.
Identifiers: LCCN 2018001603 (print) | LCCN 2018009408 (ebook) | ISBN 9781510730069 (eb) | ISBN 9781510730052 (hc) | ISBN 9781510730069 (ebook)
Subjects: | CYAC: Camps--Fiction. | Grief--Fiction. | Christian life--Fiction. | Brothers and sisters--Fiction. | Kerouac, Jack, 1922-1969--Fiction. | Humorous stories.
Classification: LCC PZ7.1.S242 (ebook) | LCC PZ7.1.S242 Jac 2018 (print) | DDC [Fic]--dc23

Cover design by Kate Gartner
Cover illustration by Pete Ryan

Print ISBN: 978-1-5107-3005-2
Ebook ISBN: 978-1-5107-3006-9

Printed in the United States of America

Interior design by Joshua Barnaby

This is for you, Mom.

I miss you like mad.

JACKED UP

SUNDAY

♦

Jack Kerouac was sitting cross-legged on the end of my bed. Again.

"BOO!" he said.

"I hate it when you do that."

"I didn't scare you, Nicolas," he said, skipping across my name and dropping the *s*. I rarely heard his accent, except at the end of some sentences. Or when he was cursing me up and down in French.

He peered at me with his glacier-blue eyes and took a drag on a cigarette.

"I asked you not to smoke in here," I said, reaching for the cigarette. But there was nothing to grab. Not a cigarette, not a hand.

"I opened the window," Jack said.

"My parents are going to think I'm sneaking cigarettes and giving myself lung cancer."

He looked at me, holding the cigarette loosely between two fingers. "Tell them the truth, then."

"Yeah right." I picked up the cheap blue pen from my nightstand and the mini composition book underneath it, and wrote down the date. Jack Kerouac, the great American author, had been dead for fifty years, but this was the twenty-seventh time he'd visited me in three months. I put the notebook back.

Jack looked over my shoulder at the radio on my dresser. It popped on and rolled across stations, settling on jazz. Always jazz. "I like this cat." Jack bounced his leg across his knee. "Charlie Parker."

"Just don't turn it up so high this time."

The music got louder, the saxophone crying like a lone bird.

"Knock it off." I turned around and jabbed at the off button. I sighed. "I thought you were going off to work on a new book or something." At least, that's what he'd said the last time, accusing me of taking up too much of his time, saying I didn't understand anything about beauty or art, *certainly not the truth!* All I cared about was rules and correcting everybody. *You'll grow up to be a gawddamn editor one day!* And then he stomped himself out in a fury, taking his near-empty bottle of whiskey with him.

Now, he snuffed his cigarette out in the ashtray on my windowsill and rolled back onto my bed. "When are you going to take that down?" He nodded at the poster hanging above my pillows and began reading it aloud mockingly. "'The only people for me are the mad ones, the ones who are mad to live, mad to talk, mad to be saved, desirous of everything at the same time, the ones who never yawn or say a commonplace thing, but burn, burn, burn like fabulous yellow roman candles exploding like spiders across the stars.'"

"I'm not going to take it down, I told you," I said.

He propped his boot on the poster. "Gawddamn book," he murmured, and ground the sole of his boot across his signature at the bottom like it was the butt of a cigarette. We'd been arguing about the poster ever since he showed up the night of my sister Diana's funeral. I'd been scared shitless that first time—confronted by a brooding drunk man. But now I was just irritated because he wouldn't go away.

"Well, everyone else seems to love the book," I said.

"*Poseurs*," he said.

I'd never read *On the Road*, so I didn't care so much about the book or the fact that Jack Kerouac, the guy who wrote the thing, hated the poster. All I knew was that it was "an American classic," but not the kind teachers would ever assign. The kind teenagers read to piss their parents off and prove to the world how rebellious they were.

My sister had given me both the poster and the book. I didn't plan on reading the book, not even her paperback copy, the cover bent and rubbed pale by her hands after years of rereading. I didn't care about the 1950s or the "Beat Generation." I didn't care about Jack Kerouac, some icon of nonconformity and road trips and wild nights. Some author who drank himself to death under the weight of his success, like every other literary great who put her head in the oven or a shotgun to his head. It was clichéd. Jack Kerouac and every teenager's life-changing experience with *On the Road* was clichéd.

But I wasn't taking the poster down.

Because I did care about my sister.

I missed her like hell.

I tried to shove Jack's leg over to make room for myself on the bed, but lost my balance instead. There was nothing to actually shove.

Jack smirked. I resigned myself to the edge of the mattress and tried to ignore him.

He folded his hands behind his head, and I knew what was coming. "Is today the day?"

"No. I keep telling you." Why couldn't it be someone funny like Mark Twain or Voltaire showing up in my bedroom? Why did it a have to be a moody, nagging alcoholic?

"Confession is good for the soul," Jack said.

"Is that what your nuns at Catholic school said?" I mocked.

The jazz clicked on again behind me. Maybe the same song, maybe different, but now the saxophone battled with a piano.

I glared at him. "Or was it the Jewish kids at Horace Mann?"

"Are you making fun of me?" He asked as the volume went up. "Or the Jews?" And up.

"Don't," I hissed.

And up.

"Seriously, you're pissing me off."

"Am I making you *mad*?" He winked at me, but without a smile. "The burning-madness of it."

The jazz blasted. I plugged my ears.

Just then, my door swung open, my dad on the other side.

The saxophone cried.

My dad jabbed at the radio till he succeeded in turning it off. "We need to talk."

"I just like the song, it's fine." I insisted, "I'm fine."

"It's jazz, Nick, not gangster rap." He sighed. "Your mom and I just need to talk to you." He set his hand on my shoulder and led me out of my room.

I turned around to flip Jack Kerouac the bird, but he'd slipped out the window, the way he sometimes did.

♦

A few minutes later, my parents had me trapped in the living room, dreading whatever was coming next. They sat across from me on the couch, my mom's legs tucked neatly against my dad's, her hand in his, her eyes brimming with anticipation. It looked happy, this scene. It looked all Norman Rockwell. But I'd heard their arguments. I'd heard the blame. That's what tragedy does to families. It holds a flame to what binds you, and sometimes you learn what you thought were rods of steel are actually mere threads.

I was the only thread they had left, and I knew how thin it was.

I stared. I'd figured they'd pulled me out of my room to discuss the too-loud music, or the liquor bottle my mom had found the week before (I'd snuck it in for Jack Kerouac, of course), or just the fact that I'd holed up in my room for too many days.

But no. We were on to Phase Three of the Fix-Nick-Quick Plan. If we could fix Nick, maybe that would mean this family wasn't broken.

But they didn't know. They couldn't know.

"It's already paid for," my dad announced, like a sports commentator, all loud and certain. But he was rubbing his thighs nervously with his palms. This had clearly been my mom's idea.

Counseling had been my dad's idea, back in April. And I'd done that. (We'd all done that.)

But Jesus camp?

How was a week with zealots going to cure my "depression," as the psychologist had diagnosed it? (Isn't everyone depressed when their sister dies? Does that need a diagnosis?)

The prescription had been the doctor's idea, back in May. And I'd done that too. (I think my mom was still doing that.)

But I was not doing a wrathful God and his hobo-hippie son.

"I don't want to go," I said, staring down at the brochure my dad had handed me.

Eden Springs, the camp was called. WHERE HAPPINESS HAPPENS!

"I'm already happy," I said. "I'm fine." And I cared about God as much as He cared about me, which didn't seem like a whole lot.

"Oh, honey." My mom slid from the couch and squished into my chair next to me. "We know you're happy, but we also know you're sad."

"I'm fine, Mom. And besides, I can't do a week with these people." I flipped open the brochure. "They're not even real. Look at them. They're like mannequins. It's going to be me and a bunch of plastic dolls, like, praising the Lord or whatever. Like . . ." I straightened my arms and then bent them in perfect right angles at the elbows. "Like Barbie, you know? 'Hallelujah,'" I said in a girly voice, lifting my arms straight into the sky. "'Hallowed be thy name.'"

My parents stared at me gloomily.

"You know how you have to move Barbie's arms and stuff?" I tried again. I lifted my arms straight this time.

"We get it, Nick," my dad said.

My mom slid back to the couch with my dad. Side by side, they looked like an advertisement for a leading detergent. All pastel and khaki.

"Look, we don't even go to church," I reasoned. Sure, there was a Bible in the living room. But it was on the top shelf, way out of reach, next to *Beowulf*, *The Tao of Art*, and a book of poetry by some Spanish guy. Like part of the foreign language section.

The only reason our Bible was even on my radar was that I'd heard on the bus in elementary school that the Bible had swear words. I'd wanted to see a swear word printed out for the masses, so I'd looked for the part where Jesus rode in on an *ass*. And there it was.

It turned out there were more swear words in the dictionary, though, so I'd ultimately opted to read that for more scandalous text.

"Honey," my mom started again. "We know you miss her. And

we know this summer is going to be hard. If you can't do your annual road trip with her, then—"

"Then I can be with her in spirit?"

She looked at me optimistically. "Well, yes, I suppose so."

I rolled my eyes. "Because you know she's the last person in hell—"

"Nick—" my dad chided.

"—who'd go to church camp. They wouldn't even let her, you know. Those people would not have even let her set foot on their campus. Or their revival tent. Or whatever."

"Well, yes, because it's for high schoolers," my mom pointed out. "She's too old."

"She's actually dead," I snapped, and my mom winced. What was wrong with me? It was her daughter, for God's sake. I softened my tone. "Look, even if she were in high school—and alive—she would never have gone."

"You'll make new friends," my dad recited.

"Where'd you even hear about this camp?" I glared at them as realization dawned. "Charlotte."

Charlotte was my oldest sister. Throughout her teen years, she'd been *that* girl (i.e., a lot of boys got to "know" her, Biblically speaking). Then she'd gotten involved in some youth group, graduated high school, and moved to Nebraska, or some other flat, dry state with rolling waves of corn and a high percentage of Republican voters. I'd lost track. She was cultish and hated anything with a rainbow on it (not post-Noah's ark kind of rainbow, the gay-pride kind). I'm sure she didn't even let her kids eat Lucky Charms, and it would have nothing to do with gluten.

Both Charlotte and Diana had been in middle school when I was born, and they acted like extra moms when I was growing up. They'd treated me like their doll, painting my nails and putting me in tutus. I'm sure she'd since repented for encouraging cross-dressing.

And, yes, once she'd gotten all religious Charlotte had tried to convert me. She'd dragged me to her youth group like a pet. At first it had been okay—what boy doesn't like free peanut-butter Ritz crackers and endless cups of lemonade, and being the center of all his sister's older friends' attention? But pretty soon, I'd been forced to memorize verses and perform in skits. The day a bunch of youth group kids lowered me from a ceiling to be healed by Jesus—and dropped me—I was done.

She'd never tried to convert Diana. No, Diana was clearly a lost cause. Not fit for the fold.

The sad thing was, Charlotte had five kids. I had five nieces and nephews, and I'd never met them. She'd send pictures sometimes. Now and then she'd call our parents, but only briefly. Nothing real.

So, it had been me and Diana.

And then she left me too.

I took a deep breath and looked at my parents, who at least had the decency to look a tad bit contrite about the Charlotte factor. They knew my feelings about her—regret and creepiness.

But she was still their daughter. "Honey, this camp was very good for Charlotte when she was hurting." I hated it when my parents did this, when they justified Charlotte. When they defended her.

"She wasn't *hurting*, she was—" *humping* the whole town, I wanted to say. But I didn't. We all knew she was "Charlotte the Harlot" at her high school.

"Aren't you afraid I'll end up like Charlotte? I mean, what if I come back and think you're devil worshippers too?"

"That's not how it works . . ." my mom sighed.

"That *is* how it worked."

"Charlotte needed something. She found that something at Eden Springs."

She had found God. She had found justification to hate our sister. The rest of the family hadn't been unholy enough in her eyes to hate, but we hadn't been righteous enough to love either.

"Wait," I said, holding up the brochure. "Did you *talk* to

Charlotte?" She hadn't even come to Diana's funeral. She'd called us maybe once in the months since Diana died. "Did you call her? Or did she call you?"

My dad's face folded up all neat. "It'll be fun. End of discussion."

He wiped his palms on his khakis and stood up. My mom stepped toward me and touched my cheek. They both walked out of the room.

"Why would you listen to her?" I asked no one.

But I thought I knew. Just to hear her voice. Charlotte and Diana were nothing alike, but their hearts beat the same blood. When you lose someone, you find the closest thing to that person and hold on.

♦

I left the house. I wasn't going back to my room, where Jack would be waiting, broody and antagonistic. And I wasn't going to sit with my parents. They'd always loved their daughters, but Charlotte had loved God and Diana had loved women. And Charlotte's God did not love women who loved women. It was a love pentagon, which seemed appropriate given Charlotte was certain Diana was in hell. And my parents had thought they could love both of them anyway.

My parents didn't hate Diana. She was their daughter, pure and simple. But every time Charlotte had come up and they'd told Diana "just let it go," or "she'll grow out of it" (like she was a bed-wetting schoolgirl), it had been like arsenic.

I walked around the garage, through the gap between the building and the neighbor's fence. At the back of the yard stood a handful of tall fir trees that shaded a green Volvo.

After my sister died, I had avoided the car, avoided the shadows where it sat altogether. After a while, I was able to walk by it, but I kept my eyes down, always staring at my feet. I didn't want to look inside the windows. I was afraid of suddenly seeing her there—maybe what she looked like after she died in it, or what her rotting corpse would look like now. But I was also afraid of *not* seeing her behind the wheel. Where she'd always been.

I snapped open the door and slid inside. Just me, the hollow silent interior of the car, and not even the smell of her anymore. Not the patchouli oil she wore or the coffee she drank too much of. It used to smell like her. In the way that clothes and bedrooms and anything smells like someone. The smell you especially notice when someone leaves.

Diana bought the car when she'd turned sixteen, and she'd planned to hand the keys over to me on my sixteenth. I still had a year to go, but I didn't want it anymore. It just sat in the yard under the dripping fir trees, the interior smelling of mildew, the rain slipping through the poorly sealed windows and the two little holes in the roof.

I leaned back on the ugly, plaid driver's seat and stared at the roof, the small places where the rain always seeped in, so tiny that I couldn't see the sky through them.

On the day Diana died, I hadn't been paying attention.

She'd walked into the house—she'd still had a key even though she'd moved out years before. After a few minutes without one of my parents hollering for me to do this or that, I'd figured it was my sister. I'd pulled myself away from the old-school Atari game, *Asteroids* I think it was, to walk upstairs and find out what she wanted. She'd been so erratic by then, and I remember feeling dully irritated with her. Just under the skin.

She'd been planning to move to northern California to work as the gardener at a spiritual retreat. And she hadn't really been hanging out with me much, which—yeah—had started to piss me off. We'd go listen to some music at the coffee shop, but she'd be on her cell phone the whole time. One of the last times we hung out, she just left me to go hang out with her girlfriend, Leah, trying to make up for some feud between the two of them. Diana hadn't hung a picture of her and Leah up at work, and Leah had been pissed. Diana had argued that Leah didn't understand how conservative it was there. She wouldn't get fired, but she'd be second-guessed and scrutinized.

"Leah's right, just hang the picture," I'd said. "Nobody cares." Then I'd joked, "You're being gay." We both hated that phrase. *That's gay. This is gay. You're gay.*

Diana hadn't laughed or rolled her eyes with me that time, though. She'd put her head in her hands. "Nick, you have no idea how small this world's box is. You've never had to try and fit in it."

She was right. That's what I would tell her now, if I could. And I'd tell her that I didn't know how small the world was because she made it big for me.

But she was gone, and the world had shrunk and shaded.

♦

Jack was waiting for me back in my room.

"I have to pack," I said. "Why are you still here?"

"Are you going to tell your parents about what happened? Before you go to this religious camp of yours?" He eyed me from under his heavy brows. His black hair was glossy, perfectly in place.

I ignored him and got my suitcase out of my closet.

He kept on behind me. "Yes, the Great Editor must pack his suitcase full but leave the truth out!"

"I can't just tell them and take off."

The truth was, I was never going to tell my parents. I was never going to tell anyone.

When I turned around, the window was open wide, and Jack was gone. Thankfully, the empty bottle of liquor and pack of cigarettes had gone with him.

MONDAY

♦

My alarm didn't go off—probably Jack messing with the radio—but my parents cajoled me out of bed, lest I arrive late to my own salvation.

I threw on the T-shirt I'd picked out to protest this whole camp thing. It featured a doe-eyed cat and read EVERY SINGLE TIME "YOU'RE" IS MISSPELLED "YOUR," GOD KILLS A KITTEN.

I didn't make it halfway down the stairs before my dad said, "Change your shirt."

"Why?"

He raised his eyebrows.

My mom came around the corner. "Honey . . ." She looked a bit misty. Maybe she always did.

"Freedom of speech," I said. "Freedom to be hilarious."

"You don't have the freedom to be a jerk," my dad said with a chuck on my shoulder.

"Honey, you don't want this to be your first impression," my mom added.

Actually, I did. It was best everyone at Jesus camp knew that God's role in my life had been relegated to punch lines on grammar T-shirts. But, whatever. My parents weren't going to change their minds. I'd made my point to them, at least.

I changed into my GOT MILK? shirt. The "got" was crossed out, and "Do you have any" was scribbled over it. I had a plethora of nerd shirts thanks to Diana, who'd thought my obsession with correctness in English usage was fun and quirky. Unlike Jack, who found it infuriating and smug.

I didn't talk on the drive to the church. I just watched the houses get closer and closer together as we made our way toward the center of our small city, which is situated just south of cool (Seattle) and just north of mentionable (Tacoma).

When we arrived, I carried my backpack to the check-in line.

My dad rolled my suitcase over to a cluster of others, as directed by a guy in a lime-green T-shirt that cheered HAPPINESS HAPPENS HERE! in rainbow-colored letters. (Rainbow! And to think, my homophobic sister chose this camp for me.) There was a heart over the *i* in "Happiness."

At the front of the line, a girl and boy with the horsey smiles that dentists dream of handed me my own T-shirt, and I vowed to save it for Charlotte. A thank-you gift.

My parents lingered behind me. I hugged my mom. I was quite a bit taller than her, but still too skinny to offer much comfort. Her shoulders shook lightly beneath my arms, and I realized she was crying. Christ. I felt bad for her pretty much all the time. My dad put his hand on my shoulder, and then pulled us all in for a big hug.

Like most parents, they were naïve and misinformed. Having spent the evening before discussing the relative merits of confession with a dead author, it was clear I needed antipsychotics, not Jesus. But of course my parents didn't know what was going on with Jack Kerouac. I didn't even know what was going on.

My mom cried a bit more and hugged me again before my dad half carried her to the car, and I waved to them as they drove away. And then I was alone.

Except for the fifty other kids teeming around the church.

I was struck by the sheer volume. The squeals, the guffaws. They'd all pulled their Happiness camp shirts on over whatever they'd worn, and their parents fumbled with cell phones to take pictures. The girls nearly snapped their moms' wrists to get the phones back and hyperanalyze the photos.

"Not good."

"Oh, my gosh, look at my face."

"Weird raccoon face."

"I need a new face!"

"Cute!"

"Oh, my gosh, tag me! Tag me!"

And then the Instagram bender. The Snapchat binge and purge.

I felt a tap on my shoulder and turned.

"Good morning!" The suitcase-director in the Happiness camp shirt held out his hand.

I shook it. "Hi."

"I'm Jason!" He continued to pump my hand.

"I'm Nick."

The overenthusiastic stranger pulled me into a side hug. "It's a blessing to have you here. T-G-I-J, am I right?"

"Perhaps . . . ?"

"Thank God it's Jesus!" He squeezed my shoulders. "Right?"

"Right . . . I guess. But redundant." I thought Jesus *was* God.

"Ha! You from Valley Christian?"

I was trapped in his embrace. "No, Mountain View High School."

"So glad to have you! You ready for an awesome week?"

I shrug-nodded under the weight of his side hug.

"It's gonna be awesome!" He threw his hands into the air, then shouted toward the group, "Because HAPPINESS . . . ?"

"HAPPENS HERE!" everyone shouted back, even the parents, cheeks pink with abandon.

"Awesome, awesome!" Jason laughed ever so joyously. He slapped my shoulder, unaware of the brute strength of his enthusiasm.

Jason stood next to me, hands together, smile beaming as he looked over the throng of teenagers. I waited for more conversation. When nothing happened, I, too, looked over said throng of teenagers and their hundred-watt smiles.

Suddenly, I realized: I was *that* kid. The awkward kid with no one to talk to. The Shadow Kid. The parent's shadow, the teacher's shadow, the camp leader's shadow, the one whose face beseeches his peers to please, please, please be his partner for the science lab. The one who writes poems in Elvish for his English teacher.

I was not a super popular guy by any means, but I'd never been *that* kid before.

Although, my name in Elvish is Turwaithion. Toor-wye-thee-on. Of course I looked it up.

"I guess I better get on the bus," I said. I had to escape from my role in this drama. And from the PCP-strength of Jason's cheerfulness. Luckily, he moved off to herald more campers.

I headed over to the line of four buses: three regular school buses and the ubiquitous short bus.

The chanting continued. Like a commune. Like a cult. No wonder the camp was held in Oregon.

"HAPPINESS!"

"HAPPENS HERE!"

"HAPPINESS!"

"HAPPENS HERE!"

"HAPPINESS!"

"HAPPENS HERE!"

I weaved through the "members of the movement" and approached a high schooler who looked particularly power hungry with his clipboard. His floppy black hair and eyeliner contradicted his Happiness camp T-shirt. "Which bus do I get on?"

Goth kid looked at me, read the front of my shirt. "Where's your camp T-shirt?"

I held it up.

He nodded. I waited. We locked eyes. And then, with the help of his intimidating eyeliner, he won the T-shirt standoff. I slipped the camp shirt over my own. In exchange, he pointed to my bus.

I was on the short bus. Of course I was. I did, in fact, have a religious disability. There was no federal No Soul Left Behind Act for me, though. Just the short bus on earth and hell in the afterlife.

I mounted the steps, and the bus driver held out a piece of paper toward me. I tried to take it, but he pinched it tight, eyeing me dubiously before he let go. "You chewin' gum?"

"No."

His lips tightened. Then, "You sure?"

I opened my mouth, lifted my tongue. "Any other cavities you want to see?" Pun intended. "Cavities, get it?"

He didn't get it, or he wasn't impressed. "Go sit down," he said.

I spotted a seat at the back of the bus and walked down the aisle, avoiding eye contact with the clan of short-bus unfavorables:

1. a girl in a wheelchair
2. a boy with a broken arm
3. a girl with too-red lips (but superhot)
4. a girl with a red bandana on her head (but prettycute)
5. a twin brother and sister
6. a girl who I later watched pick her nose for hours. At this age, nose-picking struck me as a disability, so assigning her to the short bus made sense.

I fell into my seat and peeled the Happiness T-shirt off. Then, I pulled my cell phone from my back pocket, opened my text messages, and scrolled to the feed between me and Leah.

All the messages from her were old, from before my sister's funeral. I hadn't talked to her since. I tapped out a new message: You know what week this is. Bro-sis road trip week. Parents are sending me to church camp. Can we talk when I get back?

Maybe if she answered, I could explain what happened at the funeral. I could tell her how she was the closest thing to my sister I had left. My parents had Charlotte. I had Leah.

Maybe I'd even tell her the truth.

"Anything in that writing-box there?" Jack was peering over the seat in front me. I darted my eyes to see if anyone heard him. No one on the bus had even turned in my direction.

He added, "Just makin' sure you're feeling okay amidst this joy-collecting."

I shook my head, unimpressed with his word magic. "Do not follow me to camp," I whispered. If my tally marks were correct, Jack had appeared twenty-nine times so far. His visits were getting more frequent.

Bandana Girl turned around. "Pardon?"

I glared at Jack, but he was gone. "Um, do we take this to camp?" I flashed the paper the bus driver had given me.

"You have to confess," the girl said. She turned back around.

I looked at the paper. I looked at the back of the girl's head.

WTF.

Jack popped his head back over the seat and winked. "I told you so."

PRAYERS AND CONFESSIONS

Bill: Jesus? He's no son of God. He's an alien. Yeah, he came down to Earth. And, yeah, he rose again. Back to a spaceship where his little green friends live. Listen, I just drive the bus. I don't give a shit. As long as the little angels don't put gum all over the seats.

Jason: Once again, Father, I just thank you. Thank you for these kids, for sending each one of them here this week. I know You have a purpose. You see their hearts, Lord. You know who needs the Happiness. Happiness happens here because of You. And also because I did cheer in college. Ha! Praise Jesus!

Holly: If Payton wants to break up with me because he thinks I'm the Whore of Babylon, then fine. Whatever. I'll work it like the Great Harlot.

♦

Somewhere around hour three, after Jack had convinced me that Bandana Girl was a real person and not some paid pro-confession accomplice of his, after we took a break at a rest stop where I nearly hyperventilated in a tampon bag in the unisex bathroom, a mechanical shout jolted me from my anxieties. Goth stood at the front of the bus with a walkie-talkie in his hand.

He was pushing buttons and turning knobs, clearly frustrated by the crackle, then silence. Crackle, then silence.

The other bus riders weren't paying attention to his technological woes. The kid with the broken arm had his headphones in. Nose-Picker was lecturing Bandana Girl about mermaids while she passed a bottle of sunscreen to Red Lips. (Sunscreen on a bus?)

Outside, the land was flat and brown. In the distance I thought I saw a patch of green and a barn, but it could've been a mirage. Or the ghosts of the infamous Rajneeshee commune.

"Goddamn it," Goth mumbled, and everyone's heads shot up in shock and horror. Shame splashed his face, but he quickly recovered. "No, I mean that literally. Like, this thing is of Satan and deserves damnation."

Everyone around me nodded.

"What are you trying to do?" I asked Goth, who swayed with the motion of the bus.

"It's Lottery time, man."

"Which you need to explain, Stewart," Red Lips called up to him. (Stewart. Could Goth have a less scary name than Stewart?) "He's a Pamper." She turned all the way around in her seat, resting her chin on her hands and grinning at me. Wait, was she flirting with me?

"A Pamper?" I asked.

Bandana Girl chimed in: "Pamper. Diaper. Baby—"

"You're a new camper," Red Lips said, side-eyeing Bandana Girl. "Pamper, camper, get it?" Her eyelashes got all batty.

Rhyme was the lowest level of humor in my book. But this girl was the highest level of hot, so I didn't roll my eyes.

"So, like, are you from Mountain View?" she asked.

The kid with the broken arm was suddenly watching me. His eyes flicked to Red Lips, then back to me. Red Lips smirked at him. Smiled at me. Smirked at him.

Oh, is that what was going on. Broken Arm and Red Lips—a drama couple. Or a drama ex-couple.

"It's the Donkey Lottery," Stewart interrupted, then slammed the walkie-talkie on the seat twice, like he was un-jamming a stapler.

I reached for the walkie-talkie and Stewart handed over the cheap, plastic, China-crafted toy. "See this button here? It's to change channels," I explained. "This button is to talk. You just kept changing channels every time you tried to talk."

I knew Stewart had found the right channel when I heard crackly cheering through the speakers. He turned the volume way up until the tinny sound threatened to rupture my eardrums. What was I *hearing*? The last screeching death throes of a donkey being sacrificed to God—the donkey that "won" the lottery? Like that Shirley Jackson short story we read in English, where the winner was stoned to death?

I tried to plug my ears, and then I saw the mouths of my fellow passengers begin moving. They were chanting.

Hee-haw Hee-haw Ha Ha Ha,
On a donkey, no need to walk.
Hee-haw Hee-haw Ha Ha Ha,
Just like Jesus, no need to walk.
Haw-hee Haw-hee He He He,
Who's gonna win the lottery?!

And then they started shouting, "Meeeeeee!"

"Meeee!"

"Meeee!"

And I recognized the screeching from the walkie-talkie. What I'd thought were the death throes of the donkey had just been the campers' desperately gleeful responses to an apparently not-rhetorical question. Bandana Girl set down her book and improvised a little dance to go with the chanting.

I did not join their sacrificial rites.

Finally, they ended their chant in laughter and applause—my fellow passengers just as delighted as those I could hear from the other buses through the walkie talkie. Then everyone on the short bus got quiet, looking expectantly at Stewart. He held out the walkie-talkie.

"Genevieve!" shouted a voice—I recognized Jason's—through the speaker.

Someone squealed on the other end before being drowned out by my bus and the rest of the campers. "Hee-haw . . . Hee-haw . . ." they brayed. And this time it was not a chant; they actually sounded like donkeys.

"Chris Cooper!"

The boy twin across the aisle startled me with a shout and a fist pump, and I heard the deep tones of, "Cooooop! Coooooooooooooooop!" from the speaker before they were again drowned out by the brays of my short-bus compatriots.

"Hee-haw . . . Hee-haw . . ."

So, now I knew that guy's name, and that my bus was not completely ostracized.

"Kaitlyn J.!"

Squeal!

Bray.

I still had no idea what was going on, but my busmates were on the edge of their seats. Literally. Rubbing their sweating, anxious palms into their thighs.

"Nick S.!"

My bus friends whooped.

"Isn't that your name?" Bandana Girl asked.

"Is that you?" the twin sister chimed.

"Nick Sampson, or the new kid?" Goth called through the walkie-talkie.

I didn't know whether to be excited or terrified.

The walkie-talkie crackled. "Sampson," Jason said flatly.

My fellow passengers groaned and looked at me with pity. I was not the Chosen One.

"Hee-haw . . . Hee-haw . . ." The tinny chant echoed through the walkie-talkie.

Then the bus stopped.

♦

The driver cut the engine, the bus parked right in the middle of a dirt road. Dust billowed up from below the tires. Through the yellow hue, I saw only more yellow and brown. We were in a canyon, just as barren and lifeless as the land we'd driven through to get here.

I was going to die with my fellow travelers, à la the Donner Party. Except, instead of freezing to death, we were going to bake. Which camper would I eat first?

The door to the bus opened and Jason bounced up the steps. "T-G-I-J! Am I right?"

Squeals and cheers from the other eight people on my bus. I was sure this was more convincing on a normal bus of thirty-five.

"Coooooooop," he growled. "Chris Cooper, my man! Praise Jesus!"

Fist pumps from Chris. Glares from his sister. I could almost see the devil on her left shoulder shank the angel on her right.

Jason looked at her, and he must have caught on to her disdain. "Jesus has a plan! Next year for you, Christina!"

Christina? And Chris? Had their parents totally lacked creativity, or just thought that was a cute idea?

I caught movement from outside my window.

Four donkeys stood docilely next to the camp counselors

holding their reins. The donkey-toting teens donned long white robes and sandals. Several other counselors stood next to wagons loaded with our luggage and yoked to pairs of Clydesdales.

Chris Cooper retrieved his backpack, slipped it over a shoulder, and followed Jason off the bus.

The rest of us grabbed our belongings and stepped off the bus. Well, the girl in the wheelchair didn't step. We waited for her while she whirred slowly to the ground.

It was when we finally walked (or rolled) around the bus that I understood what the Donkey Lottery was. The campers I could only assume were Genevieve, Nick Sampson, and Kaitlyn J., as well as our own Chris Cooper, each scrambled up onto the back of their own donkey.

They were not in robes or sandals like the teenage counselors. They did not have a beard or halo like the real Jesus riding on an ass into Jerusalem. But that was definitely what was being simulated there.

I stifled a laugh and looked around for someone with whom I could commiserate, but I saw only earnest and enraptured faces. Even the prettycute Bandana Girl appeared at peace with it all. There was nothing ironic going on here.

And then we started down a dusty road into Eden Springs, in the blazing afternoon sun.

The road went on forever. I was without water. I was without food. I was without the sunscreen that had been passed among my busmates.

It didn't take me long to consider prayer.

♦

I knew we'd arrived in Eden Springs when I spotted a long line of counselors, a tunnel of them, a *gauntlet* of them, all in robes and sandals. They each bent over and picked something up off the ground, and then they started waving the things. And I saw the whole donkey metaphor had not been played out.

As the donkeys walked through the gauntlet, the robed counselors waved palm fronds. The rest of the campers followed those on donkeys through. Triumphant smiles abounded.

Surely they knew the end of the story, the part where the notorious donkey-jockey got taunted, maimed with a cat-o'-nine-tails, mocked, and stabbed in the skull with thorns. And that was before he finally asphyxiated on the cross and was pierced in the side. You know, just to make sure he was not playing dead.

I was hot and dehydrated. My skin was pink with a burn. I walked around the gauntlet in order not to endanger these well-intentioned Christians with my homicidal disposition.

And then I was at camp. Which was, indeed, a paradise when compared to the walk.

Green grass everywhere. Somehow a breeze. In the distance, a pool and waterslides. Perfectly leaved trees. Paved sidewalks. Freshly painted cabins with porch swings.

Someone in a robe handed me a Dixie cup of water, and for a minute I didn't care about his costume. I shot the water like I'd seen Jack do with cheap tequila.

The same someone handed me another cupful, and another, all the while just smiling, glowing really, as he watched me drink and drink. And then he said something and pointed to a banquet table stocked with vegetables and sandwiches and more water.

Another counselor, this one a girl with her long blond hair pulled back using twine, handed me a plate. I didn't even have to dish up. She served me.

Music shouted through loudspeakers. Modern music. Finally, something normal. I sat down in the grass and ate my sandwich. The bread flaked like it was fresh from a bakery. The vegetables must've been plucked from a vine moments ago, so juicy and perfect.

Everyone else was milling about the grounds, newly energized, hopeful. We had water. We had food. We would not have to resort to cannibalism.

I was thrilled and relieved and . . . Yes, happy!

Happiness *did* happen here! At least for the near-death desperate.

I lay back in the grass, the cold smooth green grass, and looked at the big blue sky.

When I looked around the camp again, people had their cell phones out and were taking selfies.

Chris was taking a selfie with his donkey and disciple.

Another camper leaned in with a bunch of palm-toting counselors.

I took another bite of my sandwich.

A camper stood next to a woman—another one of the counselors? She definitely didn't seem like one, the way she was dressed. Or *not* dressed. Black lace and red silk. Her dark hair wrapped up with perfect ringlets hanging down over her shoulders and those breasts. I stared at those breasts. I didn't think I'd ever seen anything like them. Were we at church camp or the Playboy Mansion? The camper took a selfie with her.

I finished my sandwich as the boy moved away and another boy moved in for the next selfie.

Then, as my blood sugar normalized, my senses returned.

I saw everything.

Oh, dear gawd.

Next to the breasty woman lay a man on a mat. Dirty and haggard, he didn't get up. The campers took selfies by lying on the ground with him.

This could not seriously be what I thought it was. Perhaps it was only my post-traumatic stress from being forced into Bible skits by Charlotte's youth group.

Another man, with a cane, wandered around the camp with his eyes closed, bumping into campers. They didn't mind. They took selfies with him and the "blind" man smiled for the camera.

Oh, it was indeed what I thought. This was not PTSD.

Another woman, face horror-stricken, was only wrapped in a sheet, a Jewish rabbi nearby glaring at her, a pile of stones by his feet. They paused to take selfies with the just-arrived campers. Sometimes the characters posed together, sometimes apart.

I spotted a disciple with a coin purse and a noose dangling from his neck. Judas.

There was a man robed in purple, velvet finery. He stood by a sign that read, PICTURES WITH PONTIUS! Wow, the camp even repped the Romans.

Next to him, a character from *The Walking Dead*. Huh?

And then I saw Jesus.

I knew it was Him because He was surrounded by the masses. The Harry Styles of this band of religious figures. Like, hair and everything. But Jesus's hair was flattened by a crown of thorns. And, oh yeah, there was a tree-sized wooden cross behind him, stuck in the ground. He wore only a loincloth. I worried about the security of his junk.

When I was eleven, my parents took me to Disneyland. Before going on the rides, which is all I'd cared about, we'd walked through the village with all the shops. And there had been characters everywhere. Alice in Wonderland and Mickey Mouse and the Beast and Cinderella.

That was what I was seeing now. Bible Disneyland, every character alive and greeting the campers. But this was more Rob Zombie than Disney.

Suddenly, I was certain I was hallucinating. My Dixie cup must have been laced with shrooms. Perhaps this was some neo-Jonestown-cult-mass-homicide plot wherein hundreds or thousands of kids perished in the name of Jesus camp. Did cyanide make you hallucinate? Did I drink anything at the church before we left?

But no. Those were real donkeys. Real palm fronds. Real breasts on the fake prostitute.

A robed and sandaled counselor stood over me. "Somethin' for the PC Box, my man?" He held out a box, padlocked shut, with a slit on top.

"Uh . . ." Tithing? We had already overpaid to be here. But whatever. The disciple-counselor looked homeless, so I'd just tell myself he was buying himself some whiskey to keep the DTs away. I stood up, reached into my pocket for a dollar, and slipped it into the box.

The counselor squinted at me, but then shook his head and walked on. I heard someone laugh behind me and turned.

Bandana Girl. Her book still in hand.

"That's not a tithing box. That's the PC Box," she said.

"Politically correct?"

"Prayers and Confessions." Bandana Girl grinned. "The paper you got when you got on the bus. I told you, you have to confess. You have to write down a prayer or confession and then put it in the box."

"What happened to the good old days of talking to a priest?" I asked.

"You're Catholic?"

"Ha. No. I'm not into confessing anything." I looked around for Jack Kerouac, hoping he'd heard me. Actually, I was hoping he wasn't at camp at all, but that was likely too much to hope for. I didn't want Jack interrupting while I talked to this prettycute girl. "I'm just saying, at least with a priest, it's only you and some guy who's so old he won't remember anything you say anyway."

"So you're worried about it being written down?"

"I'm not worried about anything. I just don't want to do it." The pitchiness of my voice gave me away.

She laughed. "You look petrified."

"Well, did you see the zombie back over there?"

"That was a leper. Maybe you do need some help in the politically correct department."

"I'll write that down as my confession."

"That's cheating. You've already confessed it to me. Anyway, you'll get used to camp. It's actually fun." She smiled. I eyed the book in her hand.

"What're you reading?"

"I'm not." She opened the book and (*gasp!*) there was writing all over it.

"You broke the cardinal rule DON'T WRITE IN BOOKS." Dear gawd, she probably ran with scissors.

"I was marginalizing it," she explained.

"Literature is not to be marginalized." I glared. "Unlike zombies. They need to be put in their place pre-apocalypse."

She laughed. "I'm just writing in the margins."

"That's called annotation."

"If you're a nerd." She raised her eyebrows and nodded toward me. "But, then, nerds would wear grammar T-shirts."

I shrugged. "Or read a book on the way to summer camp."

"You cannot deny your attire. I have already denied reading. I was *marginalizing.*" She opened her book to a random page and pointed to some scribbling. "It's a play on words. The fact that I am writing in the margins—and more so, *what* I am writing—marginalizes the text." She flipped the book closed. "Thus, marginalizing."

"And that's not nerdy at all." I smiled; she smiled back. Then we both watched the prostitute walk by, followed by a girl wearing a bikini of leaves. It was hard to tell Eve from a tree-hugging working girl. "So, what book was that?" I continued.

"I'm working on Steinbeck right now." She showed me the cover—*The Grapes of Wrath.* "I already did *Of Mice and Men* and *The Red Pony*, but this takes way longer. And needs way more."

"But you're not reading them?"

"I've already read them. But I go back through and write in the margins. Like, things to think about and questions and *aha!* moments. That way, the next poor soul to suffer through torture-by-classics may find some reprieve in the snarky or insightful remarks of a classics-survivor." She laughed. "I mean, have you read the turtle chapter?"

"It's symbolic."

She snorted. "And boring. I made up a bunch of *Why'd the turtle cross the road?* jokes."

"That's literary blasphemy."

"Yes, I'll be going to hell. Me and everyone on Wattpad."

"What do you do with the books after you've defiled them?"

"Pay the fine to the school for destruction of property and sneak the book back into the pile for next year."

"Poor kids never get to read the untainted story," I joked.

"What? No way. I feel bad for the twenty-five kids who *don't* get the marginalized copy. I think I'm going to publish a line of them, like those books For Dummies. Except it'll be called something like Classics for Bored Kids."

"I guess it's a step up from SparkNotes."

"It's a stepladder up." She laughed. "I'm Natalie, by the way."

"I'm Nick."

It got quiet between us. Clearly, we had met our quota of clever for the day.

Then Natalie held up her paper between her finger and thumb. "Okay, well, I'm going to walk over there now. You know, drop this in the box. Because that's what we do here at camp." She sauntered away, smiling back at me. "Do it, Nick . . . You have to do it . . ."

I pulled my own paper from my pocket and waved it at her like I might actually do something with it. I wished I'd had something else interesting to say to keep her around. I wished I'd asked for a copy of *The Bored Kids Guide to The Red Pony*, or something.

I watched her drop her paper into the PC Box. And I wondered what sort of prayer or confession a girl like her would write.

♦

No one can blame me for checking the mattress for hay when we got to our cabins. Jesus was born in a manger, and I thought there'd be something of that experience in our sleeping quarters. Straw, the donkeys, three creepy old men gifting herbs, Mary's placenta.

I peeled back my sheets, checked the bathroom, looked under the bed. I wasn't sure what I was looking for, but I didn't want any surprises. Visits from Jack Kerouac were unpredictable enough; I didn't need unexpected Bible metaphors.

Finding nothing unusual, I sat on my bed and rested my head in my palms and wracked my brain for Bible stories. What skits had my sister forced on me as a child? Would an ill man be dropped from the ceiling? The pig with the demons in it, did it go into a house before it ran into the lake to drown? I had to know what was going to happen, what could happen.

My cabinmates rolled their suitcases in, took out Twizzler packages and cans of Monster, and shelved everything in cubbies next to their beds.

A short, skinny kid unpacked kale chips and Vitaminwater. He gave me a critical once-over. "Are you homesick?"

"No," I said. "Just a headache."

"Sometimes I get homesick, but then I just take a rest and do some problems in my math book to calm my nerves."

"That's messed up, Charles," a boy said as he walked out of the bathroom in swim trunks. Then he looked at me. "Are you the kid from Mountain View?"

I nodded. "Are you all from Valley Christian?"

"I'm not," Charles said. "I'm homeschooled."

"Thus the math book to find your Zen," I said.

Nobody laughed.

"I'm Matthew," the kid from the bathroom announced. "You want to go down to the waterslides?"

"Is that what we're supposed to do?"

"Did you already drop a prayer or confession? Then it's free time," he said. "God gave us free will, and we get free time to practice it."

I couldn't tell if he was saying all that in earnest or not, but I was certainly ready for the pool after the near-death experience of walking to camp.

"Free time isn't until after the Silent Three," Charles corrected.

"Yes, Charles, yes. But, let's get our stuff on so we're ready."

"The Silent Three?" I asked as I unzipped my suitcase and dug around for my swim shorts.

My cabinmates answered:

"It's hell."

"Hell comes before Eden in this case."

"Three silent hours of hell."

They still hadn't answered my question.

I pulled my beach towel out from under my clothes. Someone gasped. All moaning and groaning stopped.

Charles stood at my bed, mouth agape, Matthew at his shoulder, face grave. The other boys slowly moved into a semicircle around my bunk.

"Harry Potter . . ." Charles whispered.

You could barely see Hogwarts on the towel anymore, it was so faded. "Yeah, it's kinda old—" I started.

"And Satanic," Charles said.

I laughed. Nobody laughed with me.

"It's a book," I said.

"About magic," Charles insisted.

I assessed the other six boys, all of whom stared at my towel dubiously.

"I'm sure it's fine," Matthew said. "The rules don't actually say you can't bring magic paraphernalia to camp."

"Did you bring a voodoo doll?" Charles asked me.

"Why would I bring a voodoo doll?"

"Why would you bring a Harry Potter towel?"

"Because it's a hundred years old, so my mom won't kill me if I leave it here accidentally."

"But you've read the books?"

"Yeah, when I was, like, ten."

Charles pursed his lips. "This is bad. This is a bad sign."

A couple of the other boys went back to their bunks, apparently not *too* concerned.

"I'm sure it's fine," Matthew said again. "It's just a book to you, right?"

"Technically, it's just a freakin' *towel* to me."

"The language," Charles groaned. "I might need to call my mom. I might need a cabin change."

"Shut up, Charles," one of the boys said from behind his closet door.

Just then, Jason popped his head into the cabin. "Gentlemen! It's gonna be ACES today, praise God. The sky shines blue, the slides await!"

No amens chimed back.

"Happiness does not seem to be happening here. Lay it on me, my friends with a capital F. What's goin' down other than those smiles?"

Charles pointed at my towel.

Jason pursed his lips. "Neal is a Pamper, Charles."

"Nick," I corrected.

"Right, right." He waved me away. "Do you remember your infancy in Christ? In camp? Conviction is like a tulip slowly pushing through the earth. Dormant, then slow, and then boom! Pop of color!"

This is what I was afraid of. If, in their eyes, a fictional character on a towel was a ticket to hell, then I can only imagine what they'd say about Diana. "It's a towel. About a book. I'm sorry. I don't care. Can I trade with someone?"

"I'm not trading!" Charles near-shrieked.

"No, I meant with the camp. Is there an extra?"

"It's already springtime for this tulip! Am I right? Awesome, awesome! I'll find something in lost and found. Just use your towel wrong side out for now. No worries, Nea—Nick. Got it that time!" he said with a display of jazz hands. "We don't judge."

"Amen," Charles said.

"Really?" I said to Charles.

A face appeared behind Jason. And I was actually relieved to see someone I knew. Or kind of knew. It was the kid from the bus with the broken arm.

"Payton! P-Dog!" Jason shouted.

"What's up?" Payton said and rolled his suitcase between Jason and the door. He eyed me as he walked by, then took the last lower bunk. There was still an upper bunk left.

"What's *up*? Fist pump for Christ, is what's up!" Jason fist-pumped. All by himself. "Not to mention, the smiles in this room now that we've solved the Beach Towel Dilemma! Amen. Let's get to the pool. It's awesome out there, folks! HAPPINESS!"

Silence.

"Gentlemen, it's day one. Let's try that again. HAPPINESS!"

"Happens here," a few mumbled.

"It's just hard, Jason, with the towel still in the room."

Matthew put his hand on Charles's shoulder. "It's fine."

Jason held out the PC Box. "Any last-minute Ps and Cs for this bad boy before I put it in the sanctuary?"

I thought of Natalie. How easy it was for her to just drop her paper in the box. Then I walked into the bathroom to put on my swim trunks. When I returned, Jason had left.

There were seven of us left in the cabin:

Me: the devil-worshipping Pamper.

Matthew: who quickly took me under his wing (of an angel, obviously).

Charles: math savant and HP-hater (likely a Slytherin).

Payton: who ignored me altogether except for the occasional dagger-tossing glare. (*He's on scholarship*, Matthew whispered. *Everybody knows the scholarship kids.* Matthew was not on scholarship. He was a state tennis champion, for God's sake. Tennis players are never on scholarship.)

Stewart the Goth.

Chris Cooper: a.k.a Cooooooooop: The Chosen One. The Donkey Jockey. The Prodigal Son.

Dan: our counselor, who was at a meeting.

From the clock by the counselor's bed, I surmised I had eight hours left till lights out. Anyone could survive eight hours, right?

But it was the first three hours I had to worry about. The Silent Three. Death by boredom. Hell did come before Eden. And there were demons. Or at least one.

PRAYERS AND CONFESSIONS

Charles: Dear Lord, thank you for this week. May Your holy plan for me reveal itself, and may I pass my AP Euro test, if it be your will. And my AP Chem. Though I probably don't need prayer for that one.

Dan: I worry about these kids. They're such puss—sorry. They need Your strength, Jesus. Life doesn't get any easier than in their entitled little worlds. Real life is war. Or at least a battlefield. Thanks, Pat Benatar. Yeah, one of my dad's favorites.

Matthew: Forgive me for renaming all my songs on iTunes. I mean Drake to Lecrae doesn't seem that bad, but Jason Derulo to Chris Tomlin? It's just lies. I feel bad for using talented Christians as a cover for my sinful listening habits. But, dude, my parents blame secular music for my downfall.

Jason: These kids can be tough, Papa. But I know you're with me. It's because of you that I can keep this smile pasted to my face. And because of all those summers at drama camp! Ha! Praise Jesus!

♦

"You will not believe who's here," I heard from behind me. A fence rattled and, lo and behold, Jack Kerouac was scaling the chain link. He flopped over the fence and squatted beside me.

"What are you doing here?" I whisper-hissed. We were all supposed to be silent for three hours to ruminate on Jesus's sacrifice, which the Stage-Jesus had described in slasher-film detail before sending us on our way. The beating, the crown of thorns, the death, the three days in the tomb while His disciples mourned. "I told you not to come."

"And miss all this?" Jack looked out at the masses of teens, who had so far not exhibited any signs of ADD.

Some had their Bibles open in their laps. Others had journals and pens and lay in the grass, scribbling their reflections. Some had their eyes closed in prayer.

"Where's that little white paper you got? The one the girl on pretty road asked you about?"

"The *girl on pretty road*? You mean, the one with the bandana?"

"The one that got you all wondering and dreamy."

"Her name's Natalie."

"The very one." He nodded. "Where's the paper?"

"I put it in the box."

"Untrue. It's in your pocket."

"Why do you ask if you know everything?"

"I'm evaluating your truth-saying."

He pulled a pack of cigarettes from his jacket pocket.

"Are you seriously going to smoke at Jesus camp?"

"They were a gift."

"Who would give you a gift here?"

"I got connections." He lit his cigarette. "Like I said, you wouldn't believe who's here. Muhammad and Buddha. Some old Indian fella—"

"Native American."

"Sure, yeah. He talks like he's got a barrel in his belly, all round and echo-like. I got these here from a fine young woman called Ereshkigal."

"Oh yeah?" I mocked. "And where's Jesus?"

"Well, He's with them, obviously. All friends, doing their thing, one man on earth at a time."

"Right." I rolled my eyes and snarked, "Then, please, say hi to my sister."

"I can't do that. I've already told you."

"How convenient."

"Believe what you want." He took a long drag and exhaled. "You can be such an arrogant little shit."

"Can you at least smoke downwind?"

He surprised me by standing up and sitting down on the other side of me.

"Look at all those beautiful people, Nicolas. Imagine the depths in their hearts, the secrets."

"I don't want to know their secrets."

"All that truth flying around their heads like birds." He was staring off, unfocused, slipping into his poet-self. I wondered for a moment if it was only tobacco he was smoking.

"And we go on shooting it down," I said in mock poet-stoner voice.

He snapped his head in my direction. "Ah hell, what's that supposed to mean?"

Jack was always digging around my psyche, and usually I just walked out of my room to get away from his prying. But I was stuck in pretend prayer, so I told him what I thought. "I mean those truth-birds are being shot down by our word-bullets."

"Ah yes. Metaphor on, Nicolas."

"Seriously. All our words shooting out of our mouths. Always trying to tell everyone this or that. Hunting down the things we want to say. The things we want people to hear. Just leaving dead bird truths all over everywhere. Nobody knows how to say anything right."

He clicked his tongue at me, obviously disappointed by my pessimism. He fingered his cigarette while he stared out at all the campers sitting around, all meditative. "Man, you are rolling fast down sad hill."

"I should've realized what was happening with Diana. I should've known. She should've told me. Maybe she did. Maybe words just fail us."

"We misuse them, misunderstand, misrepresent, miss the target," Jack singsonged. "And now we're back to it. This is about your sister."

"Of course it's about my sister." It was always about my sister, and he knew it. He was prodding me. This is why I hated talking to him. Because his words were sharp, and all my packed-up-and-put-away sadness was going to spill out everywhere.

"Well, I can't always be sure. You've been all curled-over obsessing about Leah."

"Because she's alive! My sister's dead. I can't talk to her." I sighed. "Leah's what's left of my sister. And to Leah, I'm what's left of Diana."

"I know—yes—I do know."

I felt deflated. "At the funeral—"

"Oh yes, I saw what happened at the funeral." Of course he did. Stalker.

"That's what I'm saying. That's all it was. Just grabbing on to what's left."

Jack smoked, pondered.

A cricket started off in the dry grass. Someone cleared his throat. The wind picked up the leaves, hanging there like paper coins, the light shifting the color of them.

"Nicolas, that's what we've got. Words. That's all we've got.

And if that chasm from soul to soul is as wide as the Grand Canyon, and perhaps it is—ah hell, maybe even wider—then we gawddamn better have a bridge. That's what our words are. They're the bridge from me to you, from you to your parents, from you to those lovely girls you met today—"

I rolled my eyes.

"—and that bridge might be rickety-rackety, broken, dangerous to cross. But, ah man, that's all we have." Jack stood up, brushed off his pants. "Diana is walking a different road now—long gone and down—and there are no more words or nonwords to puzzle on and figure out."

I looked up at him. "But I was wrong. I didn't understand what Diana was saying."

"No, that's not it, not it at all," he said, shaking his head. "There is no right or wrong. There's just what you do, and what happens after."

The tears needled. "I don't like this *after*."

"You have something to say, Nicolas, and those words are gonna tear you up or rot you from the inside out if you don't tell it out. That's a worse *after*."

My throat tightened. I swallowed to keep all the words and all the sadness down. I looked back out at the people with the books and the pens, all the words.

Jack walked past me, following the fence up the hill. "I don't think I care to sit around and witness your tearfall. There are such times when a young man needs some privacy. But I think you might've heard me this time."

I was not going to cry at church camp. The cliché was too much.

Charlotte would've been too pleased.

I swallowed the thick sadness in my throat. I took out my pen and composition book, scratching two lines on the Jack Kerouac tally page. I'd seen him thirty times now.

Flipping to a blank page, I held the pen over the paper.

It hovered.

Then I wrote it down. Just to see how confession felt. The words screamed back at me, rattling around on the page like prisoners. I ripped the paper out of the notebook and stuffed it in my pocket.

♦

A microphone screeched from the center of camp. I looked down the hill into the field, where a counselor stood in the center of the grassy area and tapped on the mic. *Thump, thump, thump.* "Test." *Screech.* "Can you hear me?" *Screech. Thump, thump.*

The Silent Three was definitely over.

I stood up and headed down the hill toward the counselor calling us to join him. The characters were coming back out of hiding. The leper. The blind man. The lame man on his mat. Jesus milled about. Music blasted from the speakers.

I felt a tap on my shoulder and turned to find two counselors, both with long, dark hair, smiling down at me. Both wore robe-like garb, and one had fake wrinkles drawn on her forehead and around her mouth. I hadn't seen these two when we'd first arrived.

"Have you seen Him?" the young one asked.

"Who?" I asked.

"My son, the Son of God!" the old one said.

Mary Magdalene and Mother Mary?

"He's over there." I pointed.

"Come closer," they urged, all smiles.

I swiped at their hands, unwilling to be part of this skit. Unwilling to drink the Kool-Aid.

They tugged at my T-shirt.

"I got it. I'm going." I batted Mary Magdalene's hand away. Both girls fell out of character, struck by my unwillingness to play make-believe.

They lifted their robes to keep them from dragging on the

ground and sauntered over to another camper on the outskirts, a girl who willingly followed them into the swarm. I weaved through the campers and characters.

The phones were back out. Mine registered no service, and I wasn't about to join the throngs for the photo shoot. But I watched.

A group of about ten campers posed with some famous sinners, who stood next to signs the camp had clearly provided to help the Pampers get it. I didn't need the signs for all the characters. You didn't need to go to church to know the guy with the noose around his neck was Judas. But there were more difficult characters to peg, like the two thieves from the crosses, plus Barabbas. And the adulteress and her sheet again.

And then I saw Jack, photo bombing the campers, his fingers making bunny ears behind Barabbas's head. I walked quickly toward him. He saw me coming and darted away like an unruly toddler.

He sauntered across the lawn, and I followed him. I took the paper out of my pocket. I'd show him I'd done it—I'd written it down—and then he could leave. He'd done his job, got me to confess.

But then the music clicked off and everyone turned toward a stage. I couldn't see what they were looking at.

The chant from the church that morning started up again.

"HAPPINESS!"

"HAPPENS HERE!"

Jack had vanished. I shook my head and walked back toward the crowd of campers.

A man ascended some steps with a microphone in hand. "Gooooooooood afternoooooon, Christiaaaaaaans!" A sad attempt at an impression of Robin Williams in *Good Morning, Vietnam.* Way out of character, because the man with the mic looked less like Robin Williams and more like Robert Redford in his prime. He'd been peeled right off an Abercrombie & Fitch poster. He was the guy they hired for Viagra or Crest commercials.

Everyone cheered and shouted and whooped.

"Where are my Returning Champions?! My reigning Super Bowl Christians!"

Cheers and whoops.

"Where are my Pampers?!"

Delayed whoops from a few, including the Marys fangirl, prompted by a nudge from Mother Mary.

"Are you ready for a Christastic weekend?!"

Earsplitting cheers.

Christastic?

I was finding it hard to know if my parents had signed me up for church camp, drama camp, or cheer camp.

"Then let's pump it up! Fist pumps for Christ!"

They all threw their arms in the air and pumped their fists, chanting.

Fist pumps for Christ!

Fist pumps for Christ!

These people had an infinity worth of cheers.

The Marys stood at the back corner of the stage, fist-pumping along with them. Their enthusiasm would've been more convincing if their beloved Jesus hadn't died at the end of this story.

The pastor guy gave them each a high five and the three of them exited the stage just as the prostitute walked up, carrying an enormous Bible—like if the Bible took steroids.

Joining her on the stage were two counselors, a girl and a guy, both wearing Hammer pants and gold chains. It was not MC Hammer music that echoed through the canyon, though, but Sir Mix-A-Lot. I recognized the notes of "Baby Got Back," and I waited for God to send lightning bolts and strike us all dead. Then I saw the girl put the mic to her face and, glaring at the prostitute character, begin her rap:

Oh, my gosh, Becky, look at her Bible.

It's, like, so big.
She looks like one of those Jesus followers.

The girl stepped aside, and the boy started rapping. As he did so, counselors walked among the crowd, distributing Bibles. Some campers held out their own big Bibles.

"Fun, right?"

I turned around.

"Did I scare you?" Natalie laughed, and her eyes flashed. "Boo!" She shimmied to the beat and sang along.

I like big Bibles and I cannot lie,
You other followers can't deny
That when a friend walks in with a shiny leather case
And those pages in your face—

"And, look, you've got your confession ready, even," she said, nodding at my hand.

I looked down. There was the paper, in my hand. I crumpled it, freaked that it might fall on the ground, or she might grab it.

"Here!" Natalie called to Jesus, who was walking through the crowd, carrying the PC Box.

I tried to turn around. "That's okay," I mumbled. But then Jesus was right there. His dark eyes waiting, the slit in the box wide open. Natalie smiled and looked at me expectantly. And there was Charles, walking behind Matthew, headed right toward me.

Deep in the Book we're reading,
I'm hooked and I can't stop needing—

Matthew put his hand on my shoulder. "Hey, dude, hurry up. Let's hit the pool."

"He's got to drop his confession in first." Charles pointed at my clenched fist. Was this payback for Harry Potter?

The paper wilted in the heat of my hand. Natalie's smile never wavered. Jesus shifted his weight. Patience was barely his virtue.

And Jack appeared, leaning up against the fence across the field, smoking, watching, waiting.

I took the paper out of my hand—"Oh yeah, this. Sure."—and uncrumpled it. Folded it once, twice. Slipped it in the box.

My churchboys tried to warn me
That Book you got makes me so holy—

They rapped on.

Later, I would think about the sheer number of secrets dropped into that locked box.

But at that moment, a counselor took my cell phone, and everyone else's, exchanging them for Bibles.

My soul died a little.

Please forgive them, Sir Mix-A-Lot. They know not what they've done.

♦

"Behold Eden Springs, Nick," Matthew said as we walked through the gate to the pool. "I know Eve was totally nude in Eden, but this is a close second."

He tossed his beach towel on a deck chair. He surveyed the sea of half-naked campers like a captain taking stock of his ship. Meanwhile, I kept my eye out for Jesus and the PC Box.

"Asstastic," Matthew said, more to himself than me. "Everywhere, fine, fine ass." He yanked his eyes away from the fine, fine ass. "I know that's what you're thinking. I can see you making your *ass*essments."

I'd actually been pondering how much money I could pay Jesus to let me pull my paper out of the box. And wondering where I could stash my Harry Potter towel to avoid further scrutiny. But I said, "I was thinking *tit*illating. Literally titillating."

"Yes! I love me some SAT vocab!" Matthew shouted. "This dude's going Ivy League!"

I laughed and folded my towel into an inside-out bundle so that no one could see the boy wizard.

Matthew shoved me. "Quit doing your laundry and see the sights!"

They didn't tell you on the "What to Pack" list not to bring a Harry Potter towel. They also didn't tell you not to bring your tarot cards, your crystal balls, your voodoo dolls, or your statues of Aphrodite. They didn't tell you not to bring alcohol or cigarettes or cyanide tablets or LSD or knives or guns either.

And they didn't tell you not to pack bikinis.

Apparently not all temptation is equal.

"Titillating!" Matthew repeated, beaming at me. "Nick's a boob guy."

I wasn't a boob guy. I wasn't an anything guy, really. I mean a hot girl is a hot girl. But even Diana used to give me a hard time about my lack of romantic experience. *You should be able to diagram the female anatomy at least as well as a sentence, buddy,* she used to say. *And not because of health class worksheets.*

And of course Jack was chagrined by my lack of sins of the flesh. I imagined him sitting in a tree with binoculars, pedophile-like, staring down at all those leggy ladies.

Next to me, Matthew's voice took on the Martin Luther King Jr. boom. "I have a dream, Nick. I have a dream that one day, in the sweltering heat of Eden Springs . . . well"—he went back to his own voice—"I don't know how the speech goes. But pretty much there're two girls to every guy, so that's my dream."

As he stood there in his swim trunks with his tennis player–lean physique, I was sure that there were more than two ladies for every Matthew. More like thirty-two girls for every Matthew, and negative eleven girls for every Nick. After adjusting for those numbers, I needed Homeschool Charles to figure out how the odds played out for the rest of the guys.

I continued Matthew's rendition of "I Have a Dream" scandalously, at least as far as my memory would serve. "Let freedom ring . . . from the mountainsides."

"And prodigious hillsides."

"And curvaceous slopes."

Clearly, MLK had been a boob guy.

And Eden Springs was worried about my Harry Potter towel.

Matthew hollered out to the swimmers and sliders, "I love you, Eden Springs!" He threw his arms into the air and whooped. The counselors, the campers, everyone looked over at him. "Fist pumps for Christ!" He yelled once more. A couple kids pumped their fists. "Hells to the yes."

A girl with a book—she was too far away for me to make out her face—looked over and gave a slight wave. There was only one girl with a book. Natalie. I waved. Then I remembered that I was standing next to Matthew.

"Is that how they do it at Valley Christian? MLK-turned-porn?" I asked, pretending I hadn't just thought prettycute girl was waving at me.

"Hells to the no, Nick. My parents pay for me to go there so that I can be 'positively influenced' by all these blessed lovers of Jesus. And then the private-school girls take their clothes off for one week at Eden Springs, and it's all worth it."

Natalie was in a bikini, just like most of the other girls, but it wasn't the bikini. It was the way the light shimmered off the pool and winked from her sunglasses. It was the way her painted toenails bounced to the pop song blasting from the speakers. It was the way the navy blue of her bikini bottom lay against her pale thigh.

Frankly, it was the way she read—or wrote in!—a book by the pool, while everyone else played volleyball and chicken and Marco Polo. "I get it," I said to Matthew, just to say something.

"Oh no, young Nicolas, I don't think you do. My life lacks the titillating pleasures of your public school experience."

"There's nothing titillating about my experience, personally." My only experiences with girls were awkward things you needed to apologize for.

"Ah, but Nick, there's at least the possibility . . ." His voice fell away in reverence. "My experience is pent-up and buttoned underneath starchy blouses." He grabbed my arm, and I stopped pretending *not* to stare at Natalie. "Speaking of asstastic and titillating both . . ."

It was hard not to see who he was talking about. Long golden legs, long dark hair. White bikini. Red lips. "Ho-Lo."

It was the superhot girl from the bus. "Ho-Lo?" I asked.

"Her name's Holly. Ho . . . well, that's obvious. Lo, as in like J-Lo."

"Jennifer Lopez? She's our mom's age."

"Don't overthink it. We couldn't figure out how to combine her name and Kylie Jenner's," Matthew said, watching Holly saunter to a deck chair.

Watching Holly was like watching one of those slow-motion shampoo commercials. Slo-Mo-Ho-Lo.

Matthew interrupted his own reverie: "Speaking of fast girls." He led me to the waterslides. "The Jezebel," he said, pointing to the slide's name.

I laughed. At the top, kids lay on their bellies on mats and readied themselves for a race straight down the yellow slide to the water below.

"Head first, that's how she likes it," Matthew quipped. "Right, Holly?" he called over to her.

Holly looked up. Matthew waved innocently. Holly just looked away.

"The line is long," he said to me, "but it's worth it."

I laughed because he was funny—supersmart funny.

"I mean, I'm sure Payton thought the wait was worth it, but he clearly got sick of the long line of male suitors she entertained," he continued.

I didn't really know this girl Holly—though to hear Matthew chatter on and on, others seemed to know her quite well. Just like Charlotte.

I didn't want to think about my oldest sister. I loathed how she had treated Diana after coming back from Eden Springs. I despised that this camp, with its list of rights and wrongs, had snipped the threads that tethered my sisters to each other. I detested that nothing on this earth could tie them back together—not even regret after Diana died, if Charlotte felt that at all.

"Yeah, this line's too long," I said. "Let's catch this one later."

We headed over to the Belly of the Whale slide. Along with a couple other kids, we flipped in loops and circles through the dark tunnels on the extra-large tube. Over and over, I raced down that slide, and I refused to think about Charlotte, and I refused to think about my confession.

Matthew and I spent the rest of the afternoon at the pool, mostly going down the seven waterslides. We jumped off the ten-foot platform-cliff into the deep end of the pool. And when we'd had our fill of snacks and ogling and water sports, we walked back to the chairs to grab our towels and head to the showers.

Except, my Harry Potter towel was gone.

Matthew rubbed his hair dry with his towel while I searched the pool deck. It had cleared out a bit as people left to get ready for dinner. Goth was lying out in a pool chair next to Nick Sampson—my Donkey Lottery nemesis—and the wheelchair girl. Charles was talking to a group of bikini-clad girls. I headed over to him, sure he'd swiped my towel. Maybe burned it. Like the Joan of Arc of beach towels.

Then a hand on fell on my shoulder and spun me around. Jesus. I immediately panicked. Had he read what I'd dropped in the PC Box? They'd all assured us that nobody read them. And I'd seen the size of that padlock but . . . what if?

"You the kid with the towel?" he asked, his voice lacking the God-boom one might expect.

I nodded. There could be only one towel of import.

He handed me a brand-new—really, there was a Polo-brand price tag on it—yellow towel.

"I already wrote about this and put it in the PC Box," he said.

"About the Harry Potter towel?"

He nodded. "A prayer," he said and waved me away. "No need to thank me, man."

♦

The evening service in the sanctuary, where I'd expected venomous snakes and raising of hands and healing of the crippled, was oddly normal. The speaker from the morning, the guy who had welcomed us into camp, turned out to be the pastor, Pastor Kyle.

He looked nothing like any pastor I'd ever seen. Though, in truth, the only ones I'd ever seen were featured on the nightly news. The ones accused of child rape. All pornstache and thick glasses.

But Pastor Kyle looked like Adonis. Like Paul Walker (may he rest in peace). After seeing the plastic-perfect kids modeling on the cover of the camp brochure, I was prepared for his tanned body and white teeth, and yet I found the pastor's beauty—yes, that's what I said, beauty!—unearthly. I'm sure he led a lot of campers to God; girls would follow this guy anywhere. And boys? Well, they'd just follow the girls. I mean, everyone knows the Adam and Eve story.

"I know the Silent Three was an amazing time for you. I know the Lord was with you in your time of reflection and prayer. All those sins and secrets, friends." He talked about sin, as they all do, but without the hellfire and brimstone I was anticipating. We would have another chance with the PC Box tonight, he told us, gesturing to an older woman on stage, who shuffled off in her too-short shorts—presumably to retrieve it. Then Pastor Perfect told us a story from his own childhood where he did something wrong. "But that's a mute point," he said, "because Jesus saves!"

For God's sake, Jesus needed to save him from his grammar.

"Moot," I said to Matthew, who sat next to me, rapt. I nudged him. "He meant it was a *moot* point."

He shrugged me off, apparently not interested in the irony of a point in a speech, which you say *so that people can hear you*, being mute.

I felt like the pastor's grammar failings had to be a sign that the universe was balancing itself, though. Like, Pastor Kyle couldn't have it all. To have those bright teeth, he needed to sacrifice his understanding of the English language.

I had the latter, thus my need for braces and a tan.

While everyone jotted down some scripture that flashed on the screen, I took out my little composition book, turned past the Jack Kerouac tally sheet, and started a list: MUTE—MOOT, I wrote on the next page.

The older woman scuttled back onto the stage, interrupting Pastor Kyle's massacre of vital grammatical rules. She stood on her tiptoes, gesticulating and whispering something into the pastor's ear. The pastor leaned down, pushing the mic as far away from her as possible. Then she hurried away, nearly tripping down the stairs.

"Okay, my Champions," he said, but it lacked his Lord-lovin' fervor of moments before. "Now, there is no need to panic." Which is a sure way to incite panic. Immediately there were whispers, murmurs, *oh god, oh god, oh god*. "There's been an incident."

Eyes darted. Faces paled.

Was it a terrorist attack?

Another 9/11, on West Coast soil?

A president assassinated? (Actually, that one might warrant a celebration—at least, for the eleven Democrats in the crowd.)

"We're hoping someone will come forward immediately." Pause. "We'll get to the bottom of this atrocity." Pause. "Happiness will happen here, despite this grave situation." He was getting his evangelical groove back.

He cleared his throat.

There was a collective intake of breath.

"Someone has stolen the PC Box."

♦

You know those movies where the plane flies over unsuspecting civilians (often in rags and farming rice paddies or shepherding goats, because people in rags are worth more emotionally in film and worth less in wartime economics . . . at least to the people pulling the trigger)? The propellers beating against the sky, loud and violent. Then the whistle of the falling bomb and the explosion as it hits the earth.

And then the vacuum of all sound. The silence, complete and irrevocable and soul sucking.

Pastor Kyle's words dropped down on me. And then the heat. My nerves flashed fire through my arms and face and left me tingling, then numb.

Someone was going to read my confession. My brain scrambled for the words I'd scrawled on that paper. What did I write? What did I say? I mean, *exactly*. Could I explain it away? Could I make it a joke?

The campers were silent. Blank eyes. Clenching jaws. They were in their heads. *What did we write?* Exactly? *Oh no. But did we write the name? Did we say* our *names? Her name? His name? Their names?*

Shit. Shit. Shit.

And then the flush of shame as we realized what we wrote. *Exactly.*

The sound filtered back into our brains, our faces blanching, our eyes searching those around us for sympathy.

I looked for Jack. Not because he had stolen the box. But because this was his fault regardless. I shouldn't even have to care. I *wouldn't* care, if it hadn't been for his constant blathering.

The one time I really wanted him, and he'd vanished.

Who the hell stole the box? Suddenly, I wasn't seeing potential sympathizers in the crowd around me. I was seeing culprits. We were all seeing culprits. Our shame had faded to fury, our eyes narrowing. Who the *holy hell* stole that box? Our confessions, our secrets, the things we refused to say aloud to people, not even in the dark.

I looked at Matthew, but he stared at the carpet, unblinking. Passively terrified. I don't know what he'd written on his paper, but no way he'd stolen the box. That, or he was a fantastic actor. Was he in drama at his private school? Did he say that? No, tennis.

Payton's face had turned rage red.

Holly's mascara was running.

Charles watched me, nose flaring.

He'd picked me as the culprit, clearly.

Eyes flashed from face to face. We searched for the offender now, not the sympathizers.

"It's okay, I didn't write my name on either of mine," a girl in pink shorts said to her friend behind me.

I turned.

"Neither did I," her friend said back, and then her mouth fell open. "But I wrote his. I wrote *his*. Oh, my God." She slid back down into her seat and hid her face in her hands.

Murmurs, condolences, rumors washed through the crowd.

I saw Natalie then, just behind pink-shorts girl and her friend. She scanned the back of the room, mouth slightly open—searching for something, maybe. Or someone. She was agitated, but not crying like most of the girls. She brushed her hair back and pushed through the aisle. I watched her turn around once more. She took us all in, scanned the whole room, then she walked out the door.

♦

I told Matthew I needed to go to the bathroom and then excused myself down the row of campers. Most of them were out of their seats, standing with their arms around someone else who thought they had it worse than the next person. Groups had formed up the aisles and in front of the stage. The hugging, the tears.

I stepped out into the night, the door closing slowly behind me, trapping the chatter and prayer and sobs in the sanctuary. I stood in relative silence. The wind whispered its own secrets through the leaves of small trees. I listened for footsteps. I peered into the shadows cast by light posts surrounding the field. Natalie was nowhere.

No. Natalie *was* somewhere, and I wanted to find her. Maybe it was worry. Maybe it was curiosity. Or maybe it was suspicion. Maybe it was all three.

I walked the path through the middle of camp, scanning the field, the empty porches rolling out from each building. There was no one. Every camper, counselor, pastor, worker was in the sanctuary dealing with the fallout of the PC Box theft.

I turned to face the cabins. Maybe Natalie had snuck out to be alone, to figure out her own mess without the crying and condolences, without the *it's so much worse for me though* sentiments that (accidentally?) slipped out or emanated from superficial hugs.

I didn't know which cabin was hers. Light poured through the curtains of some windows; others were dark. I knocked on the first cabin door, waited. No answer. I skipped steps up to the second floor and knocked. No answer.

When I turned around to head back down the stairs, a silhouette of someone walking toward the hillside caught my eye. I couldn't tell if it was her. I couldn't even tell if it was a girl or boy. But I hurried down the stairs and jogged across the field anyway.

The hill turned out to be more like a cliff. It was dry, rocky, sagebrush-covered terrain, clearly not maintained by the crew who kept Eden Springs green and fresh. Unauthentically perfect, just like humans prefer. Nothing's perfect—but it can at least look that way, right? Facebook, Snapchat, friendships, marriages, dinners, family vacations, gardens, houses, kids. I thought about my own family. Façade after façade.

There was no sign of a trail, or of the person who'd been walking up it. No sign of anyone else outside, either. They were all still locked away with their sorrows, it seemed.

I walked along the hillside and toward the barns, and realized there was an old, barbed wire fence surrounding the camp. The terrain, the cliff, the fence. Clearly I wasn't supposed to leave, even if I found the trail. And neither was the person on the cliff. But there must have been way to get up there.

Suddenly, I heard the scrape of rocks. A shadow moved behind the barns. I changed course again. Slinking along the wall of the building, I looked for Natalie. I looked for any shape.

And then I found it.

It was a donkey.

It shifted its weight, sending more rocks down the embankment. The donkey barely registered my presence. It was probably exhausted from carrying the lucky lotto winners to camp.

I leaned up against the barn. I had no idea what I was doing, besides looking for a curious, pretty girl.

I wondered if Natalie had left the building because she knew something about the PC Box. There was no other reason to slip out so quietly. And, unlike everyone else, she hadn't looked traumatized. She hadn't been crying or hugging.

What were the odds that Natalie had done it?

But then I thought, maybe Pastor Kyle was behind this. Maybe it was all a trick. I'd heard one time about a church where the pastor had arranged for gunmen to burst into the building. They'd lined up members of the congregation and asked them if they believed in God. The idea was to see who would deny Christ at gunpoint. I don't know what happened. I don't know how many people stood their religious ground. I do know that no one got killed, but it was still some sick shit.

Maybe that's what Pastor Kyle was doing. I mean, this camp went all-out. Maybe this was all leading up to some kind of (divine!) intervention. Maybe our parents were all going to show up, sit at tables with us, and talk us out of our drug addictions, drinking problems, and gambling issues.

But I had no idea how I'd find out if he was doing that. And for the moment, Natalie was the one who was acting suspiciously.

The donkey shifted, closed its eyes.

"Have you seen a girl? She's about this tall . . ."

The donkey continued his silent treatment. Useless.

"Jack?" I asked the night. He was constantly telling me what to do. For once, I could actually use his intrusive line of reasoning. "Jack."

He didn't appear.

"Are you Jack?" I asked the donkey. "Because he is a total jackass, so you kind of fit the bill. No offense."

The donkey said nothing. Clearly no offense had been taken.

"Hey." A hand landed on my shoulder, and I spun around.

It wasn't Jack or Natalie. It was the Jesus character.

"What're ya doin' out here?" He didn't sound at all holy. He sounded like a regular man, like at the pool earlier.

"I'm looking for someone."

"There ain't nobody out here." He sounded like a regular *hillbilly* man.

"I saw somebody come out here, so—"

"Like I said, there ain't nobody out here." He was like Jesus appearing on an episode of *Duck Dynasty*.

"Okay . . ." I wanted to ask him what *he* was doing out here. Jesus was born in a manger, and I was in fact standing next to a barn, but this dude was a wee bit bigger than an infant and had no signs of frankincense or myrrh or Bible-times diapers.

I eyed the man. As Jesus, he carried the PC Box around all day. He could very well have stolen it and hidden it out in the barn.

"Lemme walk ya back," he said, suddenly all friendly. And, quite frankly, acting a little suspicious.

Jesus followed behind me as we walked around the barn. I craned my neck to peek into the shadows, hoping to catch a glimpse of the box. His hand landed on my shoulders and he ushered me forward a bit more quickly.

He was an older guy, probably in his thirties. Hair pulled back in a ponytail and beard a little gray. His skin was pale, too pale for the real Jesus. And he didn't even bother with bronzer.

"You know Jesus was from the Middle East, right?" I snarked.

He looked down at me, but kept his hand on my shoulder till we'd both stepped out onto the grassy field. "How ya know I ain't?"

I fixed my eyes on the hillside, searching for signs of movement, and pondered how to answer. I wanted to point out the obvious, namely his hillbilly accent. But—who knows—maybe hillbilly accents were a thing in the Middle East. Maybe the goat herders of the Middle East sounded a lot like the crawfish hunters of rural America. Maybe there was a global hillbilly community. An Iraqi *Duck Dynasty*. Mexican *Duck Dynasty*. Tibetan *Duck Dynasty*. A dynasty of *Dynasties*!

Hillbilly Jesus probably wasn't going to follow my train of thought, though, so I answered, "Because of Donald Trump and the Muslim ban."

"Touché." He laughed. Whoa. Hillbilly Jesus used a French

word. Was he trying to impress me? Shepherd me into his flock with his broad sense of language and culture? What's French for *gag*? "How you likin' camp?" he asked.

"It's fine," I said.

There was no sign of Natalie at all anymore. Not up on the hill, not down here in the field.

"Listen," I said, "I can find my way back from here."

He ignored me. "You on scholarship?" he asked.

"Me? No. Why?" I mean, I didn't go to some rich private school like most of the kids at the camp, but my family was doing just fine. "Do I look like a poor kid?"

"No, but yer attitude is poor."

Oh, jokes! Snarky bastard. "Well, clearly they don't pay you enough here, because your Jesus accent is poor."

Jesus laughed and laughed. "I asked about scholarship because I was wonderin' if yer on work crew."

"Uh, no." I tried to walk faster, to shake this guy, but he kept at it.

"Hey, it ain't bad. Some of yer friends over there are on my crew."

"Doing what?"

"I'm Jesus by day, custodian by night. I was feedin' the donkeys jus' now. Toilets next." He nodded toward the sanctuary. "Yer friends help out."

"Well, I don't need the money."

He raised his eyebrows at me. "Maybe you jus' needda work."

I got the feeling he was calling me an entitled ass, but I decided to go the way of a docile donkey and take no offense. "Okay, cool, thanks."

Then he added, "An' forget that business with the towel. Have a good time. You got yerself a new towel, donchya?"

"I never cared about the towel," I said. I could feel nerves tugging at my insides. I was running out of time. "I care about that PC Box."

"That's some messed up sh—uh, business." Jesus raised his eyebrows and swiped a hand across his forehead.

I wondered if he'd been in that barn turning too much water into wine. Maybe Jack had been in there with him. "Are they going to do something about it?" I asked, hoping I could shake him before we got to the sanctuary. I wanted to get on my detective way.

"What're they supposed to do?"

"Search the camp? Appeal to the goodwill of kidkind? Interrogate campers, cabin by cabin, with bamboo up the fingernails? Crucify someone?" My helpless fury stirred. "I don't know. *Something.*"

The camp had managed to provide me with a Polo towel in order to conquer such evil as magic, but they had no plan for the evil of stealing. And, as always, Jesus was some white dude. The hypocrisy confounded me.

"Look, it's going to be okay."

I shook my head, defeated. He didn't understand, and it was clear I wasn't going to be able to go anywhere tonight without this character.

"Everything happens for a reason."

Oh, gawd. Not that platitude. Hypocrisy *and* naïveté. The reason bad things happened was that people were bad.

"Besides. It ain't so bad. John 1:9, Nick."

Hillbilly Jesus quoting the Bible. Whoa. Actual whoa. Too bad I had no idea what he was talking about.

We were halfway across camp when the doors to the sanctuary burst open and all the campers poured out of it. Some bass pumped through the speakers and out the door, but I couldn't tell what song was being bastardized this time. The campers were in pairs and groups, and I could hear them laughing and singing.

Maybe they'd found the box. I quickened my step, leaving Jesus to clean up after the humans and the asses.

♦

Matthew was nowhere to be found. Natalie was still AWOL. Everyone was forming groups and sitting in circles on the well-lit patio, Bibles and notepads open on their laps. Holly was the last person to come out of the sanctuary. She somehow didn't look like the girl I'd seen at the pool that afternoon. She was smaller somehow, chin lower, eyes downcast. It didn't take away from how sexy she was though.

Bold as it was to approach Red Lips, something about Matthew's rumor report at the pool that afternoon made me feel like I could. If she'd Netflix-and-chilled with every other guy, she could talk to me, right? "What's going on?" I asked her.

"Nothing. How're you?"

"No, like, what are we supposed to be doing now?"

"Oh." She looked around. "I don't know. I was in the bathroom." She sounded different than she had on the bus. Different than at the pool.

That's what it was: she sounded real. No Pampers/campers rhymes. No lipstick. She was shell-shocked, like the rest of us. The disappearance of the box had knocked us all down a peg, I guess.

"Are you okay?" I asked.

"I just. You know. What people could say." She looked back at the sanctuary door. "What people *do* say."

I thought of how Matthew had described her. I wondered if it annoyed her. But she had to know what it looked like, the way she dressed, those red lips.

"Maybe—I mean, probably—I need to just pray about it," she said, and she sounded sincere.

"Where've you been?" someone asked from behind me.

Holly looked up, and I turned to find Payton. I remembered the way he had glared at me on the bus. Oh no.

We answered simultaneously:

"Barn."

"Bathroom."

"Together?" The WTF on his face made the reason for the question clear. But it was a stupid one anyway. Obviously barn and bathroom meant we were not together.

"I was looking for you," Payton said to Holly. "We're supposed to be in groups."

Holly's demeanor changed back to Red Lips from the bus. She crossed her arms and stepped a little closer to me. Double down on the *Oh no.*

Step away from the nerdy kid, Ho-Lo, I wanted to say. I like chess—not that I'm going to tell anyone that—but please don't make me your pawn in this game with Payton.

Saved by the Goth. Stewart walked over. "Anyone see Natalie?"

I said nothing. I was standing in the middle of a romantic showdown of some kind between Payton and Holly, and Natalie may or may not have been scaling a dusty cliff, and I didn't want any part of it.

Goth led the three of us to the group of kids from our bus: brother and sister (Chris and Christina, Christastic!), Wheelchair Girl, and Nose-Picker.

"We were just debriefing about what happened tonight," Goth informed us.

"What are they going to do about it?" I jumped in.

"What do you mean, what are they going to do about it?" Goth asked, crossing his arms over his chest.

Clearly he'd misunderstood my tone. "No, I mean, I *want* them to do something about it. That's what I'm saying. I'm *keenly* interested in their plans."

The group eyed me.

I said, "Look, are we going to look for the box, or are we going to interview people, or what?"

"That's what the pastor is working on. We can only control what we can control." Goth sounded like the counselor my parents sent me to. "Let's talk about how we're feeling. How are we doing right now?" So, so counselor-y.

And so that's what we did. For about thirty minutes. Chris. Christina. Nose-Picker. Goth. Holly. Payton. Everyone's feelings, not surprisingly, could be summarized this way: super-duper-Chris-tastically pissed and scared.

I wanted to punch a wall, sitting there. It was like counseling all over. But it was so stupid. I'd done this all before, and here's what I knew: Talking about feelings doesn't change anything. It doesn't change your sisters, and it doesn't change your parents, and it doesn't change anything that's happened in a family. It doesn't change the weight of your parents' marriage on your shoulders.

But my confession, so recklessly stuffed into a box that was now missing, could change what remained of my family.

I had to find that box.

Just as I moved to get up, Goth knelt in front of Wheelchair Girl. I'd forgotten about her. I assumed she hadn't written a confession. I hadn't seen her write one, and I didn't know if she could. She hadn't spoken. From what I could tell, she communicated with her eyes. "Monica," he said, and touched her arm. Goth asked her yes/no questions, and her eyes moved right for yes, left for no. Yes, she was having fun. No, she was not sad. No, she was not scared.

I envied this girl one thing. And it was that. She was not sad, and she was not scared.

I was both of those things. All the gawddamn time.

And then Natalie appeared, joining the group with her light step. And, of course, a book in her hand. "Sorry. I'm really sorry. I had to get out of there after that debacle. I did some praying. And I really think it's going to be okay." She sat next to Nose-Picker and gave her a side hug.

They all did the hug thing. I did not. I watched Natalie. I looked for signs of dust on her knees, on her shoes. I didn't buy her story about needing to pray.

"I really do think it's going to be okay," she repeated. "Not just for me. For everybody here."

"Well, praise Jesus, then, right?" And just like that, Holly turned on the super chipper voice I'd heard her use on the bus.

It seemed our debriefing was officially over. Natalie spotted Pastor Kyle and headed his way. Goth sat quietly by the girl in the wheelchair. The kid he was hanging out with by the pool earlier came over and sat by them. Payton wandered over to another group, but he kept his eye on ours. Well, on Holly.

Holly glanced at him.

"Is that your boyfriend?" I asked her.

"No." Then, quite loudly, "He's my *ex*-boyfriend."

"Are we praising Jesus for that?" I asked. "T-G-I-J and all that?"

She kind of laughed. The smile on her face seemed honest again. She was pretty in that moment. Pretty in the way being *real* makes someone pretty.

She flipped her notebook closed, and I noticed the guitar design on the front.

"Do you play the guitar?" I asked.

She considered me. Then, "Um, yes."

"You do?"

"What, is that hard to believe?" she asked, still smiling.

"Are you, like, in a band and stuff?"

She blushed and looked away. "I wouldn't call it a band. I play with a couple of people, yeah. If we had a drummer, we might be a band."

"That's so cool." It *was* cool, and it made her even hotter. She had the perfect body, *and* she played an instrument.

She rolled her eyes, "Yeah, well," she said, dismissively, but she was smiling. "I play mostly by myself. I actually like to write songs too," she continued, "but I've never really tried to sing any of them. I don't sing. Like, really don't sing. But, I think—" And then she stopped.

I turned to see what she'd seen. Payton. Her eyes darkened for just a split second before she asked, "Do you want to pray with me?"

She and I hadn't moved. We still sat cross-legged on the ground while the others milled about. I started to decline, but she grabbed my hand. "Lord, Your power is so great, so grand, and so big. So, so big." She talked too loudly. She definitely wanted everyone (especially those with broken appendages) to hear. Her other handed rested on my thigh. "We are just so blessed. Thank you for bringing Nick to camp, Jesus. Funny Nick." She held my hand quite tightly. The other one brushed my shorts against my leg. "Thank You for breakups and the rough roads and the hardships. All the hard, *hard* things." Her hands squeezed the parts of me she touched. "In Your name, Amen."

She opened her eyes, and they flashed golden mischief. Shit. I was waxing poetic.

"A—" I croaked. Jesus. My voice hadn't cracked since eighth grade. "Amen."

Holly looked back at Payton, and smiled even more triumphantly. Then she stood up, brushed off her shorts, and walked off toward some other group.

I stayed where I was, abandoned to think about big and stiff and firm and hard, and her hand making it so. I could not move.

Natalie was staring at me, and her wry smile was growing. Now we'd both seen something we didn't want the other to see. I'd seen her leave the building, and she'd seen the effect a hot girl's hand has on a virgin grammar nerd, known as Turwaithion to his Elvish buddies.

"Do you need a book?" she said, holding one up. "You know, for your lap?"

"Where'd you go tonight?"

She narrowed her eyes, a touch of her smile remaining. "Why are you asking?"

"Because I saw you leave."

She laughed.

I continued, "Why did you leave right after the box was stolen?"

She bent over in laughter. People were watching. "Wait, are you interrogating me?"

"No, I'm just asking."

"Is it weird that I'm flattered by your suspicion?"

"Uh, yeah."

"What's my motive?"

"I have no idea."

"You're a terrible detective, Nick." She explained, "The motive is the path to reasonable suspects."

"So what's your motive?"

"You're so bad at this!" She laughed some more. "I need to marginalize some Sherlock Holmes for you."

She was right; I did need that book. Thankfully I no longer needed it to cover my lap, but I did need some crime-solving mentorship. "Look," I said, "it's just that I didn't even want to put my confession in that box, and now it's gone."

"Then why did you do it?"

Because of you, I wanted to say. Her bright eyes. The eager way she'd called over Jesus and the box. The way she danced to the songs. The way she believed in it all. "Because everyone else was," I said, immediately regretting it. "And yes, I jump off bridges when my friends do."

She laughed. "I'm going to tell you a secret, even though you are the worst interrogator on this planet."

"Okay."

"I just got accepted to City School. Have you heard of it?"

"No."

"Okay, well, it's a public school, but you have to apply, and you have to sign a contract and stuff." It surprised me that she would switch from a private school to a public school. "It's a school of the arts."

"Oh, you're into the arts?"

"Well, yeah, like design. I want to go to Rhode Island School of Design. Have you heard of that?"

"No."

"That's right, you're about grammar." She smiled. "I want to do some kind of design with books. Like covers or something."

"Or marginalizing."

"Exactly." She laughed, and then it died away. "Anyway, I have a confession in that box that violates that contract."

"Why are you telling me this?"

She sighed. "Because you're not the only one with something to lose."

My turn to sigh.

I appreciated the fact she was trying to make me feel better, but she didn't know.

Later that night, as I was walking back to the cabins, I thought about what I could lose. What she could lose. She was worried about school, but there were lots of schools. This confession was about my family. You only get one.

And then I realized, Natalie may have told me a "secret," but she still hadn't told where she'd gone that night.

And there was no doubt in my mind she'd done that on purpose.

Gawd, I really was a terrible detective.

◆

Back at the cabin, Matthew and I found everyone except Charles sitting around in a circle. Jeez, this camp had a lot of sitting around in circles.

But this circle was a little different. Donkey Lottery Winner Chris and Goth sat in the center, both with their fingertips resting on the plastic planchette of a Ouija board.

I had been hoping Payton wouldn't be in the cabin yet, but he was there, all flared nostrils, pursed lips, and dropped brow line. I wanted to say, *Mr. Neanderthal, talk to your girlfriend—ex-girlfriend.* But he could probably kick my ass even with a broken arm, so instead I inquired about the "demon worship" going on center-cabin.

"It's the Holy Ghost we're after here," Chris explained.

"It *is* the Holy Ghost. It already said it was," Payton barked.

"How old are you?" Chris asked the board.

I watched, but nothing happened. So I went over to my cubby and grabbed my toothpaste.

"Holy shit," someone said.

"Holy Ghost, you asshole," someone else said back, laughing.

I looked over and saw Chris's and Goth's hands moving with the planchette.

"It's just going in circles," Payton said. "You guys are pushing it."

"No, it keeps going back to the A and then the Z," Matthew said.

I watched as my bunk mates theorized.

"A-Z."

"Azzz . . ."

"What starts with A-Z?"

"From A to Z?"

"Infinity," I interrupted.

"Yeah, A to Z. The whole alphabet. Infinity," Matthew confirmed.

"No," I said. "The thing is making the infinity sign. Watch it move." I pointed.

Silent, we watched the ivory-colored game piece move around

and swoop down and to the right, around and down and to the left. A sideways eight over and over.

Goth pulled his hand back, and the planchette stopped moving immediately. "No way," he said.

"Ask it something else," Chris said.

Matthew sat next to Chris and put his fingers on the planchette. "Is there a God?" Matthew asked.

"Whoa, right off like that?" Payton said.

"What's it gonna say?" I jested. "It's the Holy Ghost. It has to say yes, or it has no credibility."

And, indeed, it said yes.

Then it spelled out "A-L-L H-O-L-Y."

"All holy?" Chris asked.

The planchette moved on. We watched as the letters spelled out "E-V-E-R-Y-T-H-I-N-G."

"What an existential game," Charles mumbled from his bunk. He looked like he'd been crying. What had he written in his confession?

"Fine," Chris said. "When am I gonna die?"

"Shit, you guys are not messing around," Payton said.

The planchette slid across the board to land on the eight. Then it crept in small circles for a moment before sliding back to the two.

"Eighty-two. Not bad," Chris said.

Payton shouldered Matthew out of the way and took a seat next to Chris.

He placed his two fingers on the planchette with Chris's. "What's your name?"

"Holy Ghost doesn't need a name," Chris chastised.

But the planchette moved. "J-"

"E-"

"A-"

"N-"

"Jean?"

"The Holy Ghost is a girl?"

"It's obviously not the Holy Ghost, dumbass. I mean, *Jean*? That's not even biblical."

"It is now."

The planchette continued to move.

L-O-U-I-S. My face got warmer with every letter.

"Louis? Do we have two ghosts? Jean and Louis?"

What we had was a French-Canadian dead man.

The planchette was moving to No.

"This is dumb," I said. "Ask a new question." I could not let the board reach the last name, a name most of the guys probably would recognize, even if they hadn't read his books.

K-

E-

R-

"Ask a new question," I said, a little too loudly.

O-

"Like what?" Chris asked.

U-

It was still moving, but they couldn't keep track of the letters if I kept talking.

"Like anything that's not boring, like a name. Like who cares about the ghosts' names? Obviously we have a man and a woman."

The planchette stopped.

"Okay," Chris said, his tone serious. "Tell us a secret."

"Not that," I said in a panic. I had to stop Jack from answering that. "I mean, you can just get those in the PC Box."

Damn it. Why did I always keep talking way past the time for shutting up?

Heads whipped in my direction faster than if I'd admitted to tossing puppies in a blender.

"Do you know where it is?" Charles asked, upright in his bunk now.

"I'm joking, for God's sake." But they kept staring. "Keep going."

Chris cleared his throat. "Tell us a secret," he said again. Matthew looked around at the group. The planchette didn't move. And then it did.

It started out doing the infinity sign and then it stopped on S.

"This better not be about me," Goth said. I was confused till I remembered his real name: Stewart.

The planchette moved to the I.

S-

It landed on the T.

I took a step back.

E-

R.

It stopped.

"Seriously. This isn't helping," I said, making sure not to look anyone in the eye as I grabbed my toothbrush.

In the bathroom, I brushed and brushed and brushed. I stared at my complexion in the mirror: the purple half moons under my eyes, the way the fluorescent lights pierced the skin and revealed everything underneath—the blood, the bone, the grief, the guilt.

Is this what confession felt like? I didn't want people to know what I stored in the dark parts of my psyche. I did not want lanterns and headlamps searching in there for the hidden things.

The door swung open, and I spit my toothpaste into the sink. "What's wrong?" Matthew said.

"Nothing. Just tired."

Matthew eyed me.

"You guys done out there?" I asked, nonchalant.

"Must be you," he said.

"What?"

"Nobody else out there knows anything about a sister."

"Well, Chris might. His sister was pretty pissed when he won the Donkey Lottery on the bus." Matthew leaned against the wall while I rinsed my toothbrush. "Do you seriously think the Holy

Ghost hangs out on the Ouija board, whispering secrets like some middle school girl at a slumber party?" I said.

"No. But you're the one who snuck away at the mention of a sister."

I rinsed my mouth out, my teeth more than clean, my gums brushed raw.

"And, dude, you're awfully defensive," he added.

I sighed. "It's not really a secret."

Matthew waited.

"Just nobody here knows."

"Knows what?"

"My sister died. That's the thing. That's why I'm here."

"Because your sister died?"

"Pretty much. My parents thought this would be better than mourning at home because that's just awkward. All that silence and tears."

Matthew squinted at me for a beat, then grinned. "Yeah, I hate it when people act all sad when someone dies."

We both laughed.

Matthew brushed his teeth while I took a pee. When I came out to wash my hands, he was done and sitting on the counter waiting for me. "Do you really think that was the Holy Ghost?"

Obviously, I didn't. "I don't know," I said.

"It said it was."

"Yeah, but then it said Jean and Louis," I said, careful to make it two separate entities, careful to mispronounce the names into ugly hard English consonants and sharp vowels. Even though no one could Google it on their phones while we were here anyway.

"That plastic thing really moved under my hand."

"I believe you."

"It spelled out *sister* when I asked for a secret." Matthew looked legitimately shaken.

"Pretty much any noun could've led to some secret," I explained.

But obviously Jack had picked just the right word for me. I put my toothbrush up in my cubby. "But, listen, I really don't want to talk about my sister, okay? So . . ."

"Yeah, I get it," he said. "It's private."

"Well, it *was*," I said. I imagined for a moment the scene—me, my mom, my dad, Pastor Kyle, the truth. I felt the pang as though it were already happening.

♦

When Matthew and I emerged from the bathroom, the Ouija board was gone, but the group was still in a circle, and our counselor Dan had joined them. Dan was a college kid who also, as the brochure promised, was a specimen of orangish-tanned, bleach-white, four-hours-per-day-in-the-gym perfection. The unfairness of it all. Perfect godly lives. Perfect football champions. Perfect complexions. And then there was me—nerdy blaspheme.

I hated Dan.

Especially when he told us to sit down.

In something called a "Trust Circle."

"What happens in the cabin stays in the cabin," Dan said, as if strippers, shots of tequila, and lucrative poker games were imminent.

He summed up the story of Jesus and then demanded that we share our own anecdotes of mischief, like the pastor had done during his sermon.

Were we really doing this right after the PC Box got stolen?

Apparently so.

Charles: didn't do the dishes once when his mom asked.

Matthew: lied to his girlfriend. (*Lied next to her, if you know what I mean*, he said to me later. *Lay*, I corrected. *I know*, he said, *but bad grammar is part of the punch line.*)

Stewart, a.k.a. Goth: had fallen in love and gone out on a secret date.

I got the distinct impression no one was totally trusting the Trust Circle, because these stories were lame. But who would? The worst of our truths were out there somewhere with someone of questionable intent.

"What about you, Nick?" Dan asked.

I looked at Matthew. Did he tell Dan about my sister being dead? It wasn't a secret, but I'd said I didn't want to talk about it. And I certainly wasn't going to share that in the Trust Circle.

I thought of one of the nights Jack and I stayed up too late, one of the nights he actually made me laugh instead of making me mad. The night he told me he'd lost his virginity to a prostitute.

"I drank beer a couple weeks ago," I admitted. "I snuck it into my room."

Charles nodded, his suspicions confirmed.

Payton perked. "I got shit-faced a couple weeks ago too."

Charles gasped. Dan *tsk-tsk*ed.

"I didn't get shit-faced," I clarified.

"Language," Dan snapped at me.

Really?

"Oh, because you're better than me?" Payton glared at me.

"No, I just wanted to clarify."

"Just admit it. You think you're better than me. I saw you out there with Holly."

"Wha—" I started.

"Okay, let's pray," Dan said. He did. We did. Or, at least we all bowed our heads and closed our eyes. I closed one eye, lest Payton attack. "Now, speaking of doing bad things . . ."

I eyed Dan—with both eyes now—finding his segue odd for Jesus camp.

"We've got some pranks to pull, gentlemen. As most of you know."

Matthew nodded vigorously and leaned in.

Charles left the Trust Circle and climbed into his bed. "This is when I go back to my workbook."

"We know," Dan said, rolling his eyes. "Nerd," he added under his breath.

"Okay, Nick," Dan said. I was the only kid new to Dan's cabin. "This is a Christian camp. But it's still a summer camp. Thus, pranks must ensue. There are some rules to these camp pranks, however." Dan looked around. "Gentlemen?"

The other eight campers recited the rules:

"We will not physically or emotionally hurt anyone.

"We will not spend too much money on any one prank.

"We will not damage the camp property or the property of others.

"We will not harm children or puppies, but rodents might suffer.

"We will not overshadow the purpose of our time here, which is to worship our Lord Jesus."

"Good. So, tonight I've got a new one for us. The Garbage Can Cleanup."

We all changed into black clothing, which apparently had been on the camp packing list for glow-in-the-dark mazes and Frisbee golf, or something, but Dan had also employed them annually for his cabin's pranks. He'd been doing this for three years.

As he explained the tradition, I suddenly realized I'd actually been blessed to have this asshole as my counselor. He was giving me direct permission to be out and about, all over the camp, under the cover of darkness.

I didn't care about the pranks. I cared about finding that box.

In the dining hall, we snagged three garbage cans. Then Dan led us to the amphitheater, where we found two more. Two more in the sanctuary. I made a mental note of nooks and crannies to search later.

By the time we slid through the dark space behind the cabins, all nine of us had garbage cans.

"We need buckets," Dan whispered. "Nick, follow me." We

snuck along the side of the sanctuary, through a door, down a hall. We opened one door, but Dan closed it fast. "Backstage." He went to the next. It opened into a small office. Shelves, a desk, boxes.

"Is this the pastor's office?" I asked, my heart beating wildly. Breaking into the pastor's office seemed like a capital offense.

"Custodian's, you idiot." He sighed. "Grab the buckets."

So, this was Jesus's domain. Well, when he was less the scrub-your-feet guy and more the scrub-your-toilets guy.

I grabbed the bucket by the door. I didn't see *buckets*, plural.

"That one," Dan growled, pointing to one half-hidden behind the custodian's apron, or jacket, or whatever. I fumbled with the bucket handle and we slipped back out the door, down the hall, through another door, and along the side of the sanctuary.

I noted more rooms, more corners to investigate. And then I saw it, in the corner, like a moth. A small, white, fluttery piece of paper. I dropped to my knee and pretended to tie my shoe. Dan spun. "Hurry up, newb." When he turned back around, I snatched the paper off the ground and slipped it into my pocket. I couldn't read it now. Maybe it was nothing but a phone number or a Bible verse, but it looked a whole lot like the papers I had seen people slip into the PC Box over and over that afternoon.

After rejoining the group, Dan led us to the far end of the campgrounds. There was a small building with a spigot. We filled the buckets with water as fast as possible, then dumped them in the garbage cans until each was three-quarters full. I kept checking my pocket to make sure the paper hadn't wiggled out. Dan chose nine cabins at random, and we rolled the garbage cans to the doors, then leaned them there to wait for morning.

Our cabin was on an upper floor, and so were half the other campers'. They would be very happy in the morning that they had to trudge up and down stairs each and every day, because it spared them from our prank. Those garbage cans were just too heavy to carry up the stairs.

Finally, we snuck back to our cabin and closed the door. We didn't turn on any lights. We followed the beams of small flashlights throughout the cabin and kept the curtains closed. If anyone spotted the tiny lights moving, they would assume people were just going to the bathroom.

I slipped out of my shorts and tucked the paper under my pillow.

Matthew leaned over the side of the bunk. "Dan's been doing this for years, and he's never been caught."

I feigned interest and crawled into my bunk. Under my blanket, aided by my own small flashlight, I unfolded the paper and read.

I realized quickly that what was written there had never been intended for someone else's eyes. It was not a number, or a Bible quote. It was simply this: *My uncle molested me. I think I'm going to tell.*

Holy crap. This wasn't some girl drama that had campers crying and hugging and hoping they hadn't included names. This was real. And it had been floating around in the hallway.

I doubted some camper had just missed the hole on the top of the box when they dropped this in. And slips of paper didn't just fall out of slots like the one the confessions had been dropped into. That box had been opened, that's for sure, or that paper wouldn't have been on the ground. Maybe this secret had blown out when the box was opened. Or maybe the papers had been moved from the box to a different receptacle.

But that box had been opened. And whoever opened it was reading those secrets.

Someone was *reading* our secrets.

I clicked the flashlight off and slipped the confession under my pillow. That little paper had been in the hall outside the sanctuary. Lots of people traveled that hall because it linked the sanctuary to the camp offices, but the closest office was the custodian's.

I thought of Jesus, who had been out by the barn when everyone else had been praying and crying and hugging one another. He'd said he'd been feeding the donkeys, but I didn't remember seeing any hay on him. Of course, I didn't remember *not* seeing any hay on him.

I tried to remember the conversation, if he'd said anything odd. He'd told me it'd all be okay; he'd quoted the Bible. John 1:9.

But Natalie had been out that night too, and she hadn't told me where she'd gone. She'd said she had a secret in that box, but she'd also urged me to put my secret in that box three times earlier the same day. Three times. Like a holy trinity.

And then there was Dan. Matthew had just said he was a master at sneaking around, never been caught. And the dude was an unrelenting prick. But nasty enough to steal people's prayers and confessions?

I needed motives. All I could see was opportunity. A real detective would know motive was more important.

I needed to get into the sanctuary. I needed to read the Bible. And I needed to get into the girls' cabins, but not for reasons Jack Kerouac would like.

♦

In the middle of the night, I stumbled across our already-messy cabin floor to the bathroom. The light automatically clicked on when the door swung open, the fluorescents blinding. I squinted and pushed open a stall door.

"What the hell?"

Jack was sitting on the toilet, painting the wall, his antiquated suitcase tucked between his legs.

"Hello, Nicolas," he said, not looking at me. There was a half bottle of some white liquor at his feet. The cap lay next to it.

"You need to leave." I reached for the bottle, to get the cap on it and throw it away before someone saw it, but my hand slipped right through it.

"Why did you do that on the Ouija board?"

He ignored me.

"For God's sake, I put the paper in the box. I did what you said. And now it's gone. And you're still stalking me?"

He looked at me then, shook his head, and went back to painting.

"Ugh," I sighed as I let the stall close behind me. I stood at the urinal. "Jean-Louis," I mumbled, murdering the French accent all over his name.

When I turned back around, I couldn't hear anything or see his feet under the stall door. But when I pushed it open, he was still there.

I leaned in to get a look at what he was creating. It was a red and black, very sharp, very gory depiction of the crucifixion of Jesus.

"What is wrong with you?"

"I'm Catholic," he said, and then he let out a short, bitter laugh.

TUESDAY

◆

Our first alarm the next morning was Dan. Six a.m. "Going for a run! Who's going with me?"

Mumbles, grumbles, heads under pillows.

"Athleticness is next to godliness!" he shouted.

"Athleticism," I mumbled.

"You're the one who wanted the wake-up call," he said right in my ear. I swore I heard him call me a douche before walking out the door.

My head throbbed thanks to Jack, who had left me wondering late into the night what it would take to get him to leave me alone for good.

Dan shouted one more time outside my window, but I rolled over and went back to sleep.

The next alarm was the first scream. I opened my eyes. Matthew was scrambling to the door. Chris behind him.

Crap. I'd meant to get up with Dan so that I could check out the sanctuary before the first sermon. Now I'd have to sneak around after breakfast.

I heard another scream. I sat up while my cabinmates laughed. Guffawed, really, till they lost their breath with it.

I rolled out of bed and walked out onto our deck. Matthew leaned over the railing. Charles hung back, lips pursed.

"Yessss!" Matthew said as a garbage can of water fell inside the Zion Cabin to our right. No screams, just expletives from the boys.

"This is your handiwork?" Charles asked me.

"Well, Dan gets the credit," I said.

"This does not glorify the Lord."

"Charles," Matthew said, "if you have an issue with it, why do you keep signing up for Cabin D? Cabin Dan? Cabin Of-the-Devil?"

Charles shook his head and walked back inside, the slamming of the cabin door punctuated by a third scream.

Matthew and I stood at the deck and enjoyed six more screams and ensuing expletives. For a minute, I considered telling him about the confession I'd found the night before. The guy was smart; maybe he could help. But something held me back.

I thought about Holly, how he'd made jokes and told me things and I'd laughed and played along. Was it the same thing? Maybe I didn't want Matthew to know I had a secret.

There was that feeling about Charlotte again. And Diana was right there too. She wasn't like Holly and Charlotte. She'd dated some, but she only loved Leah. And that was enough for people to pay too much attention.

Diana had gone out on a date one time in high school. She'd tried to pass it off like she and the other girl were friends, but someone had seen them kissing. It wasn't even like Charlotte and Holly. It was just a kiss, and she hadn't meant for that secret to get out there, either. But everyone had talked about it, and it had caused giggles and scrutiny and worse.

I knew about the gossip because Diana had gotten beaten up so badly for it. I had still been a little kid, and her face had been so swollen she'd looked like a monster. I was afraid of her. She was bruised and broken because her whole being couldn't fit in the world's small box.

No, I couldn't tell Matthew about the confession I'd found. I knew what would happen to my family if my parents found out about what I'd written. I could only imagine what would happen to this kid's family if they found out about this uncle. It was up to that kid if they would eventually confess. That was their truth to set free or to tame.

We headed to the showers, and on my way I checked the bathroom stall. Jack had responsibly cleaned up his ode to the Renaissance.

By the time we were ready to head to the cafeteria, Charles was fully absorbed in his math workbook. We waited for him to find a derivative, and then we left, Charles a few steps behind.

As we walked into breakfast, the counselors were singing Vanilla Ice's "Ice Ice Baby." Or rather, "Christ Christ Baby."

Dan served us eggs and bacon. Counselors all around the room served their campers—if I remember correctly from the brochure, it was something about demonstrating servitude. Dan's face was all scrunched up in disdain. I hope Jesus hadn't made that face at the Last Supper.

As he poured our orange juice, Dan asked, "Where's Stewart?"

Payton pointed. Goth was sitting next to that same guy and Wheelchair Girl.

"Stewart, your love triangle can wait!" Dan shouted across the dining hall. "Dude, I thought he and Nick broke up."

I about choked on my orange juice. "He's gay?"

"Gay as the day is long," Dan said. "Why, you got a crush?"

"No, I'm just—"

"Tongue-tied with desire?"

Goth meandered over, and I stared till he was in his chair.

I looked around the table, at all the guys just chewing their food, not one of them bearing stones or torches or pitchforks or other implements of the riot before the exile. I had no problem with him being gay. I was just shocked nobody else seemed to have a problem with it. I was at Jesus camp, after all. The very one that converted Charlotte, the Queen of Homophobelandia. So I had pretty much just assumed that Eden Springs would be filled with more Royalty of Judgment.

I was genuinely shocked, but in a good way. Like the universe just got a little bigger and warmer. I didn't know how to explain that, so I finally said, "I was just curious."

"Bi-curious?" Matthew laughed.

Dan didn't seem to get Matthew's joke. He had his own. "You heard about the cat that died of that?" Dan said. "Curiosity killed the cat?"

I didn't look at him. I just chewed my food. "Curiosity's not a disease," I mumbled, my mouth full of egg casserole. "It's not malaria."

"So be it. It's a fatal car crash. A school shooting."

The flame of hope I'd just felt flickered. He really was an asshat. A racist, misogynist asshat with decent pranks and my key to searching the campus. He turned around and said something to one of the girls in too-short cutoffs. Then, back to us, "All right, you pansies! We got our schedule for the week. We've got crafts in fifteen. Ropes tomorrow." And the next part he whispered, "And dirty work every night."

My cabinmates stood up. I stayed seated. Matthew sat back down next to me. "He's a douche. Dan the douche."

"I was just asking," I said.

"Which is as deadly as a zealous antiabortionist. Stop doing dangerous things, Nick. Questions bad. Curiosity bad. Only happiness happens here!"

I laughed.

"Okay, let's go craft!" he added.

I started after him, then remembered my morning mission. "I have to go do something really quick," I said.

"Do something?" He looked around us in a wide, dramatic circle. "Oh, I didn't see Holly here this morning."

I had to think about that for a second. "Wow."

"I know, dude. That's what she's gonna say when she sees your tiny manhood."

He turned around and skipped away, laughing.

He would make Kerouac proud on so many levels.

◆

I pushed the sanctuary door open. The dark and the AC cooled me off. The door closed behind me, and I couldn't see anything. I waited for my eyes to adjust for a moment.

It didn't take long for the stage to take shape down front, a sliver of light from behind a curtain illuminating it. This is where Pastor Kyle had expected to see the PC Box last night. It had obviously traveled down the hall after being stolen and opened. I would start in the sanctuary and move backward.

I walked down the aisle to get a closer look around the stage. The box wasn't off to the side or on the ground in front. Not that I really expected it to be. But wouldn't that be a prank of sorts? Just steal the box for the night, freak everybody out, then put it back. But no. If that confession had fallen out of it, that meant the box was definitely opened.

Shuffling from backstage startled me.

"Hello?" I waited.

Nothing.

"Jack?" I asked, a little quieter.

I looked up and behind me into the sound booth to make sure no one was there before making my way around the stage and up the stairs. I wasn't really doing anything wrong, but this is what empty rooms do to me. Even if a teacher hands me her keys to get something from her classroom, I'll unlock the door and step in, and there will be this tingle of nerves, of guilt. The silence, the darkness, the lack of witnesses. It's the temptation to be tempted. Like standing on a cliff and wanting to jump.

My footsteps echoed as I made my way to the closed curtains. I peered between them to glance backstage.

"Hello?"

Still nothing.

I pushed the heavy fabric aside and slipped through.

I walked behind a screen. Looked on shelves. The door that led to the hallway where Dan and I had been the night before was propped open with a bucket.

Disappointed I hadn't found the box, I walked through the curtain and back onto the stage.

"Hey, you're not supposed to be in here," an older kid called out from the back of the auditorium. As he walked closer, I saw his counselor badge.

"I was just doing some prayer stuff."

"In the sanctuary?" The kid said as if this was baffling. "It's for skits."

The irony was not lost on me. "I know. I just—"

"Where are you supposed to be?"

"I'm on my way to crafts."

"Crafts are outside."

"I know. I just—"

"Who's your counselor?"

Please don't get him involved. "Dan."

"What's your name?"

"Nick."

"So, listen, buddy. Nick—" He stopped and his mouth dropped open. "Oh . . . Nick."

"Yeah . . . ?"

"You're here for prayer?"

"Um, well—"

"For the devil-worshipping stuff."

Harry Potter again. "Is this about—"

"Listen, I can lay hands. I took a class."

Oh, hell no. I wasn't going to let him pray for me, let alone touch me while he did it. "I'm a verbal person, not kinesthetic," I said. "I learned that in class."

"I get it, I get it." But he stepped closer as he said this.

"No, seriously."

"Yes," he said and reached for me.

"I mean, no hands. I have a rash."

He stopped, hands in the air like a traffic cop. Breathing deeply, he reached for me again. "Jesus healed the lepers."

I stepped back. "You're not Jesus." Then, for good measure: "And I'm not a leper."

If the Harry Potter gossip had traveled that fast and turned into devil-worship, God only knows what would become of the leper comment.

"So, you don't want me to touch you?"

"Just pray for me from over there." I pointed to a corner. "I'll be back after crafts to let you know how it all turned out."

♦

I spotted Matthew easily enough and headed over for crafts. At the Creation Station. No, I'm not joking. That's what it was called. *The Creation Station.*

Crafts. Nobody does crafts, except kindergarten kids in colorful classrooms and kindergarten kids in church basements. But Eden Springs was bringing it back old-school—gangster rap and childhood experiences alike.

I could see as I walked over that our cabin had been paired with a cabin of girls, which made the whole crafting thing that much worse. Boys don't craft, and our incompetence is made ever more obvious when juxtaposed with girls—who do craft—crafting.

Matthew patted my stool. As soon as I settled in it, someone slid *The Grapes of Wrath* across the table. Natalie smirked at me. I hadn't even noticed her and another girl sitting there.

"Care to read?" she asked.

"Do I look like someone who would read during a riveting session of crafts?"

She read my Bad Grammar Makes Me [sic] T-shirt.

"Yes. Definitely yes."

Matthew looked at me. "Do you two know each other?"

"We're old dance partners," she said.

I flipped absentmindedly through the pages of the book. "And nightwalkers," I said, and made eye contact.

Natalie's smile disappeared and then reappeared. "Nick always needs a book when he prays. It makes him feel grounded."

Really? Matthew looked at me.

I shook my head.

"Sorry it's not Sir Arthur Conan Doyle or Agatha Christie," she added.

A counselor dropped large piles of clay in front of us, and everyone at my table got to work. I eyed Natalie for a bit. She was beautiful and happy this morning, not at all the aloof girl I had seen walk out of the sanctuary. She was the breezy girl who told everyone it would be okay even though our secrets were out, and sincerely meant it. The one who hugged the girl who picked her nose—All. The. Time. And she understood that we were sparring to see who'd tell the truth—the whole truth—first. But we'd have to continue later, sans audience.

I looked down in front of me, at the beige mass of what looked like Play-Doh.

Clay at the Creation Station.

"What am I supposed to do with this?" I asked. Recreate Adam and Eve? Remove ribs? Breathe life into little dolls?

"Kim, slide that over here," Matthew said to the other girl. It was a menu of clay-crafting options.

I read the list: plate, handprint (à la kindergarten), coffee mug, candleholder, and wait a minute—"An ashtray?"

"Just 'cause you smoke doesn't mean you're going to hell," Payton said, glaring at me.

"I thought the body was a temple?" I asked.

"Play nice, Nick," Natalie said.

"My grandfather smokes," Charles said.

"And you're worried about my beach towel?" I mumbled.

"Satan and smoking are very different things. My grandfather is a godly man." Charles grabbed his pile of clay and moved to a different table.

Natalie smiled at me. "I heard about you and the devil towel."

"Who hasn't?" I looked at the kids around me. "Here's what I don't get."

Matthew leaned in. Kim looked up from her mass of clay.

"First off, the girls and their bikinis are no problem, but my towel—which actually covers the body—is satanic. Second, just about every counselor serving food in the lunchroom is female. Has anyone noticed it's like 1950 here? And now it's cool again to smoke and James Dean is all that and all the hot housewives look like you?" I pointed to Natalie with that bandana in her hair.

"Wait, did you just point at me?" She smiled. "You think I'm hot?"

My face flushed, and I attempted to dig myself out of a pit of embarrassment. "All the girls serve us in the dining hall and poolside, like we're JFK and they're Marilyn Monroe about to sing us 'Happy Birthday' with their bathing costumes blowing in the wind, full ass exposed. And no one thinks this is odd?"

"You didn't answer the question about thinking I'm hot," Natalie said.

"And the gold chains and gangsta rap? Seems kind of racist," I continued.

"Last year, it was cowboy boots and country," Payton said.

Matthew smirked. "You sure had a lot to add to our MLK speech."

It was about boobs, not race, I almost said. Oh, gawd, was I just as bad? I looked down at my clay, formless and impotent.

"Make a handprint for your mom, Pampers," Matthew said. "It'll soothe the hypocrisy blues."

"You're just placated by bikinis." I decided on a candleholder, and stewed in my idiocy as I rolled my clay out flat, following the directions.

"So many bikinis, I'm easy to please," Matthew singsonged.

"Save your rhyming for the poetry session," I quipped.

My table laughed.

"Proverbs Slam is tonight," Matthew said.

"No effing way," I said.

"You're right," Matthew laughed. "No effing way."

Natalie beamed. "Oh my gosh, please can we start that?" I couldn't tell if she was even joking. She concentrated on her clay and massaged something to life.

That moment felt like an in with the table. Like maybe we could broach the subject and solution of our secrets. Surely they wanted to get to the bottom of this instead of twerking to rap-turned-gospel and kindergarten throwback time. "So, last night—" I started.

"Like Demi Moore, right?" Kim interrupted. She had wrapped her arms around Payton to help him sculpt despite the cast on his arm. "In *Ghost*. Have you seen that old movie?" Her lips were right by his neck.

At this point, nobody cared what I had to say. Even I barely cared. All eyes turned to watch the amateur porn going on across the table.

"I never saw that movie, but you make it sound good," Payton said, their hands working the clay. He caught me watching them and smirked. Then he looked around the crafting area, no doubt searching for Holly. He spotted her at the same time I did. She stood at the edge of the covered area, hands on her hips, watching it all.

Payton got up from his stool, but Holly marched over to our table.

"Oh, hey, Holly," Kim said sweetly. "Did you come to play?"

Holly rolled her eyes. "I don't even have my guitar."

Kim laughed. "That's not the kind of"—air quotes—"*playing* I was talking about."

Holly's mouth dropped open. Before she could say anything, Payton took her by the arm and led her away. As they got farther away, I could see her hands whipping through the air while she talked. I didn't know if she was crying or yelling.

"I can't believe she still even comes here," Kim said, sitting back in her stool. "Whatever. Jesus loved the whores too."

Matthew laughed. "Are you talking about you or Ho-Lo?"

Kim glared. "Duh, who do you think?"

I squinted at her. She was the one who'd just made a (sex) scene at the crafting station, and she was making a crack about Holly?

Natalie sat watching the scene, then looked down at her clay project.

I wasn't about to step in. I didn't know these people, and I definitely didn't want to be a part of this. So I changed the subject. "Did your cabin get hit last night?" I asked, careful that I didn't look guilty. "You know, with the pranks?"

Natalie shook her head extra hard, like she was clearing it of the Kim ugliness at the same time she was answering my question. "No. We're on the second floor. Only the first floor got it."

"Oh," I said, and my voice cracked. I am no better a liar than I am a detective.

"This looks like a pile of shit," Matthew said, staring at his project, and thankfully changing the subject yet again.

Charles gasped from the neighboring table.

"That's the point, isn't it?" Natalie said.

"'Pile of Shit' is not on the list of options," Matthew said, holding out the menu of craft choices.

"Everything we touch turns to shit," Natalie said.

She had no idea.

"I think that's the point," she added. "Of this whole Creation Station business. Like, God can create the real stuff. You and me, if we try to do it alone, it's going to turn out like . . . well, like your pile of shit."

"You people and your overthinking things," Matthew said. " I'm just bad at crafts."

We worked our clay a little longer.

"I'm out," Matthew dropped his clay on the table. "I'm going to weave some socks out of grass." He walked over to a station where, in fact, grass-weaving was taking place.

"I don't think you can really make socks there," Natalie said to me. "Place mats, yes, but socks seems a bit far-fetched."

After a while, Payton returned to our table, shoulders slumped. Kim watched him, but he didn't look up. He mumbled something and took his clay over to Charles's table.

"I do like your outfit," I said to Natalie, trying to cover up the earlier awkwardness, the public announcement about her hotness. "How you look like you stepped right out of that World War II 'We Want You' poster."

"Wait. I look like the old guy with the pointy beard and accusing finger?" Natalie asked.

"No, you know. The one with the lady flexing her biceps." I flexed my biceps. "'Yes, We Can!' That poster."

"'Yes, We Can'? That's Obama, Nick."

Kim laughed.

"I thought he said I was hot earlier," Natalie said to Kim. Then, to me, "I look like a black man with a pointy white beard? An Obama/ Uncle Sam mash-up."

"Obama's kind of hot," Kim said.

"Not with fluffy white hair, he wouldn't be," Natalie chastised.

I shook my head. "No, you know who I'm talking about. The one with the full red lips and dark hair all pulled up." I gestured toward Natalie's face. "And she has those cheekbones and bright eyes. And she's strong, but not masculine. Even though she's flexing, she's feminine. And she looks out at everyone all strong and dares you to do the thing . . ." I trailed off, noticing Kim and Payton watching me. "Whatever the thing is," I mumbled. "You want to do the thing."

Even drop your worst secret in a box, lest you disappoint the courageous girl hailing Jesus.

Silence as Natalie and Kim stared at the flush eating up my face.

Natalie smiled. "Her name's Rosie the Riveter."

I nodded. "Yeah. That one."

Natalie held up a clay piece. "I'm done." I recognized a frowning face molded there. "I made the drama faces." She held up another molded face, this time smiling.

"Are you in drama?" I asked.

She smiled. "Aren't we all?"

She kept looking at me, so I pretended to fix something in my candleholder-to-be. "I meant at school."

"No," she said, standing up. "No, I'm not." She picked up the two drama faces, one in each hand.

She and Kim stood up and walked away. Payton walked behind them. Kim called something over to him, but he just waved it away. Maybe she apologized. Or maybe she said another mean thing. Matthew sat down next to me again.

"We can put your candleholder on this." He held out a small square of unevenly woven straw.

"What happened to the sock idea?"

"This is it. It's a two-dimensional, sock-like mini place mat."

"It's not even shaped like a sock."

"Don't be so critical. Your candleholder looks more like the model of a vagina one might find in an anatomy classroom."

"They have models of vaginas at Valley Christian?"

"Or, look"—Matthew flipped the vagina-shaped candleholder upside down—"a penis."

"It's like a mood ring," Matthew said, flipping the clay back and forth, "but it's only got two moods. Penis . . ." Matthew flipped it over. "Vagina."

We headed over to the basketball courts.

"Kim and Natalie. Titillating and asstastic, respectively," he said, grabbing a ball.

I took the ball out of his hands and got lucky on a shot. Matthew watched the girls round the corner till they were out of sight. He wasn't Pastor-Kyle perfect, but he was tall, broad shouldered, and funny. I was sure he had no trouble with the "fine ladies."

I, on the other hand, couldn't say anything normal, as evidenced by the Crafting Station debacle. And I couldn't even get Leah to talk to me again—even though I wasn't interested in her the way I was interested in Natalie. I just wanted to apologize. Or something. I wanted to know she was still there.

"Kim's obviously into Payton, though." Matthew continued. "Fool's errand, that one. He'll never give up what Holly's puttin' out."

"I thought they broke up."

He scoffed.

"What about Natalie?"

"Natalie is not a slut."

"I didn't mean *that*."

"Oh . . . I see. Yeah. She's hot. Like, in a cool way." Matthew grabbed a basketball. "And smart." He laughed. "Yeah, I could see how you'd be into that. She's no doubt Ivy League-bound. Parents have tons of money, is what I heard. I think her brother's on a row team at the University of Washington or something."

I didn't correct him about the Ivy League thing, or tell him that she planned to attend RISD, the number two art school in the nation. "She doesn't act like a snob."

"Oh, no, I'm not saying that. I'm just saying. She's smart and rich and perhaps"—Matthew took a shot and it swished into the net—"out of your league."

Pretty much every girl was out of my league.

"I think I saw her walking up on the hill yesterday. It was weird." I didn't tell him it was right after the box was stolen.

"Yeah, dude. She's kinda weird. Does her own thing. Just kinda a closed book."

The ten-minute whistle sounded.

"A closed book with a hot cover," Matthew added and tossed the basketball over to the bin.

PRAYERS AND CONFESSIONS

Dan: My dad's not going to AA anymore. Yeah, so. I'm thinking of hiring some singing strippers to come bang on his door dressed up as those princess fairy girls from *Frozen*. They could sing some "Let it Go" carols. It's like the theme song for AA. Like that slogan, "Let Go and Let God." Maybe that would get his attention and he'd go back to AA. And then maybe my mom will move back home (if I promised there'd be no stripper encore).

Payton: I didn't break up with Holly for the stuff she's done. I broke up with her for what everyone *says* she's done. I guess that makes me a jerk, but I don't want to deal with all the rumors.

Pastor Kyle: Thank you for the Sampson & Delilah salon idea. What camper doesn't love a good pedicure, where your feet are oiled and dried with hair, just like Mary of Bethany did for Jesus. And Sampson and Delilah? Come on, that's clever! Even if Delilah was a bad guy.

Matthew: Please forgive me for how I've blamed my parents in all that stuff. Please forgive me for how I treated Sarah. And maybe also for the MLK porn speech. That probably wasn't cool. But it made Nick laugh, and I like that guy.

◆

"The Disciplettes," Matthew explained, nodding toward a large group of girls that had gathered at the outdoor amphitheater. They shouted something, got into a formation, ran out of it. Shouted. They were all dressed in matching skirts. It was a cheer squad. Each sweater had a capital *J* for Jesus on the front.

"BE SO RIGHTEOUS!

"B-E SO RIGHTOUS!

"B-E-S-O-R-I-G-H-T-E-O-U-S

"BE RIGHTEOUS!"

The Disciplettes leapt and danced and cartwheeled for Christ. Charles flitted among the girls now, talking very intently to the bounciest, likely condemning them to an eternity in hell for their tight sweaters.

The bass pumped from the speakers in the amphitheater, calling us over to our cabin groups. The rappers came to the stage and made a disaster of Young MC's "Bust A Move":

This is a camp for all you followers
Tryin' to do what the Lord does tell us.
Avoid lukewarm and get super zealous,
Leave nonbelievers feeling jealous.

The rappers had done their part, and the whole camp started singing:

So open your Bibles because the Word does prove,
Jesus is here to bust a move.

I did not sing with them. But I spotted Natalie, singing and hip wiggling with Kim and a couple other girls. After a few verses, she suddenly bent over with laughter.

That's how Diana and I used to laugh. Till it hurt. Till our sides cramped, and the hilarity rendered us silent and shaking. Till our parents would yell at us to *keep it down in there. Cease and desist. Enough of that racket.*

Natalie caught me watching her, and I looked away just as Pastor Poseidon came up to the stage. He joined the rap, his bright teeth a lantern of truth. Counselor-servants wove among us with cups of what looked like wine. But it was just grape juice. Because laws.

"Fellas!" Douchey Dan called us over to him.

"With an F," I said, more into my Dixie cup than to anyone.

The rap ended, and Pastor Liam Hemsworth instructed us to sit in the grass. As we did so, Payton kept his eyes on Holly, who seemed to be looking around for someone. She caught my eye and waved.

I felt a stir of disgust and pity. I hadn't for one second thought Holly's extra prayers and attentions the night before had meant she was actually into me. I knew she'd flirted with me to get to Payton. This was her game, and Holly was *that girl.* The punch line of promiscuity jokes, Matthew's and Kim's and probably the whole camp's.

But she also played the guitar and wrote music, this girl that everyone gossiped about. She sat alone in her bedroom strumming songs she made up in her head. I couldn't figure out how both the sweet artist and the slutty girl could be a part of this one person. Could she keep both? Could she *be* both? At the same time? Maybe some parts of us have to move out to make room for the new parts.

Look what Charlotte had pushed out to make room for God.

"Ladies and gentlemen," the pastor said. "Jesus does INDEED bust a move! Jesus was so fun (such a party animal!) that he turned a hundred twenty gallons of water into wine at his mom's request." He was careful to add an emphatic, "Not that we condone underage drinking," yada yada. "But in this doggy dog world, we need someone on our side!"

I was pretty sure he didn't mean Snoop Doggy Dogg, though the camp's dedication to nineties rap did make me wonder. "'Dog *eat* dog world,'" I said aloud to no one in particular, reminding myself to add that to my list under MUTE—MOOT.

He talked about Jesus, and Hillbilly Jesus came to the stage and mimed a Bible story. The pastor concluded with an update: they had no leads on the location of the PC Box, and they were still debating whether or not to create a new one.

A new one? WTF?!

I looked around. Head nods. A couple amens.

Hell no.

I started to head toward Natalie, but just then a hand landed on my shoulder. When I spun, Jason stood there with Pastor Abercrombie & Fitch. Dan walked over.

"Where's your stuff?" Jason asked in a tone that said no happiness was happening here.

"What stuff?"

"You don't have anything with you?"

"My candleholder," I said, pulling it out of my pocket.

Dan cough-laughed. "Is that a candle in your pocket, or are you just happy to see me?" he said.

Jason glared him into silence.

Suddenly, I heard a scraping behind me and turned around to see an older man dragging a large piece of wood across the concrete. "First one of the camp," the man said.

Jason nudged me over to the man. "Turn around," he said.

I did what I was told and saw that the piece of wood was actually a large cross. Before I could even process that, they were situating the crossbeam against my back and across my shoulders.

"You've got to be kidding me," I said.

Nobody said anything.

The men just nodded at each other and let go, sure I could hold the thing. It wasn't too heavy, not like the one I supposed the actual Jesus had carried. But then, I hadn't been whipped to near-death like the actual Jesus.

Plus, they probably wanted to avoid a lawsuit for spine injuries.

"What's this for?" I argued. Was this really happening?

"Transgression," Jason said.

"What'd I do?"

"Walk it on over there," Jason said, pointing to the sanctuary.

The campers close to me watched, nudged their neighbors. Heads turned like a wave of falling dominoes to get a look at the spectacle. I didn't want to make out the faces of anyone I knew, but I saw Natalie, her smile fading. Goth was right there too. Holly was so close, she started to reach out to touch my shoulder, but then seemed to think better of it. Culpability was contagious.

I walked, my cheeks burning with humiliation, which I supposed was the point. But I thought the crown of thorns had been for that. The cross had a more practical purpose: execution.

I didn't dare look again at the campers, who were no doubt fist-pumping for Christ at my exit.

When I reached the grassy lawn, soft with fresh water and hidden divots, the cross got harder to drag. But I didn't fall down. Not once. Not thrice, like the holy man himself.

After I crossed the lawn, the four men led me down the sidewalk to the side of the sanctuary. They lifted the cross off of me. Jason and the older man carried it through the door to the backstage area.

Pastor Prince Charming led me a bit farther. Dan followed us into a room with two desks and a bank of computers and phones. There was a sign above it that read BABYL ON.

I stared at all the phones. I hadn't seen mine since the day before. None of the campers would know if anyone had texted or called or emailed or tagged them in a post for nearly a week. I wondered for a beat if Leah had answered the text I had sent from the bus.

Dan cleared his throat. He and the pastor waited expectantly.

"What'd I do?" I asked.

"I think you know," Dan said. He'd been with me all morning, basically, so I doubted *he* actually knew. But he was enjoying his authority. As he delivered that line with his arms crossed over his chest, it looked like he'd been practicing in the mirror.

The pastor put his hand on Dan's shoulder and asked if he'd give us a moment of privacy.

I waited for a lecture.

"Nick, I like you, and I know it is God's will that you are here. I don't get the sense, from what happened here today, and what happened in the cabin yesterday, that you do."

"It's a beach towel."

"Irregardless," the pastor said.

I opened my mouth to correct him, to tell him *regardless*, but I thought better of it. There'd probably be some kind of follow-up punishment for my contempt. What happened to campers who had already carried their cross? Were they nailed to it for a second offense?

"But today it is not a beach towel."

I looked at him dubiously.

"Yesterday was a beach towel. An oversight, you argue. But today . . ." His words faded out. He shook his head.

"The candleholder? I didn't mean for it to look like a vagina." The pastor looked puzzled. "Or a penis. Or whatever part you're seeing."

"This isn't about a penis." At the mention of the word, the pastor's face curdled into the antithesis of an Adonis face. "Or a vagina."

"The sexism comment at the Creation Station?"

The pastor shook his head. "We can't move forward until we confess our sins and hold ourselves accountable."

"I did confess my sin!" I pulled my hair back from my forehead. "I put it in the box. The box you said was stolen."

"Now you've hit the nail on the hand."

It's *nail on the head.* Nail on the head. Nail in the hands was Jesus's fate. I looked around for someone, something that made sense.

"Where's the box?"

"What?" I rubbed madly at my hair. "How would I know?"

"Young man, calm down."

"I'm not going to calm down. I didn't steal that box! I didn't even want my confession in that damn thing, and now it's there and I'm shitting my pants and you're accusing me of stealing it."

"Nobody's sh—defecating." Pastor Hot Stuff put his hands on his hips and took a deep breath. "I was told you threatened to steal the PC Box last night during the Trust Circle."

"Are you talking about the Ouija board thing?"

"There was no mention of a demonic relic."

"Other than my towel," I sighed. "Look, I was *joking* about stealing the box." I was sure Charles had brought this bit of information forward.

"And this morning, a very reliable source said that you were in the sanctuary alone, sneaking around backstage before crafts."

"Yeah, *looking* for the PC Box," I said.

Pastor Ryan Gosling considered me. "I didn't want to have to do this." He handed over a piece of paper, and my heart beat against my ribs. Somehow they must have found my secret. They'd probably already called my parents.

I unfolded the paper. And it wasn't mine.

It wasn't mine.

But it was the one from under my pillow. It must've fallen on the floor when I made my bed or rummaged through my clothes this morning.

"If you didn't steal the box, how'd you get this?"

"I found it."

"Where?" Pastor Kyle would make Natalie proud with his grilling.

"In the hall, outside the sanctuary."

"Why were you there?"

Oh, crap. "I was in the sanctuary this morning, and I went out in the hall," I lied. Despite Dan's douchiness, I would not snitch. I would not tell him about the pranks.

The pastor eyed me.

And then it occurred to me. "That could be my confession. How do you know it's not something I wrote?"

"Because the person who wrote that confession came to us as soon as the box was stolen."

"What for?"

"To pray, Nick. And to ask for advice."

I thought of Natalie searching for Pastor Kyle the night the confessions were stolen, how she'd left our circle to seek him. I'd watched him pray with the kids who were crying. I saw him hug them, pat their shoulder, sit with them.

"Well, I didn't steal that box," I insisted. "I found that confession. I don't know how to prove it, but you have to believe me." I handed the paper back to him.

He sighed. "The Lord calls me to trust you." He pursed his lips. "For now, that is."

I exhaled. I hadn't realized I'd been holding my breath. "Can you please go tell the masses that I've been exonerated?"

He thought for a moment. "I will tell them you bore the cross for a different transgression."

I could see campers walking down the path outside the window. These kids thought I'd stolen the box. I didn't really care what Pastor Kyle told them. I didn't care about the towel or the clay vagina, or whatever other minor thing I'd done. But I did not want people to think I stole their secrets. It was enough that I was already an outsider. I didn't want to be despised.

I thought of Diana for a second. Of what it must feel like to doubt what people were thinking of you, for the connections between you and others to be so tenuous. To feel so apart from the crowd, to not know who condemned you and who accepted you. I didn't want to feel that.

The pastor looked a bit contrite for a second. I thought maybe he'd apologize then, but he didn't.

We were all choking on apologies. Even the reverent.

"Can we use those phones?" I asked.

He cocked his head. "Well, now, phones are for emergencies at camp."

"The PC Box is kinda an emergency."

He started to say something.

"I just want to talk to my family," I said, hoping that sounded appropriate and true.

"That's the thing, Nick. We're trying to disconnect you from your family here at camp. Only for a bit, so that you can get in touch with your real Father. Your Heavenly Father."

I could only stare. Disconnect us from our family? "I'm upset," I said. "I'm embarrassed." These two things were true, but they weren't really why I wanted to use the phone.

Either that clued him into my imperviousness to his holy intentions, or he succumbed to whatever guilt he felt about his wrongful accusation. "Okay. This is obviously an emergency," he said, lifting the receiver of an old phone that actually had a cord attached. He looked at me and waited.

I told him the phone number. Outside the window, Payton and Holly walked by. He had a hose over his shoulder. She had a computer bag. They didn't even glance inside. I wondered if anyone knew where I was.

Pastor Kit Harington (the hair was wrong, but the jawbone was right) put the receiver to his ear, and I thought for a second he was going to do the talking, in order to make sure I wasn't checking in with my dealer or pimp or something. But after the first ring, he handed me the phone.

It rang and rang and rang, and I thought about that confession I'd found. Whoever that person was, they had sought out someone to confide in. I wanted to talk to Leah.

But the phone just kept ringing.

I hung up. I had hoped she would answer if she didn't recognize the phone number. I didn't want to talk to Pastor Kyle, even if he was probably an okay guy. I wanted to talk to someone who actually knew Diana.

My confession settled back in my throat.

But I didn't hand the phone back to Pastor Kyle. I didn't want to go back outside yet. The haze of accusation still lingered. I wanted to talk to someone.

And if I couldn't talk to Leah, then there was someone else I wanted to hear from. Someone I hadn't talked to in months. I didn't need to apologize to her like I did Leah. In fact, the reverse was true. I wanted to hear an apology. If I had to be at this camp, she should at least have to explain herself. After breakfast that morning, when I had realized that there were Christians on this planet—and even at this camp—who weren't pink-swastika-carrying homo-haters, I kept thinking about her. Eden Springs welcomed Goth, who was openly gay. It welcomed Dan who, while a bully, didn't hate Goth. It also welcomed Charlotte years ago, and I didn't understand how she became the way she was, and why she couldn't accept people for who they were.

Or maybe I just hadn't understood *her*. Maybe I just needed to hear her out.

"Um, can I try a different number?" I didn't tell Pastor Kyle the new number was for someone else entirely. But this was actually for family, so I didn't feel too bad.

The phone rang three times before she answered.

"Hello?"

"Hey."

"Who's this?"

"Your brother."

Silence.

"Really?"

"Yes, Charlotte. It's Nick."

"Wow. Nick. Hi. How are you?"

Awkward is how I was. I hadn't talked to her since before the funeral.

Charlotte had called the house after the funeral. She'd asked for me after talking to my parents. But I'd refused. But as I stood there at Eden Springs, with the old phone to my ear, I thought about how maybe refusing her calls was something like Leah refusing mine. I thought about Diana trying to talk to me in those last few weeks. How I'd been too irritated with her to really listen.

Maybe when people reach out to you, you should reach back. Like Jack said, our words are our bridges.

"I'm good, I guess," I said.

Maybe her apology was lodged in her throat.

"I was just calling to say hi," I continued. "I'm at that camp you sent me to. Well, the one you told Mom and Dad to send me to."

"That's great. I thought you'd like that."

Really? "Yeah, it's great." Lie. The apology, the explanation, nothing was forthcoming. Maybe she needed a hint. "I was wondering if I could ask you something."

"Sure."

It was silent as I tried to think of the exact words, to build up the courage for any words at all. How do you ask for an apology? It wasn't even for me. She owed it to Diana.

In the background, I could hear her kids—my nieces and nephews—arguing or playing. It was hard to tell the difference.

"Nick?"

"I'm here." And then I just asked it: "Why didn't you come to Diana's funeral?"

Silence. I watched Pastor Kyle shuffle papers, put pens in boxes. Then she said, "You called me from Eden Springs to ask me that, Nick?" Her voice was high-wire tight, and part of me wanted to take the question back. I didn't want to hear the wrong answer. I didn't want it to be what I'd thought. I wanted Charlotte to be better than I'd thought.

I didn't want that hope-flame to die out completely.

"Well, I've been wondering for a while, but—why didn't you go to the funeral?"

A deep sigh through the phone lines. "Nick, you know why. I didn't approve of her lifestyle."

And there it was. "Her *lifestyle*?"

"Or how she died, frankly."

"How someone dies is a matter of approval?" The pastor looked up. I turned around so that he couldn't see my face. I knew my eyes would give away my desperation.

"Suicide is a sin, Nick. And so is homosexuality. And the last thing I'm going to do is go to some funeral where people think I condone that."

"It's Diana. It's your *sister*." This was not the reaching out and reaching back that I'd expected. That I'd hoped for.

"And I sure as heck didn't want to have to see that Leah person. Her . . ." Charlotte couldn't even say it.

"Her *girlfriend*, Charlotte. And you didn't even know Leah."

"How cool her girlfriend is doesn't make the sin less of a sin. Suicide and homosexuality, Nick."

"It's how you die and how you're born," I nearly shouted. I could feel the pastor watching, but I refused to turn around.

"We *choose* whether or not we go to hell. She chose."

I couldn't believe I was related to this person. "Did you choose to be such a bitch?"

And here it was again.

In that millisecond of silence, I heard the decrepit bridge between me and Charlotte collapse, falling into the rushing river below, debris breaking on the rocks on its way down.

"Okay, Nick," I heard my sister say, and the pastor was reaching around me to grab the phone, an echo of Charlotte: "Okay, okay, that's enough."

"It's not okay," I said to both of them. "None of this is okay. It's not fine. None of this is fine. Not you, and not you. I'm not fine."

And I wasn't. I'd had two sisters my whole life, and now I had none. And I was stuck at some camp for God, and He was the one who'd stolen them both. He stole Charlotte, feeding her some kind of bullshit where she could trade in being judged for judging others. And He stole Diana entirely. He swiped her off the earth.

Charlotte had already hung up, but I gripped the handset and kept saying the truth, "I'm not fine," aware that there were tears on my cheeks. By the time the pastor wrested the phone from me and said good-bye into the receiver, I was panting.

He stood there, red-faced. "Let me appraise you of the situation."

"It's *apprise*," I said, pressing the heels of my hands to my eyes. "The word you are looking for is *apprise*, not appraise. Appraise is to assess value. Apprise is to inform."

"I don't know what that phone call was about, Nick, but I do know that cursing out a family member—anyone at all—is disrespectful and certainly not the will of God."

The flood of anger was sinking back into my brain matter, leaving me too rational. Too aware of what I'd just done.

"I can tell you're struggling, Nick. Is there something you want to talk about?"

I looked at this man, who likely had never had a problem in his life. Perfect complexion, perfect teeth, perfect physique. God had given him everything and taken nothing. He'd been blessed by God since slipping out of the womb with a perfect smile through a painless birth.

Was there something I was struggling with, besides the fact that he'd forced me to walk across campus carrying a cross for a crime I didn't commit? At least I'd just given him something to tell the campers. That I'd carried the cross for cursing my sister out. Definitely not following the Golden Rule.

I shook my head. "I'm sorry," I said to the pastor. "I'm fine."

Before sending me back to my cabin for a big-kid time-out, he put his hand on my shoulder and closed his eyes. His lips started moving, and I could tell he was praying.

I didn't have the energy to shrug him off.

Apparently the story about my rash hadn't reached him yet.

◆

When I opened the cabin door, Jack Kerouac stood in the middle of the room applauding.

I stared at him. Finally, the clapping slowed to nothing.

"Is this ovation for swearing at my sister?" I asked.

"I liked that, indeed." Jack appeared on the top bunk above me. "But, more so, you have them convinced you'd actually steal something."

I sighed and walked over to my bed. "I wouldn't do that."

"Oh, that I know. That's your problem."

I grabbed my notebook from my backpack and sat on my bed. I added a tally mark for Jack, as well as DOGGY DOG WORLD and IRREGARDLESS and APPRISE/APPRAISE to my list of verbiage faux pas.

He looked over my shoulder to see what I wrote. "One of your problems."

Jack's legs dangled over the bed above mine. He held a licorice stick between his fingers like a cigarette. He dropped an open bag of Twizzlers down to me. I took one, chewed on it as I lay back on the bed.

"You got any of that piss-beer like the other day?" he asked.

"Seriously?"

"Sadly, no. Unlike the handsome pastor, I do not think you'd risk a rule for a fun time."

"It's not a fun time when someone is reading all of our shit. You know that, right?" I kicked at the top bunk. "The stuff about my sister is in that box. I'm in full panic mode down here and you're bummed I didn't steal the gawddamn box myself." I sighed, chewed my licorice. "For God's sake, what is so wrong with being a rule follower?"

"Oh, Nicolas . . . these words. This idea. This is your soul-leech." He sat before me now, a sofa chair appearing suddenly underneath him. He was going for the full philosopher effect now. "You're not meant to be a *rule follower* at all. You're not supposed to *follow* rules. They're not a trail up a mountain. They're not even a sidewalk through a dirty city. Rules don't *lead* anywhere. They're tools, is what they are. Yes, yes. You learn them, know them, pick them up, and put them in your pocket. Use them when the time's right. But good lord, do not follow them. You follow what you love."

"Are you done?"

"Well, one more thing. Don't pick up too many rules either. They're heavy as stones. And you gotta travel light. Yes, you do."

I lay back on my bed and closed my eyes, imagining soft leeches crawling around in my chest, searching for a little life left to suck out of me. "You stole the box, didn't you?" I said.

"Now, *I* would do that. But I did not."

"But you talked about how you wanted to know what was going on in everyone's heads. You just said that yesterday."

"I cannot steal that box any more than I can walk into a store and purchase a fifth of whiskey."

"Then who did? You said you see everything."

"I saw you call Leah."

"Yes, because I needed to talk to her."

"I know what you want," he said quietly. Kindly, in fact.

I sighed and admitted why I'd called Charlotte. "I wanted my sister to apologize."

"You can't ask for people to react any way, this or that. Not apologies, not forgiveness, not grace. You can only extend these things."

You can reach out, but you can't expect them to reach back.

"There a radio here?" Jack asked, suddenly across the room, peering into cubbies.

I shook my head.

"No cigarettes, no beer, no bebop, no women, nothing to do but roam and ramble and stare out into this vast expanse of half-naked girls—"

And he was back at it. "You can leave."

"—most of whom are available for sweet breath and lips and words—"

"You can leave," I said louder.

"—none of whom are Leah."

"You can leave!" I sat up straight in my bed and threw my pillow.

But Jack was already gone.

I lay back on the bed, but I was too angry to sleep. I had to carry a damn cross for something I didn't do. It was humiliating, and everyone saw. And even if Pastor Pettyfer (sans British accent) told everyone I didn't do it, they would only half believe him. You can't take that back. The accusation lingers, the condemnation a veil between you and everyone else.

And Charlotte. Here I was at Jesus camp with gay people, and my own sister couldn't wrap her mind around homosexuality. Not even to understand her own dead-and-gone sister. Not even to go mourn her at her funeral.

And then Leah. If she would just let me apologize. If I could just talk to her, to hear the way she talked. Just like Diana. If I could just say good-bye at least. But her absence just festered. To my parents, Charlotte was what they had left of Diana. I understood why they had spoken to her after the funeral—she was their only daughter now. She was all they had left. And to me, Leah was what I had left.

♦

When my sister died, I spoke at her funeral, which was held in an old cathedral near where she lived. She didn't go to St. Mark's—she wasn't a practicing Catholic—but she liked to go there on Sunday nights for Compline, to hear the sonorous chants of the choir. To listen to the rites, to ponder her mortality. She'd brought me a couple times. I had lain on the floor of the church, which you could do, and allowed the organ notes and the choir's voices to slip into me and resonate in my chest. I loved it there, and when she died I knew it was the only place for her funeral, but I had worried that the priest would have nothing to say because she didn't fellowship, or whatever, with the congregation.

I stood up there, looking out into the mourners one last time in search of Charlotte, indignant that she hadn't come.

I told the story of how, for my tenth birthday, Diana had kidnapped me and drove me in the green Volvo to the coast. She'd planned it with my parents, but I hadn't known that till later, when it was getting dark, and I had been afraid that my parents would be worried.

"It's okay," she'd said. She always said that to me. "You're fine. I'm going to take care of you."

She'd parked her car on the beach, where the loamy waves beat against the hard gray sand. We had woven through the clumps of seaweed, crab shells, and barnacle-covered driftwood, picking up every sand dollar we could find, turning each over and over and inspecting the pale disks. It had taken a long time to find ten sand dollars that hadn't been broken apart by the seagulls. We'd put them in a yellow plastic bucket that Diana had pulled from her trunk, and then in a falling-apart cottage she'd rented for the night. We'd painted each sand dollar with a different scene, a scene that represented one wish for every year I'd lived.

"If only you had ten lives," Diana had said. "You are ten-lives cool, Nick. Maybe one-hundred-lives cool. You're bigger and better than the rest of us."

She was crazy, and she said crazy things I barely understood. I told her so.

"I hope you live ten lives in this one. Live till you lose your breath."

I didn't quote that conversation in my eulogy. Instead, I'd just said, "Diana was a mad one." And then I'd meant to recite the Jack Kerouac quote that was printed on the poster on the wall, but I couldn't. My throat squeezed shut till I couldn't breathe, and I tried to talk and a sob came out, and my mom, whose mascara had run all over her face, came up to the podium with my dad and held me up as I walked back to the pew.

At the wake, I sat by the fireplace and looked out at all the beautiful women my sister had known. Her girlfriend—or ex-girlfriend—Leah sat down in a chair next to me and put her arm around me, telling me what a beautiful job I'd done.

"She *was* a Roman candle," Leah said, choking on her own tears at the end. I loved Leah for many reasons, least of which was her finishing the Kerouac quote with me.

Her hair flowed down her shoulders and she wore this tight black dress like she was going to a cocktail party. Leah was beautiful, and I had no childhood memories without her in them. She'd been my sister's girlfriend for a decade. I was fifteen, and she was twenty-three, and we were lost. I couldn't feel what held us together. I didn't know if it was a thread or a branch or a steel rod. I just knew I needed her to not leave me too.

When Leah had broken up with my sister, I hadn't cared that Diana had been sad. *I* had been sad.

And I had been mad at Diana for whatever she'd done to cause the breakup. It had to have been her fault. Diana had been too much a butterfly. Leah had been on more solid ground. Leah had read books. She'd talked about them. She'd cooked dinner. Her interests hadn't waxed and waned. She'd had a job. She'd had a *career*.

The day my sister died, Diana drove to Leah's house. I don't know if she drove out there to talk, to win Leah back. Or maybe she'd always intended to punish Leah for ending it. Maybe there had never been a conversation one way or the other. Maybe there had never been any hope for either of them. Maybe the plan all along had been punishment, never atonement.

It didn't matter. Leah was punished.

Because my sister shot herself, and Leah had to see it. And see it. And see it. And see it. And see it. For all the long years that she would live. She would be punished.

Diana was a mad one.

And I was mad at her.

At the wake, Leah started talking, started retelling that day.

"It's my fault," she said. "I should've just talked to her, or pretended I still wanted her . . . It's my fault." And then she just kept on saying it, repeating it like a mantra, like the prayers any of the left-behind say. Like my mom said, like my dad said.

It's my fault.

It's my fault.

It's my fault.

But they were wrong. They didn't know.

Leah cried, her mascara snaking in sad rivers down her cheeks that somehow made her more beautiful. Desperate and beautiful, and I still loved her because I just always had, because she was always there. And I knew then that I wouldn't see her again. She would leave me too.

I walked around the house, sipping off people's abandoned cocktails. Everyone seemed to drink strong at wakes. Soon, I was stumbling to the bathroom to take a piss. I was holding walls for balance, and then Leah was there, in the hall by the bathroom door.

She'd cleaned off the mascara, but her eyes were still glassy, from drink and sadness.

"It's my fault," I said with a heavy tongue. I almost told her then. About the gun and the bullets.

But, instead, I leaned forward and kissed her. I didn't wait, and she didn't stop me. She opened her mouth, and I tasted her, the warm darkness of what it meant to love her. And the love mixed with my tears and her tears. And I loved her like my sister did, kissed her like my sister did. Sadly and wholly.

The only time I cried.

The only time I was being true.

"It was all sin and holiness," Jack said from the corner of the room.

♦

I was awoken by the door bouncing open against the wall and my cabinmates storming in.

"It's because of his towel," Charles said. "Even if he didn't steal the box."

There was only one towel worthy of this level of attention.

"I don't even have my towel anymore," I said from my bed, startling them all.

The guys—Charles, Chris, and Payton—turned toward me.

"Oh, hey."

"What's up?"

"You okay?"

Charles continued, unfazed by the fact that I'd heard his accusations. "But you *did*. You did have the towel. And you brought it here."

I looked meaningfully at Chris, but didn't say anything about his Ouija board.

I sat up on the edge of my bed. "Next it'll have brought a plague."

"Like smallpox," Chris said.

"Don't be ridiculous," Charles said to Chris. "That's been eradicated."

"Probably swine flu," Payton offered, straight-faced except for the twitch at the corner of his mouth that Charles clearly didn't see. Whoa—he was on my side. I felt a sting of guilt for the Holly stuff. Did he know people said stuff about her?

"Ebola," Chris said.

"I'm serious," Charles said. "All of this—the PC Box—this is what happens when you bring the relics of demonic worship to camp."

"Fine. What do you want me to do? I got rid of the towel. I didn't steal the box. I mean, I'm super pissed too. I have a confession in there."

"Maybe. If your confession is still in there," Chris said.

"What do you mean?" I looked from face to face, every one of them drawn. "What are you talking about?" I felt my throat tighten in panic (or cardiac arrest—as opposed to the symptoms of an imminent plague).

"Look outside."

I stepped out onto the porch. About fifty political signs were stuck into the hillside. Campers walked back and forth on the lawn in front of the fence. Reading, waving, pointing, while the counselors frantically plucked the signs from the ground.

"Mine wasn't there," Payton said from behind me.

"What are those?"

"Confessions," Chris said.

My face flushed. "Printed onto signs?"

"No, printed on paper and taped to signs."

I squinted to read, but I couldn't see from where I stood. At least they were taking them out.

"Mine was on one of those," Charles said.

I heard him. I understood him. It explained his indignation.

But mine could still be out there.

"It was pretty easy to tell it was yours," Payton said to Charles. "We all know you love the Disciplettes."

Charles's eyes darted from Payton to Chris. "But you didn't know I wanted to be one."

"Yeah we did," Chris said.

He swallowed, looked at me. He wanted me to make him feel better, but I couldn't.

I kept my eyes on the scene. The barbed wire fence clearly indicated the hillside was off-limits. Campers were supposed to stay on the green grass. Stay inside the Garden of Eden, lest a serpent lead you to the tree of the fruit of good and evil, and all that jazz. Surprisingly, most campers still abided the rule.

"When did those signs even get there?" I asked. The counselors kept yanking them from the ground, one by one. Gawd, I hoped mine wasn't out there.

"They were there when Pastor Kyle finished the sermon. You know, after he led you away. After they called us back."

I turned away from the few signs that remained on the hill, my cheeks still hot from panic.

"Did he tell everyone I didn't steal the box?"

The guys nodded.

"Did he tell everyone I found that confession, that it wasn't something I stole?"

When no absolutions were forthcoming, I asked, "Did everyone believe him?"

Shrugged shoulders, eyes avoiding mine. Matthew was the only one who ever stood up for me. But he wasn't here. I was the leper after all.

"You guys, it was in the hall when we were getting buckets for the prank."

"Sure," Payton said. "You'd better not post my secret on one of those signs."

The signs were gone now. If mine had been out there, I'd have to wait till it blew through camp like their gossip before I'd know about it. I'd have to wait till someone put it all together.

The guys started getting ready for the pool, slipping into their swim trunks and grabbing towels. I lay back on my bed and stared at the bunk above me. The door shut without a single one of them inviting me.

They didn't believe the pastor. They didn't believe me. That truth curdled in my stomach like a slow poison.

I took the Bible the camp had given me off the windowsill.

I hadn't stolen that box. I hadn't dropped that confession in the hall. Hillbilly Jesus had said everything was going to be okay, and he'd quoted the Bible. He'd wanted me to know something. I turned to John, flipped to chapter one, and read the ninth verse:

There was the true light, even the light which lighteth every man, coming into the world.

I read it again and again.

Why would he give me this verse? Maybe it was a clue. Maybe Jesus knew who stole the box, knew that I was onto something, but couldn't tell me. Maybe he was speaking in code. Maybe the person who did the lights in the sanctuary was the culprit. Was there a lighting person? This wasn't Broadway.

"That doesn't make sense," I said aloud.

"What doesn't make sense?" I sat up. Charles was still in the room. I'd thought he'd gone out with the other guys.

"I was just reading John 1:9, and it doesn't make sense to me." I wasn't going to tell him why I was reading the Bible. Maybe I'd get some credit for reading "the Word." You know it's bad when you're hoping for homeschool credit.

"Which one?"

"Which one, what? I asked.

"There's John, 1 John, and 2 John. Which John 1?"

For eff's sake. I'd read plain John 1.

I flipped to 1 John 1:9 and read: *If we confess our sins, he is faithful and righteous to forgive us our sins, and to cleanse us from all unrighteousness.*

I read it again. And I read it again.

I'd found motivation.

♦

I set the Bible down and walked out the cabin door. From the porch, I could see most of camp. It was eerily quiet. Some of the Super Bowl Christians were back to normal, jumping off the high dive at the pool. Some played volleyball. A couple girls bought ice cream bars from the freezer bike rolling around blaring Christian rock. I saw many people walking in and out of the sanctuary. Small groups were sitting together on the patio where we'd prayed in small groups the night before. There was a line on the sidewalk to Pastor Kyle's door.

I scanned from the barns to the sanctuary, looking for that familiar, long robe. I had to find Hillbilly Jesus. He'd had the opportunity. He'd been outside of the sanctuary the night the box was stolen. His office was by the sanctuary. He carried that box around all day. And now motivation—he was a guy who played Jesus. A guy who had a bad accent, who scrubbed toilets by night. A guy with no actual power, who had found a way to *really* play Jesus. A written confession was one thing, but putting it out into the world, making us accountable to everyone. To Christ. That was a thing. I'd read about it on the Internet. And that's what he was doing. Charlotte would've been all about it.

The counselors were on high alert, peering into campers' faces, scanning the grounds, all a bit twitchy. Or perhaps the one riding the bike just didn't ride bikes that well.

The girls with their ice cream wandered past my cabin, and I followed them with my eyes. A guy with long hair was setting up a small table on the lawn outside the first set of cabins.

Jesus.

I went downstairs and headed for the table just as some volleyball players left their game to walk over.

Jesus was performing a card trick—an elementary one at that. He dealt four rows of cards, a girl pointed to a card, and then he picked them all up, shuffled, and stacked them in fours. He pulled out her card, apparently, because the round of golf clapping ensued.

Jesus shuffled the cards, looked around at his audience, then spotted me. "Come in a bit closer," he said. His hillbilly accent was gone. I know he recognized me—I was the Harry Potter kid, the barn kid, the carry-his-cross kid. But he was in character now, so he was all aloof and ominous, à la Old Testament God. He looked around us, chin high, hands out like he was preparing to feed us loaves of bread and fish.

I did as he said, and the girls around his table grudgingly stepped aside.

"Would you like a turn?" he asked, his voice resonating. He must've taken vocal lessons to do that. He included all his syllables, no "ain't" to be heard.

"A card trick?"

Diana had bought a book of card tricks when she was in high school. She actually made money doing kid birthday parties and setting up makeshift stands down by the Pike Place Market in Seattle.

"I can guess your card."

"I'm sure you can," I said. Anyone could learn tricks.

"Don't you wanna witness it?" he asked.

"I can watch other people while you—"

"Jack," he interrupted.

I looked at him sharply. "What?" I'd come down here to talk straight, but he'd knocked me off balance. I needed him to explain that Bible quote, but not with all these other campers around.

"Jack," he said again. "Always."

I looked around for Kerouac. Were other people finally seeing the things I saw?

"Jack of Hearts for you."

"What are you talking about?"

Jesus nodded toward me. "In your pocket."

I reached into both pockets.

There was the Jack of Hearts, in my right hand.

The audience gasped.

"Now do you believe?" he asked.

I shrugged. "I already did." It was sleight of hand. Then again, he'd transformed overnight—that wasn't just some cheap trick. What did he really have up his sleeve? I tried to hand him the card back.

"You keep it," he said, pulling a Jack of Hearts off the top of the deck in his hand. "I already have one." He shuffled the cards. "You like deception?"

"No."

"You lie to yourself," he said. Then he winked at me. "We all like deception. We like where the hunt takes us." I was sure he was talking about finding me in the barn, but it was still a weird-as-hell thing to say.

He folded up his table, slipped his cards into his robe pocket, and walked away. The girls with the ice cream cones followed him, chattering in awe. The volleyball girls waved over their friends who'd remained at the net. They all followed the man across the camp, to the end of the cabins where he set up his table once again.

I started after them. I would hunt down this deception.

"You rose from the dead already?" I turned around and saw Matthew, his hair still wet from the pool.

It took me a second to realize he was talking about dragging the cross for my punishment. "It turns out they didn't crucify me."

Matthew laughed. "Nope. You just have to do the carrying the cross bit. You won't be the last. I had to do it my first year here too."

"Whatever, it's pretty effed up."

"Kind of, but it's like an initiation."

I didn't think it was an initiation. An initiation was something everyone had to do, and I hadn't seen hundreds of kids dragging crosses that morning. Just me. And I felt that fine burning point of exclusion keenly.

"I didn't steal that confession." I regaled Matthew with the story.

"Why didn't you tell someone? Or turn it in?"

"I wish I had," I said, but that was only true in retrospect. Only because I ended up having to carry a cross. Finding the paper had not expedited my search for the culprit. And now the confessions were all over the campus. Well, except for the one I'd found. Lucky kid.

I looked over at Jesus setting up his table again, a new audience forming around him. "Why's that guy doing card tricks?" I asked.

"Dude, that's Jesus."

"I know," I said. "Doing card tricks."

"He's performing miracles," Matthew corrected. "He'll go hang from a cross on the second-to-last day. He's ripped under that robe. It's sick."

"He's not performing a miracle. He's performing a card trick that eight-year-olds learn."

"The tricks get better," Matthew said earnestly. "And he does this cool magic where he lifts a table—"

"Wait, *magic*?"

"Well, yeah, he's not *literally* Jesus doing miracles." Matthew chuckled.

"Magic. As in Harry Potter?"

"No, as in Jesus. It's different."

I looked at Matthew, who was a cool guy, the kind of guy who made this otherwise shitshow of a summer experience actually fun. He didn't see the hypocrisy. Or he'd settled in. Maybe that's what people did for a sense of belonging.

"Card trick miracles? Seriously, the garbage-can prank had more pizzazz."

"Sh, Nick, keep your head, man," he said, looking around. "I'm gonna go shower and get a pedicure or ice cream or something. Wanna come?"

"A pedicure?"

"Sampson & Delilah's Salon. It's new this year."

"Maybe later," I said. Right now, I wanted to talk to Jesus again. He'd had motive and opportunity and now he'd made that weird Jack reference and said that thing about deception. He was playing me.

I watched Magic Jesus (gone were the days of Hillbilly Jesus) pack up his card table and walk away a second time, his entourage following right behind. He raised his hands to them in what appeared to be a blessing, and they scurried away.

He walked around the sanctuary at the far end of camp and disappeared down the path by the medical building (aptly named Healing Hands!). It was the same place we'd filled the garbage cans with water the night before. Not far from the custodian's office, and the hallway where I'd found that confession. I walked quickly down the sidewalk after him. But when I rounded the corner of Healing Hands!, he wasn't there. I saw the back door of the sanctuary propped open. I didn't know if Magic Jesus was in there or the in the medical building.

I started with the sanctuary. It was lit up, and the stage curtains were open. I could hear chatter and laughter and tears. Standing at the side of the stage, I saw groups of campers in prayer or chattering lightly. Jesus was not among them.

I headed backstage next.

"Hey, what're you doing back here?" It was Dan. "Now's not the time for pranks, dumbass."

"Have you seen Jesus?"

"No, but I feel him in my heart." He thumped his chest and held up a gang sign. Or a God sign.

I rolled my eyes. "The magician."

"Look," Dan whispered. "I'm getting some shiz ready for some pranks, and you're making it look all suspicious. Go pray, or go home. He's not back here." He stood there till I walked out the door to the sidewalk.

I crossed over to Healing Hands!. The door was closed. I imagined the PC Box inside the building, broken open, with confessions strewn like straw across the floor. I tried the handle. The door was locked.

I banged on the door. Magic Jesus had to be hiding in there—unless he'd slipped away while I was searching the sanctuary. If he was in there, then he'd have to come out sometime. Jesus was essential to the pastor's sermons.

I could have sat and waited for him to come out, but I didn't. Because, just then, I spotted Natalie walking up on the hillside again.

This time, I knew it was her, not just some nameless silhouette. I could see her red bandana.

And a backpack. I imagined Jesus stuffing that backpack with confessions, Natalie making the signs with her clever designs. Marginalizing our confessions.

Co-conspirators.

I set off after her.

♦

I started up the hillside, following that familiar backpack. Yes, I could get in trouble for being on the hill, but I already *had* gotten in trouble, and for something I hadn't even done. At least the small trees dotting the hillside partially hid us from view.

We climbed, Natalie still unaware of me behind her. After scrambling up and over the ridge, Natalie kept walking, but I stopped. Not because I was out of breath. I was stunned into place by the view. Three giant crosses stood beyond the hill in a small valley in the vast, desertlike landscape. They hadn't been visible from camp, and they were huge—way bigger than the one I had to carry.

Natalie slowed as she passed between two crosses, resting her hand on the middle cross. She was not in a hurry. Not to bury the backpack or remove its contents.

I called out to her, hoping my voice wouldn't sneak out of the valley and down the hill toward camp.

Natalie turned and spotted me, clearly surprised. She didn't smile like usual, and she didn't wave.

Instead, she looked back over her shoulder, in the opposite direction from camp, as if someone else was waiting for her. I looked past her, but all I saw was more gray-brown hills of brush and short trees. The sky was turning a soft pink. Natalie turned back around to face me.

Finally, she turned on a smile, the smile of the bubbly, breezy Natalie. But I could tell that's what she'd done. Folded up whatever expression had been on her face and put on her smile like a mask. She walked a few steps toward me and called, "You do know you're breaking a rule right now?"

I caught up to her. "Birds of a feather and all that," I said, eyeing her pack.

"Yeah right." She smiled.

I shrugged and smiled back at her. "What is this place?" I asked, tilting my head back to look up at the crosses. They were at least twenty feet tall.

"Golgotha, obviously."

It wasn't so obvious to me. "What?"

"Not what. Where," she said. "It means 'hill of skulls,' or something like that. It was the place outside Jerusalem where the Romans crucified their criminals."

"Like Jesus." I hadn't known the place had a name.

"Exactly. But it wasn't just Him. There were thousands of others.

It wasn't a special way to die or anything. It was normal. Like lethal injection."

"Your definition of 'normal' concerns me."

Natalie laughed. "You know what I mean." She shifted the pack off one shoulder.

"Well, I can say from personal experience that I'm glad we've moved away from crucifixion."

She raised her eyebrows. "Oh, it still happens. Just like people are still stoned and burned and beheaded."

I imagined giant nails hammered through my wrists and feet. Hanging naked and bloody for hours, until the weight of my body crushed my lungs. The time it would take. How long you'd have to be alone in your pain.

It was the last moments of death that obsessed me, especially after Diana died. What did the brain think? What did it feel? How much did pain hurt in the last minute of life? In the last millisecond? Was it the worst kind of hurt, or did it not matter at all?

I put my hand on the thick, wooden pole that reached way up to the crossbeam. "But there are only three crosses that really matter," I said.

"Well, technically one," Natalie said, nudging me with her shoulder. Then she stepped away from me, but continued talking. "We go on a hike up here the day before we leave. You know, to help us really see the sacrifice." She set the pack on the ground.

"So you came up here early to really feel it without the masses of bored teens?"

She narrowed her eyes, looked out and away from camp, decided something. I could see it cross her face. Some concrete plan. And it was just like I'd told Jack during the Silent Three. She had some secret I couldn't know. The nonwords.

She unzipped the backpack, and I knew what was going to happen next. Those papers.

"Picnic?" she asked.

The pack, which she now held out to me, was full of food. So she was not some kind of confession-runner for Jesus.

I was relieved because I liked her, disappointed because I wanted finding my confession to be that easy. "Food is always good." I shrugged.

Natalie sat down on the ground with her back to the camp and faced the pink sky in the West. She unzipped the small front pocket and took out two protein bars.

"You like to hike?" she asked, handing me one.

"Not really. I was just following you."

She smiled.

"I like to fish, though, and hunt." I said so that she knew I liked the outdoors, in case the answer mattered. "My dad and grandpa go a lot. I'm the only one who packs a book."

"That you don't write in."

"Am I belaboring that point?"

She smiled, bit into her protein bar. "I like to hike. My favorite part of camp is the hike up here actually."

"Seems kind of like a nonevent. You just walk up a steep hill." All hiking seemed like a nonevent to me. Fishing could be boring at times, but it had a purpose. Hunting too. Though I wondered if anyone in my family would go hunting this fall. I didn't know if my dad or grandpa would be keen on it anymore. After Diana shot herself.

"No, they take us this really long way around at sunrise, telling stories, preaching, and all that. It's cool. Then we get up here and someone tells his testimony, and the sun comes up and we all walk back in the light."

"The way, the truth, and the light."

"Amen."

"So when's this hike?"

She swallowed another bit of the protein bar. "Friday."

"What's today?"

She laughed. "Tuesday."

"It's summer; they took my cell phone. Time is lost on me."

"As it probably should be all the time."

I took a couple bites of my protein bar. It tasted like berry-infused paste.

"Should I not admit that I followed you because I thought you were a nefarious confessions trafficker for my number one suspect?"

"I'm flattered yet again," she laughed. "But, wait, you have a suspect?"

I told her about Magic Jesus and his opportunity and his motivation. She listened and complimented me on my cleverness, but she didn't seem entirely convinced or deeply concerned.

"Don't get me wrong," she said. "I want them to find this person and put a stop to our secrets being out there. I really, really do. But we have to face the fact that we might not figure it out. We need to plan in that direction. We need to pray in that direction. We can only control what we can control, and I don't know if you're going to catch the guy."

I didn't like that answer. I was going to hunt down Magic Jesus. By the end of the day, if I could manage it.

"So why'd you come up here if we're hiking here soon?" I asked.

"This is the prettiest place."

We were sitting in an off-limits area, where the grass didn't grow green, where there were no slides or rap songs or ice cream bicycles or lush cabins or family-style meals. We were sitting in the dirt, looking out at dry sage and too-short trees on a dusty landscape with the horizon painted pink. We were outside of Eden Springs, the part of the desert that men built to show us the beauty of God.

Natalie was right, though. This was, in fact, the prettiest part. "My brother's about twenty miles that way," she said, pointing in the direction we were facing. The opposite direction of camp.

"You have family that lives down here?"

"He's at camp too."

"That's cool." What does a University of Washington rower do in the desert? "Same kind of camp, or . . . ?"

"He's at zombie camp," she said and took a bite of her protein bar.

I laughed. "Seriously?"

"Yeah," she said.

"Well, I guess it is the same kind of camp then. Jesus being the first zombie and all."

She smiled, shaking her head. "You're going to hell."

"Raised from the dead, walking around scaring his enemies, and his friends too, frankly."

"Lightning bolts are coming for you right now."

She pulled four bottles of water from her pack, handed me one, stuffed two back.

"You were prepared," I said, indicating the water bottles.

"I'm always prepared."

"For an apocalypse?" I asked as she took out two oranges and some trail mix. I saw a couple of cans of soup or chili or something still in her pack.

We peeled our oranges in silence. I popped a full slice in my mouth. We sat for awhile, and Natalie's smile disappeared. The one she'd put on for me. "You know what it's like to miss someone so much that you feel like you can't breathe?" Natalie asked. "Like their very absence stole all the air out of your lungs?"

The sudden question, the fact I knew exactly that feeling, stole my air.

When my dad first brought me to counseling after my sister died, the psychologist did this weird exercise where he had me tap on my sternum. He instructed me to say certain things I was thinking as I tapped. He told me, *You'll know you've hit on the truth when you cry.*

I have no idea what the chest-tapping thing was. I don't know if we hold our tear bucket under our collarbone, and bruising the shit out of our rib cage is the equivalent of punching a hole in it. Or if it's some physical distraction that lets the mind wander to what we really believe. I never cried with the counselor, not when tapping my chest or just talking.

I'd cried only once since my sister died. At the wake. Only two people as my witnesses—Leah and Jack. If Jack counted as a person.

Natalie had hit on the truth just then. Afraid to talk now, afraid months of tears would spill everywhere, I simply nodded yes. I knew what it felt like to miss someone so much that the breath was snatched from your lungs. To feel claustrophobic with loss, like the universe's walls were falling in on you. To feel trapped in a world where your favorite person no longer existed.

"That's how I feel about my brother," she said.

I ate another orange slice, chewed it a long time, focused on the movement of my jaw until I was sure I wouldn't cry. Finally I said, "You don't see him?"

"He's pretty busy with school," she said before looking away, and again I sensed words still in her mouth, tucked in her cheeks, and under her tongue. "I go to this camp because he goes to that camp. That way I can be near him."

I was obviously missing something. It wasn't just a college thing. Maybe that family black hole. "Divorce?" I asked, and the word felt sticky in my throat.

She nodded vaguely. Like Matthew said, a closed book.

"Sometimes, I just talk to him, and it's like a prayer and I think maybe I can hear him talk back. And then I think God probably calls that a sin."

I didn't really know what to say. "I don't think He judges you." I didn't know how to talk about God, so I changed the subject. "I sometimes do that with my sister. I miss her so much that I sit in her car and talk to her."

She looked away from me, her eyes settling somewhere across the valley. "You know that feeling when you watch someone walk away? They just get smaller and smaller on the horizon till they're just a flicker. And even when they aren't there anymore, you can still swear you see them. Maybe that's how you know you love someone."

"There's something my sister used to say." Gawd, I hoped Jack Kerouac wasn't listening when I quoted, "'A pain stabbed my heart, as it did every time I saw a girl I loved who was going the opposite direction'—"

"—'in this too-big world,'" Natalie finished.

I thought of Leah then. Walking away from my sister and eventually walking away from me.

Natalie's face spread out with a smile so big. Real this time. "You like Jack Kerouac?"

"My sister kind of worshipped him," I said.

"I think I like your sister." Natalie used the present tense, and I reveled in it for a moment, could almost pretend it was true. "I kind of worship him too," she said, then closed her eyes and raised her hand to the sky. "I'm just hyperbolizing. Sorry, Jesus." Then she laughed and looked at me with this kind of amazed glowiness all over face. "I can't believe you know Jack Kerouac. Like, who knows Kerouac these days? I mean, people our age anyway."

"I don't actually like him. Not his writing, and not him really. I mean, from what I know, he was kind of an asshole to people. But I can quote him at dinner parties," I joked. "I don't really even know what it means half the time."

"Dinner parties"—Natalie laughed at this—"and church camp." Then she took a deep breath and settled into this peaceful smile. "You're a funny one," she said.

She was too. The way she looked around, all bright-lights-in-her-eyes, all that delight when the pages of herself were flipping from this to that. With her hair and cheekbones all sexy and strong like Rosie the Riveter.

"I suppose you've marginalized *On the Road*?" I asked.

"No, I haven't, actually. I've read it, but haven't taken pen to page."

"No doubt it needs marginalizing for anyone to like it," I said, hoping Jack would hear that part.

"You're quite the harsh critic."

"He just talks and talks and talks, and never really says anything."

"So you've read it?"

Crap. "Just parts of it. And then, you know, my sister and her obsession."

"Why does she like him so much?"

"She wanted to join the circus and hit the road. And he did. Well, hit the road, not the circus part."

"She doesn't want to anymore?"

And I said the next part before I could stop myself. "She committed suicide."

Natalie's mouth fell open. "Oh, my gosh, Nick, I'm so sorry."

"No, it's okay. I mean, it's not okay. I just—" I stopped rambling before the rest of the story spilled out. With the way people talked about everyone at camp, maybe she'd already heard about the Ouija board. But nobody knew the rest of it.

Natalie had stopped eating and was looking at me. Really looking, in a way that made me suspicious that she might see the nonwords, and she'd read me anyway.

"My sister was this crazy beautiful thing," I said. "She kind of butterflied through life."

"Butterflied through life . . . I like that."

"New verb."

"From Urban Dictionary?"

"It is pretty gangster."

She nudged my shoulder. "Your sister was a mad one then?"

"Pretty much," I said. "And she dragged me around with her like a toy and I had some vicarious fun."

Natalie was smiling. "She danced, and you stood against the wall?"

"Well, she was always trying to get me to dance."

"At least you showed up?"

"Can't take credit for that either. She forced me."

"If it's any consolation, I didn't used to dance, or even stand against the wall. I was, like, on the other side of the wall, peeping through a small hole. I was scared to do anything."

"I can't imagine Rosie the Riveter not dancing."

"I was shy, scared."

I couldn't imagine that of the girl from pretty road. "What changed?"

"I don't know really. I guess there was something I wanted bad enough. Like, I lived behind that wall. And then one day, I walked around it. Whatever I was afraid of stopped scaring me." She was looking off again. "But honestly, I don't remember what it was."

"No epiphany?"

"Nope. I just started trying things and doing things, and finding I loved the things. And the world just kept getting bigger and bigger."

"Like what?"

"Like, the flute. I tried that. I was horrible. And fishing. Worms, gross. But I like swimming, and I like painting, and I like—"

"Marginalizing."

"I'm an expert marginalizer."

We both laughed.

"You know how they say eyes are the window to the soul and all that? For me, art is like the door out of my soul. It's safe to come out that way." She looked at me, searching. "You know?"

"Yeah, I think so."

"It's why I have to go to City School, why I have to go to RISD. It's just another kind of church, for another part of my spirit." She paused. "What about you? What are you good at?"

"Not much."

"What?! You can't not be good at something."

"Okay, I'm good at grammar."

She shook her head and smirked. "This situation is grave."

"I never met a dangling participle I couldn't nail back into place."

"You just keep talkin' sexy."

"Apostrophes, pronoun usage, split infinitives."

"So hot."

"I have very strong opinions about the Oxford comma."

"Doesn't everybody?"

We laughed.

"I never should've admitted to writing in books," she said.

"My stomach curdled to witness it."

"There are the people who write in books and then there are the people who don't."

I nodded. "I'm Team *Not* Writing in Books."

"But you're Team Secretly Correcting Grammar."

"I'm not so secret about it."

"Charming."

We sat there for a while, but I didn't want to go just yet. I liked being around her. The easy banter.

I cleared my throat. "So what do they do at zombie camp? Like, costumes and stuff? Crawl around on the ground like their limbs are falling off, perhaps?"

She looked off to where the sun was dipping below the horizon. "I guess." She started packing up our picnic garbage. "I'm gonna head back, okay?"

Her mood had changed. Just like that. "I'm sorry."

"Oh. No, it's not you." She smiled weakly. "You didn't do anything." But I had done something. Or hadn't done something. I didn't even know.

She stood up and brushed off her shorts.

"I'm gonna go the long way back, okay?" She pointed to a trail that I supposed was the one we would return by when the whole camp walked up here for testimonies. I could tell it wasn't an invitation to follow her.

"Yeah, I'll just slip down my little hill over there like a ninja."

She didn't laugh. Just swung her backpack over her shoulder and slipped her other arm through. She took a couple of steps toward the trail and then turned around. "I'm glad you broke the rules to stalk me," she said, which made me feel a little better.

I smiled, nodded, put my hands in my pocket. "Thanks for the snacks."

She waved and resumed her walk toward the trail. I looked up at the three crosses, no longer casting much of a shadow as dusk descended. I leaned against the middle one and watched Natalie wind her way into the valley until I couldn't see her anymore.

I was well aware that I was still looking for her when she was long past the point of being seen.

♦

Before Dan returned from his nightly counselor meeting, the Ouija board was out again. But this time, I had an idea. No search for the Holy Ghost this time.

"Let's ask about the PC Box," I suggested. I had returned to Healing Hands! after hanging out at Golgotha with Natalie, but found the door still locked. I'd peeked into the sanctuary, visited the barn, walked circles around the camp. Jesus was nowhere to be found, and he hadn't shown up for the evening's sermon.

Surely Jack, know-it-all and stalker, had seen who took the box. And he insisted he was roaming around camp with the likes of Jesus and Ra and the Buddha. Surely, one of them would be able to shed some light on the truth here.

Maybe Jack would talk to me through the board. Maybe he'd stop with his word puzzles.

We were all in the cabin—Chris, Payton, Goth, Charles, Matthew, and me. Chris and I put our fingers on the planchette. After doing the infinity thing like the night before, it started settling on letters.

F-

R-

A-

N-

K-

"Frank?" Chris said. "Someone named Frank stole the box?"

"There's no Frank at camp," Goth said.

Matthew added, "Though it does sound very criminal. Very 1920s mafia."

But the planchette had still been moving while we talked. There'd been something else, and we'd missed it.

M-

"Matthew?" Charles called from his bunk.

Our heads spun toward our very own Matthew.

"Dude, are you serious?"

"I'm just making inferences based on the text," Charles defended. He had that look on his face again, the darting eyes and fidgety hands. Was he concerned for us? His cheerleader confession was already public. But worrying on behalf of other people didn't seem like Charles.

Y-

R-

R-

H

"Common Core failed you," I called up to Charles.

Someone made a buzzer sound.

"That's not even a word. That's the sound you make while taking a shit," Payton said.

"It's myrrh," Goth pointed out.

"Is that even a name?" We all looked at Payton.

The board spelled out B-E-T-H.

"Beth and Frank?" Matthew's brow furrowed in disgust. "Nobody names their kids that anymore. Those are grandma and grandpa names."

"Bethlehem," Charles said. He'd been watching when we hadn't. Like before, the planchette had kept moving.

"Wait, then," I said. Bethlehem, myrrh . . . "Frankincense. I bet that's what the other word was. Not Frank."

They all nodded.

The Ouija board spelled MANGER. WISE MEN. MORMON TABERNACLE CHOIR.

This was absolutely Jack Kerouac having fun with us.

The planchette circled. Then, S- I- L- E- N- T- N- I-.

"Silent Night!" Payton shouted.

J- I- N- G

"Jingle Bells!" Again, Payton.

"F- R- O- S-"

"Frosty the Snowman!"

"Seriously, let us have a chance," Chris whined.

"It's like Name That Tune, without the tune," Payton said.

Chris added, "And with the Holy Ghost."

T- A- N- N- E- N- B- A- U- M.

"*The Royal Tenenbaums*? That's not a Christmas song."

"It's a movie. And not a Christmas one either."

"That's the German name for 'Oh, Christmas Tree,'" Charles said. "'O Tannenbaum.'"

Clearly we'd gotten too cocky. Jack had upped the ante.

The Ouija spelled FELIZ NAVIDAD.

"The Holy Spirit is going multicultural," Matthew said.

How PC of the PC Box.

The planchette spelled song after song, like a YouTube Yule log playlist.

YULETIDE.

CAROL OF THE BELLS.

THE HOLLY AND THE IVY.

The planchette stopped moving.

Payton begged for more. "Come on . . ."

"Are you serious right now?" Chris actually shouted.

I shook the game piece across the board. "I guess the Holy Ghost got bored," I said. But what I really wanted to say was, Jack is an asshole.

PRAYERS AND CONFESSIONS

Pastor Kyle: Lord, thank you for bringing these kids here to camp. Please help me guide them through this dark time, Heavenly Father. We've all experienced dark hours. And You've been there for me in the worst of times.

Dan: My dad's nightmares are getting worse. Last week I woke up and found his shotgun leaning up against the wall by my bed. He has no recollection of putting it there. Alcohol + PTSD = a negative equation. I don't need Charles's help to know that.

Holly: I'm not sorry for going to that stupid party. I just should've known better. They're always looking for a story.

♦

Dan was back and ready for action. He talked about Jesus as our BAE. We said a prayer. "Okay, let's trust it out, pray it out, and prank it out, fellas!"

"What about the PC Box?" Charles asked.

"What about it?"

"Well, doesn't it seem inappropriate to continue your pranks?"

"Yeah, seems kinda weird," Goth said.

While I didn't say it aloud, I was ready to get back out there. But this wasn't pranks for me. I was going to search for clues.

If only Charles knew. He could be the Robin to my Batman on this camp-wide hunt for justice. The Pythagoras to my Euclid.

"Inappropriate," Dan sang back in a baby voice. "Kinda weird." He put his hands on his hips and returned to drill sergeant mode. "Don't be a bunch of pussies."

So the cabin chanted the prank rules while Charles crawled up into his bunk. I mouthed *watermelon, watermelon, watermelon* so that it would look like I knew the rules.

"Lower cabins got it last night. Upper cabins tonight."

Dan led us through the darkness to the sanctuary. "Nick," he whisper-growled. "Get in there and get duct tape and superglue."

"Me?"

"You know where the custodian's office is. Now go."

Dan seemed to want me to get in trouble. As if carrying that cross hadn't been enough. "Payton's on work crew; he knows that office better than me."

"I do grounds. I don't go in there," Payton said.

But then I realized: this was something like divine intervention. I had just been given permission to snoop for evidence. Magic Jesus had had the opportunity to steal those confessions. And Dan had just directed me to dig around in his office.

I walked through the door and down the hall. I knew this time which door was for backstage and which was the custodian's. The light was on in Magic Jesus's office, but he wasn't in there. So I tiptoed in and slowly closed the door behind me, to keep any of my shadows or noise from the hallway.

I looked on the shelves. Leaf blower, several large toolboxes, toilet paper. I opened the cupboard, looked through boxes, shoved cans of paint aside. Nothing.

No doubt Jack was loving this. Two-time rule breaker.

Unlike when I'd snuck up the hill after Natalie, though, this time I had clear purpose. If Jesus was the one who stole the PC Box, it would be in this office. That little paper confession from the hall the night before would not be the only one floating around. While sign after sign of spilled confessions had already been posted, there had to be hundreds more. And this would be the perfect place to store them; no one else would be in here.

I checked the desk. Pens, Post-its, a flash drive, and a deck of cards in the center drawer. Magic Jesus's magic cards.

I opened the side drawers one by one. The top drawer had the tape. Second one had the glue. I didn't need to open the big bottom drawer. I had the supplies. But just in case.

I slid the drawer open to reveal a set of hanging file folders with campers' names on them. Maybe ten. Payton's name was there. So this was his work crew. Not surprisingly, Holly's name was in there too. Maybe she was on crew for a scholarship, or maybe she just wanted to follow Payton around. I didn't recognize any of the other names.

The door swung open.

"What're you doing?"

I whipped around, snagged my foot on a cord.

Dan caught the laptop as it slid across the desk.

"What is taking so long?" he snarled.

My heart raced. "I couldn't find it at first."

Dan situated the laptop back the way it had been. "Wanna bet this is full of child porn?"

He sat down in the chair. He was an asshole, and he was really going to check the laptop.

"Let's just go," I said.

And he did, thank God.

I hadn't been caught searching. But I also hadn't found anything. Yet.

◆

Dan explained our mission and then assigned each of us a partner and a cabin. I was with Goth, pranking Jericho.

"That's Holly's cabin." Payton balked.

"Which is why you're not going in, man-whore," Dan said.

"We'll get our hands on the box while we're in there, Payton," Goth said.

"Shut the hell up," Payton said.

"Get in, get out," Dan laughed, dragging Payton to their cabin.

"That's what he said," Chris joked.

"Or she."

"Depends on if it's good or bad."

"Depends on if it's hetero or homo," Goth said.

"Holly definitely says that to Payton."

"Hurry up!" Matthew imitated a girl's voice. "Get in, get out."

Something heavy settled inside me. I didn't care about Payton. But I kept thinking about Kim's nasty remark to Holly. "Come on, you guys," I said.

They stifled their laughter as we reached the cabins.

"Okay, but seriously. Look for the box," I said.

"We're always looking for the box," Matthew said.

"I'm not," Goth said.

More laughs.

"Okay, but seriously," I said.

"Dude, okay, we're going to."

We split up.

♦

When Goth and I reached the back of Jericho, one of the girls' cabins, we walked carefully around the side and up the stairs to the second story. This was one of the bigger cabins. Two entrances, and way more campers with stuff to mess with. More potential thieves.

I held the duct tape, aware my hands were sweaty. Goth had the superglue.

"Let's start with the glue in the bathroom," Goth whispered.

The bathrooms were farthest from the front door, our escape route. It made sense to get the hardest part of the job done first. We climbed the cabin stairs like cartoon robbers and stopped at the first door, but I signaled right, and we crept over to that door. I put my hand on the knob and nodded. He nodded back. I opened the door a crack, and Goth sneaked in. I shut the door and waited outside for a brief moment. When he didn't come out screaming, I opened the door and slipped inside.

With the curtains closed, it was too dark to see Goth's whereabouts. I waited for my eyes to adjust, listening to the sleep-breathing of the girls. One girl snored, but it was a soft sound, not like guys' snores, which always sound like we're chomping at the air.

Their light snoring was one reason why I couldn't imagine the PC Box being in a girls' cabin. Plus, I didn't know who was staying in this cabin, and I didn't know about motives and opportunities for these girls. But then I thought about talking to Natalie up at Golgotha. She hadn't seemed that interested in finding the PC Box at all. So poised, for someone whose secrets could be leaked at any moment.

I definitely wasn't going to pass up the chance to poke around.

My eyes weren't really adjusting, so I walked straight through the dark with my hands out in front of me.

Then the bathroom light flickered on, automatically triggered by the door, and Goth slipped through. I followed. It smelled like apple-vanilla-lavender sweetness.

I *really* couldn't imagine the PC Box in a girls' room.

We started at the cubbies, each with a name taped on the top. From every cubby, we grabbed one bottle or compact or comb. We put three dabs of glue on each item and set the objects back into the cubbies.

I slid Natalie's bottles of this and that around in her cubby, looked in the little zippered bag there. No evidence.

"You do Holly," Goth whispered, interrupting my search. "That's not my style."

At Holly's cubby, there was a manila folder. I didn't want to ruin her love poetry or song lyrics or whatever she was storing, so I left that alone and glued the rest of her stuff to the sides of the cubby.

"I hope this holds with the moisture," Goth whispered. "You know, the heat and the shower."

The door suddenly swung open. Goth crouched in a shower. I backed into a stall and locked it. My blood stormed in my ears.

"Sarah, is that you?" a girl asked.

"Mm-hmm," I mumbled in my best high-pitched, tired-girl voice.

She peed for a long time. More like tinkled.

Which was the third reason I couldn't imagine the PC Box here. Girls tinkle. They don't rob and steal.

She flushed the toilet, washed her hands. We remained still. After a few minutes, the lights went out. We left our hiding places and exited the bathroom, the light popping on behind us.

Goth and I jungle-crawled across the floor to the other side of the cabin to the second bathroom, where we glued more girl paraphernalia to the cubbies.

Time for the duct tape.

Outside the bathroom, we found shoes and snacks and notebooks, and duct taped them to the ceiling and to the sides of clothing cubbies.

I was disappointed to not find the PC Box. Not in the cubbies, not under the beds, including Natalie's. But I was relieved to get out of the dorm. I didn't want to get caught, and the girly perfumes were giving me a headache.

We walked back toward our cabin. "It's way too fruity in there," I said.

"No such thing."

It took me a second to get his joke. When I laughed, Goth did too.

"Can I ask you something?"

"Go for it."

I prefaced the question by telling him about Charlotte. How she was a self-proclaimed "righteous follower of Jesus" who simultaneously hated certain groups of people. "But everyone here knows you're gay?"

He shrugged. "I assume so."

"Even the pastor?"

"Yep."

"And they're just . . . okay with that?"

"It's not really their business to be okay or not okay."

"Yes, totally," I said. That was it. That was thing with the whole world judging one another. "That's what I tell Charlotte. But I swear she's on some mission. She goes on about how God hates homosexuals and all that." I air-quoted the last part, lest he think me earnest.

"Well, they can hate me and not have me at camp. Or they can love me and have me at camp. If you claim to be a Jesus-lover, there's only one choice."

"So, they accept you."

"Girl, I said *love*. They love me here." He said the last part with a lisp and a click of his tongue.

I laughed again.

I so wanted Diana to be there to laugh too. I wanted her see how it could've been. How it *should've* been. Not necessarily being at Jesus camp. I didn't really want to be here, and I doubted Diana would either. But just being *anywhere*. Being any*one*. She could've lived as big as she wanted, as openly and joyously as she wanted.

I had known Diana wasn't happy in the months before she'd died. It wasn't just the breakup with Leah. She'd never finished stretching out her own skin and realizing it fit.

"My other sister was gay." I cleared my throat. "She died, though."

"That sucks."

"Yep." It was an understatement, but it was true. "Not everybody loved her," I said, thinking of Charlotte. Thinking of the first time I ever told a kid at school that my sister was a lesbian, assuming it was as interesting and as significant as the fact that my house was two stories. But as I'd watched that girl's face curdle and pinch, I'd realized it wasn't just *being* gay that was a problem. It was also a problem to love gay people, to find no fault. To pass no judgment was to be judged too. At least where we lived. And it wasn't just Christians. The kids who beat up my sister in high school weren't doing it in the name of God. Maybe they went to church, maybe they didn't. The only certain thing was that they wanted my sister to know she was not free to love who she wanted. Or even kiss who she wanted.

They beat her up in the name of hate.

"Not everybody loves me either," Goth said, shrugging. *Their loss.*

"And Nick's your boyfriend."

"I met him here."

"That's funny."

"So, you know, they just ask us not to be in the same cabin or perform poolside gay sex tricks or start riotous gay orgies."

"But straight sex tricks and orgies are okay?"

"Absolutely."

We got to the cabin, but no one was back yet.

"So how do you know . . ."—I realized I didn't know her name—"the girl in the wheelchair?"

"Monica? That's Nick's sister."

"What happened to her?"

He looked at me like I was being a dick. "She was born."

"No, I just mean, like what kind of disabilities does she have?"

"All kinds. It's creatively called multiple disabilities."

I wanted to ask more questions, but no matter what I said, I sounded like an idiot.

"It's cool she comes to camp with Nick, though."

"Yeah. Monica is easy to love."

The guys returned to the cabin pair by pair. There was good and bad news. We'd successfully decorated the cabins, but no one had found the box.

There were other cabins. But there was also the elusive Jesus.

♦

"That was a pale shadow of debauchery."

Jack was in the bathroom again that night, sitting on the shower floor with an empty bottle next to him.

"Breaking and entering." His mouth moped across the words. "What about pretty road girl?"

"Are you drunk?"

"She's a fine, fine girl, ample breasts, brown from the sun."

"You're a pervert."

"No, no, I'm a dead man who hasn't loved a woman for half a century," he slurred.

"It's like the opposite of necrophilia."

"When will you decide to live?" he asked, ignoring my insults.

"I am living."

"You exist. You breathe and walk around and wait for whatever to happen."

"I'm doing something. I'm looking for the PC Box."

"It's the problem your sister had with you."

The anger burned in my chest. "My sister had a lot of problems, the least of which was me. So don't even go there."

"It's what your sister *wanted* for you. To live so hard you'd lose your breath from the thrill of it all."

"I'm fifteen! It's hard to live so big."

"No. You spend too much time looking for wings before you fly."

"I think being careful is part of living through your twenties. Why don't you go ask my sister about that?"

I locked myself in a stall to pee.

"Why don't you kiss that girl?" Jack said from the shower.

"Well, I'm not gonna walk up to some girl and grab her ass and stick my tongue in her mouth, like you would likely advise," I said as I washed my hands.

"Maybe that'd cure what ails you."

"Nothing ails me."

"Your spirit's a pale thing. You're formless."

"I don't even understand you half the time." I looked down at him. "Look at you. You're drunk on the floor of a church camp bathroom."

I kicked at his shoe and nearly lost my balance when my foot hit nothing.

"Why won't you help me find the box?" I asked, indignant.

"I did, I did. You don't hear the words when they drift in."

"On the Ouija? That was just songs. A bunch of Christmas carols."

"You don't see the things hiding in plain sight."

"Are you seriously going to sit there and throw my words back in my face? About my sister? Fuck you, Jack." I slammed my hand into the wall.

"You're so angry, Nicolas."

"What are you *doing* here if you're not helping me?"

Jack opened his mouth as if to speak. Then he puked all over the floor.

WEDNESDAY

♦

The next morning, Natalie was waiting at the bottom of my cabin stairs.

"Totally ignore my hair," she said. She still had the bandana, but her hair was pulled up in a bun. "I couldn't wash it. We got hit by the Superglue Fairy. Shampoo deemed inaccessible."

"Crazy," I said. I had no wit or charm. I was exhausted and angry from the night before.

She eyed me. "You certainly look well-groomed."

"Yeah? Thanks."

"But your cabin's upstairs."

"Yeah . . ." Her eyes sliced through me. She suspected me. "But my shoes were hanging on the ceiling. Laces duct taped and everything," I covered.

"Mm-hmm." Her scalpel-eyes continued their exploratory surgery.

I quickly changed the subject. "Have you seen Magic Jesus?"

"Magic"—an air quote there—"Jesus?"

"Well, you know, the robed guy who does magic," I explained. "But, have you seen him lately?"

"I've heard he's been praying with the campers and stuff. I haven't seen him recently."

"Where? In the sanctuary?"

"I don't know—Wait, what are you wearing?"

I looked down, afraid I had committed some heinous fashion crime. Or worse, left some evidence of last night's prank. But it was just a striped T-shirt.

"Where's your uniform?"

Ah yes, my nerd shirts. "I only have so many T-shirts."

"Excuses." She got oddly serious for a beat. "I wanted to give you something before—" She looked away. "Breakfast."

"Okay . . ."

"But now I doubt you can handle the necessary nerdery." And just like that, she was back. Matthew had called her a closed book. But she was more like a book that kept flipping from page to page.

"I can handle it."

"Okay, then, speaking of duct tape and hanging things from the ceiling." She handed me a book—*Sixty Scenes of Sexy.*

"I take that back," I said. "I can't handle it."

"It's perfect for you."

"What?" I looked around, afraid of witnesses, afraid of heavy crosses. "Why?"

"I think you'll have a lot to say about it."

"I don't need to read it." I was a boy. My brain wrote new chapters of erotica every minute. I just didn't know what to do with all of it.

"You said you were good at grammar and all that." She handed me a red pen. "Marginalize it."

"It's already marginal."

"Right. So you have a duty to do something with what you love." She waved her hands wide. "This world must be saved from the *shlit.*"

"Is that Yiddish?"

"Shit literature. *Shlit.*"

"I thought that was your job."

"What? No. I make the classics more accessible."

I laughed.

"I'm serious. No more of this *shlit.*"

"I cannot walk around here with this." I held the book up. "This is a crock of *shlit.*"

"Tough *shlit.*"

"The *shlit's* gonna hit the fan."

"*Shlit* happens."

"I'll be up *shlit* creek without a paddle."

"Don't lose your *shlit*. Hold on a sec."

She took off, jogging to her cabin. She ran up the stairs of Jericho, the very cabin I'd been in the night before. Had she seen me? Is that why this morning's suspicion?

When she returned, her hair falling out of its bandana, her face red, she took *Sixty Scenes of Sexy* out of my hand and wrapped it in a new book cover.

"*Twilight*? This is a piece of *shlit* too." I pushed the book back at her. "They confiscated my Harry Potter towel, for God's sake. This is a supernatural love triangle. Written by a *Mormon*."

"Mormons love Jesus too."

"She has sex in book four. They break the windows with their passionate screeching."

She smiled. "So you've read them."

"I've seen the movies," I admitted. Diana had said it was part of my romantic education. To know every woman just wanted a man-eating monster who could quote Shakespeare.

"Just take the book," she pled and started backing away from me so that I couldn't give it back. "It'll feel so good to write all over it. And honestly, it's a fun, fast read. Don't be such a snob."

"Okay, I'll take it." She was walking away, heading toward the dining hall. I called after her. "But can you please find me a different cover? Maybe Suzanne Collins or James Dashner or something?"

"I'll try!" she called back.

"Find something that hasn't been banned in public schools!"

She laughed maniacally. "Impossible!"

PRAYERS AND CONFESSIONS

Dan: I miss my mom. How does a mom just up and leave? I get that my dad's crazy. But then, you're my mom. Take me with you.

Payton: Holly thinks I broke my arm skateboarding. Right. I broke my arm in a fight with some kid who called her a slut. Look, I know what they say. Everybody does. Because even though our school is super Christian, we all hear the same rumors. But Holly's not a slut.

Matthew: I'm not stupid. I know why I say all that stuff. And I probably shouldn't. But if I just keep talking about tits and ass, then no one will think I really care about what happened between me and Sarah.

♦

I went back to my cabin to stash the book. But before I slipped it under my pillow, I flipped through it.

Natalie had inscribed a note on the inside cover:

Dearest Nick,

You are likely the Messiah of Grammar. Messiahs are called to save mortal man. Unsheath your pen (mightier than the sword, they say!) and do this thing.

—Natalie

P.S. I started it off so that you could see how it's done.

And she had, mostly crossing out repetitive words (burgeoning; sardonic) and phrases (oh dear; she twirled her hair) and replacing them with something new. For a visual dynamic, she'd doodled a picture of the sorry kid in the stationery store who had a crush on Miss Bronze (at least, that's what I figured the doodle was later, when I read it).

I didn't want to read the book, but I wanted more of Natalie. And I liked being talked to as I read. I liked being inside someone's head at the same time I was in mine. I liked being with Natalie even when she wasn't there.

After stashing the book in my pillowcase, I headed over toward the dining hall. Magic Jesus was nowhere to be found, but I spotted the Disciplettes, who had gathered near the pool. They ran around in different formations.

"GIVE ME A J!"

"J!"

"GIVE ME AN E!"

"E!"

One cheerleader was wearing pants.

Charles.

In polyester pants that matched the cheer skirts.

And a cheer shirt with a capital *J*.

Charles was a Disciplette.

Or a plain old Disciple. I wasn't sure how it all panned out with the gender differences.

I wandered over. "It's early for cheer practice," I said.

He narrowed his eyes.

"I'm not teasing you, Charles. I think it's cool," I said. Even if it was cheerleading, it was cool to him.

Charles stepped away from the girls. "Is everything okay?" he asked.

"Yeah, why?" My friendliness seemed to have caught him off guard, or something.

"You're just wandering around?"

"Well, I guess."

He scanned the camp, biting his lip. "There're no more secrets out?"

"No."

Charles nodded. "Okay, that's good."

He didn't actually seem like he'd settled into his role as a Disciple(tte) yet, but I felt jealous of him nonetheless. Charles was lucky. His secret getting out actually provided him the liberty to live his dream, but my secret getting out would be a family nightmare.

"Charles, get over here," one girl called. "We need our bases."

"I designed a stunt," he explained to me, walking away.

"Wait, you're going to throw that girl in the air?"

He turned back around, the side of his mouth turning up in an almost-smile. "I calculated the initial velocity and angle of the trajectory prior to designing the stunt."

And then he and two sturdy girls, standing in a threesome, a holy cheer trinity, positioned themselves to throw another girl into the air.

"This is not safe," I called out.

But the girl flew, and the Disciplettes caught her.

"See," Charles called back. "It's math, so it is safe."

"It's not math." I joked. "It's cheer, for God's sake."

"No," he said. "It's cheer *for* God's sake."

♦

In the sanctuary, Pastor Tom Brady kicked things off with Christian rap. I wasn't paying too much attention. Mostly I was staring at the pastor, thinking Russell Wilson would've been a better sports reference, because everyone at camp was pretty loyal to the Seahawks. After all, most of us were Pacific Northwesterners. And it's probably more responsible of me to make some multicultural comparisons when describing the unnatural perfection of the pastor. Plus, according to Twitter, Russell Wilson is a born-again virgin. But then, the pastor, though tan, tanned more orange. And didn't quite have the puppy smile of the famed quarterback.

The song changed to something slower and the screen blipped. I expected new lyrics to appear on the screen.

But the words didn't match the song at all.

It took me a second. It took us *all* a second before we realized what we were seeing.

Screen after screen after screen of confessions.

I don't know if I should tell my dad about my mom and the grocery clerk. I mean—

I pray for my dad, but he keeps hitting her. And I want to move out, but I can't just lea—

I'm called to lead my brother, but he doesn't know how much I drink. Nobody knows I—

I smoked it last time, but I know it's a matter of time before I—

I love him, so is it really so wrong—

There were screams. *Oh, my Gods*. The pastor scrambled up the aisle. A woman raced him into the sound booth. The screen went black.

Then it was just holy music and holy tears.

The pastor walked slowly back to the stage. A couple counselors moved to sit by some of the kids who were crying, hiding their faces in the shoulders of their friends. It made it worse that they cried so publicly. That the counselors rushed over. They were basically admitting that one of those was theirs—that their dad was a cheater or a wife beater, or they'd had sex or done drugs.

I was relieved my confession hadn't been there. And I was in the room, too, so they couldn't accuse me again.

Or so I thought.

Pastor Kyle apologized, prayed. As he did so, a couple girls kept their eyes open, watching me.

I looked away.

Someone behind me kicked my back. When I turned around, a kid sitting a couple feet behind me glared.

"I gotta be real with you," the pastor said. "We gotta talk about sin anyway, so I'm going to lay it out for you. We're seeing each other's sins in a way that was not meant to be. You're seeing it, and you're tempted to judge one another."

I spotted Holly. She and Payton were actually sitting next to each other.

Payton must've felt me staring. He turned, then pursed his lips and shook his head.

He thought I'd done this. But how could I? I was in the sanctuary with them.

The pastor continued, "Not today, Champions. And, Pampers, you're in the Super Bowl now. Listen up."

He pulled a rolling whiteboard to the stage and drew a diagram up on a screen. A cityscape. It even had the Space Needle, so I knew he was drawing Seattle, a city most of us had at least visited, since the majority of the audience had come from Washington, Oregon, and California.

"And this is how we all see sin," Pastor Kyle continued. "We see some sins as worse than others." He pointed to a squatty building. "Maybe this is telling a little white lie to some of you, not that big. Peeking at someone's paper on a test, maybe."

I was trying to pay attention, but I kept thinking about Payton's accusing eyes. The two girls.

"And maybe this is adultery, cheating on your girlfriend or husband," he said, pointing to the Space Needle, which isn't that tall, though it does stand out.

Something bounced off my head. A crumpled piece of paper. I didn't open it to see if it was a hate note.

"And this is murder." The pastor pointed to the tallest building, which would've had to be the Columbia Tower, since that's the tallest in Seattle.

Then the pastor paused to draw an aerial view of Seattle—a design like a plate for the top of the Space Needle. The dot in the center for the needle turned it into a breast. With a nipple.

I couldn't laugh, though.

Someone cleared his throat. I happened to look up, just in time to see a kid flip me off.

"This is how God sees sin," Pastor Kyle said when he was done with the bird's-eye view. "You can't recognize the height of any of the buildings. None of them are taller, bigger, greater than the others. Your lie is as great as the adultery is as great as murder."

And I swear he was looking right at me.

"Remember that when you look at one another. Before you judge. No matter what you see on this screen."

Amens from the audience.

"T-G-I-J!" someone shouted.

Several campers had their arms around each other. They were feeling His call.

They weren't going to judge each other for what appeared on the screen.

But they were going to judge me because they thought I'd put it up there.

"And now, you know what time it is?!" Pastor Kyle called.

Time to get ill? I wondered, anticipating the Beastie Boys.

"Time to get dirty!" he shouted. Which I did not expect. "Fist pumps for Christ!"

And the kids exploded from their seats, sprinting for the door, nearly trampling me. Matthew held onto my elbow and dragged me out. "Here comes the best part."

Right. He hadn't seen the glares or the spit wads. Even now, the other kids jostled past me too hard.

Matthew was out the door when Dan stepped in front of me. "After we get dirty," he said, jabbing his finger at my chest, "you better come clean."

PRAYERS AND CONFESSIONS

Pastor Kyle: I think about that afternoon often. I think about what I preach to kids about wisdom. I think about what I preach at the church about obedience. It seems small. Just pick up the phone really quick and take a peek. The highway is straight. It's no big deal. But that second could have destroyed a life.

Dan: I found my dad passed out at the table. The steak was burned. Smoke filled the kitchen. I went to school the next day smelling like a house fire. "Your mom needs to wash your clothes," a nerdy kid said. I smashed his face. That doesn't mean I don't love Jesus.

Holly: I don't hear them talking about me. I *feel* them talking about me. Like insects on my skin.

Matthew: I sent Sarah a card. I asked if I could see her. I don't want to get back together or anything. I just want to tell her I didn't abandon her. That it was my parents who sent the money and said I couldn't see her anymore.

♦

The doom and gloom of the sin sermon gave way to a glee stampede as campers raced to their cabins and changed into grubby clothes. Apparently, we were literally going to get dirty.

I didn't run back to my cabin. I just walked.

I thought about finding the PC Box; if I did find the box, would it matter? Would they assume I was just giving back what I'd stolen?

Our cabin was empty when I got there; everyone had already changed clothes and headed out. I considered just hiding in my bunk, but I felt like that would be admitting to something. I had to keep participating. I had to keep putting myself out there, even if it meant judgment and cruelty, because I hadn't done anything wrong.

I dug through my clothes, set aside my HYPERBOLE: BEST. THING. EVER. shirt for the next day. I didn't want to ruin it, and I wanted to show Natalie that I'd returned to the nerd uniform.

In too-short basketball shorts and a faded middle school honor society shirt (yep, I could still fit into a shirt from eighth grade. Barely, but yes), I followed a small mob of campers from another cabin. We headed past the donkey barn, where I'd found Magic Jesus that first night, to a field that I had assumed was off limits because it hadn't been watered. Dry grass and tumbleweeds meant out-of-bounds.

We arrived at a giant mud pit, an Olympic-sized swimming pool of a mud pit.

"Let the sins begin!" someone shouted.

Campers whooped and fist-pumped; Pastor Kyle beamed. I stood there baffled until Matthew called me over to our group.

We were divided into teams, each cabin split into two, for a total of thirty-two teams. We lined up at the edge of the mud pit to compete in a basic relay race.

The three kids before me surged through the mud, their faces getting splattered, their white teeth the only clean thing as they laughed, maniacal and delirious. Then it was my turn. I sank past my ankles in the mud, tiny pebbles and sticks scratching at the soles of my feet. The earth gripped me, and I pulled. I could barely move. And I was hot, and I didn't want to be doing this.

In the first relay, my team came in second—second to the other half of our cabin. Dan called directives from the side of the pit to assist us through the quagmire. He only stopped shouting at us to coach the other team representing our cabin. Either way, he was ensuring his cabin's victory.

Relay after relay, we churned through the mud, new obstacles being set up each time to challenge us.

The campers played the games, rallying to the pastor's anti-judging-sin war cry. It was like nothing had ever happened. It was like we hadn't just seen secrets flashed across the big screen. Everything they'd worried about, everything they'd done, just out for everyone to see.

They all judged each other. I'd witnessed it. They'd judged one another before anyone stole the PC Box.

They judged me.

But just like that, they could put it all aside thanks to the pastor's message. Thanks to a game. It made me sick, the hypocrisy. Right now I was on a team; in ten minutes, they'd be glaring at me again.

In ten minutes, we'd all be waiting for more confessions and prayers, more secrets. No matter the sermon, it was not okay. We couldn't ignore the consequences. The *afters*. Because there were always *afters*, and mine would damn me, far beyond their judgments.

When a counselor announced the next tournament, I walked away from the group.

"Get back over here." Dan grabbed my arm.

"I think I'm done."

"Don't be a douche. We're almost done."

His words ate at me. I didn't want to be a douche. That was the point, wasn't it? I wasn't a douche, even if they thought I was. I shook my head and walked back to my team.

I looked for Natalie, but I didn't see her. She wasn't running the latest relay with Kim's team. I couldn't find the other team that would've come from their cabin.

The next game was an individual race. There were twelve lanes marked with caution tape from one end of the mud pit to the other, like in a swimming pool. The object was to get to the other end of the pit, where twelve girls waited for us, all dressed in shining red devil leotards.

"What are they holding?" I asked Matthew. Each girl had something in her hands, but they were too far away for me to tell what.

"Prizes, for the winners. Like, there's cash and minutes to use the Internet in Babyl On and candy bars and stuff."

A whistle blew, and it was my turn to race. The first few steps were easy. Or easy-ish. I yanked my feet from the mud and got ahead of the other eleven campers. But the farther I went, the harder the mud pulled me down. The mud pit didn't get deeper, but I was definitely sinking more, the closer I got to the finish line.

It was like all the stories I'd heard about quicksand. If you struggled in the muck, you basically ensured your death.

I lifted my legs and worked my body through the mud, realizing two campers had passed me. I looked at the devils at the end of the pit, their faces all made-up with caked-on foundation and fake eyelashes. Their mouths shone with sexy-red lipstick, and their hips and breasts threatened to burst through the silky material of their costumes.

Two more campers passed me in the mud.

And ahead of me, there were twelve girls barely older than me, dressed like prostitutes. Waving around a calling card, or a piece of candy, or a dollar bill.

I stopped racing. All eleven other campers reached the end before me, breathless but proud. Slowly, I worked my legs and hips through the muck to the end of pit and pulled myself out.

I heard a whistle and knew Matthew would be plowing ahead in the lane behind me.

The devilish vixen at the end of my lane looked at me with pity and held the cash behind her back. "Here's some candy," she said in condolence, and I swore she licked her lips at me. I walked away, leaving the Hershey's bar in her pale, long fingers, painted blood-red.

Then it occurred to me: these counselors in scantily clad attire were the embodiment of sin. Not a counselor in a Freddy Krueger mask. Not somebody in a mobster suit. Not a thief, not a drug dealer, not an altar boy–molesting priest. A flirty, sexy girl.

Jeez.

Holly never stood a chance here, did she?

In the heat of the morning, the mud dried and cracked on my skin, leaving it tight. I had scratches on my arms and a cut on my shin from something in the pit. My stomach felt thick, and breakfast felt too close to my throat, from the heat or the exertion. Or the sin-and-devil metaphor.

I was done, and I didn't care what Dan said. I walked away from the pit toward the cabins.

But my devil girl stopped me, her costume glistening in the sunlight, the conciliatory Hershey's bar no longer in her hands.

"You have to clean off," she said. Her makeup was so heavy, she looked like a Shakespearean player.

"Where do you think I'm going?" I said.

"You can't go into the cabins like that. You have to go clean off first. Over there." She pointed back toward the mud pit, where the male counselors had joined the show. Dressed in long robes with crowns on their heads, each one held a green plastic hose in his hands. More Jesuses. Counselor Jesuses. "They clean you off."

One of the Jesuses approached me. "Looks like you're ready for grace."

The devil girl touched my arm. "Kneel."

I was tired of their games. Tired of the fact that they didn't seem to be doing anything about the PC Box except blaming me. The fakeness of all of it. And the hose in his hand looked distinctly like a snaky penis.

So I said, "No." I did not want to kneel before him and be washed clean by his pee-jizz.

The devil and Jesus exchanged a look.

"I'm not going to get on my knees." I reached for the hose.

Jesus stepped back.

"You have to ask him to clean you off. Just kneel," the devil-girl continued.

"I'll just spray you down real quick," Jesus offered in a softer voice, like he knew I was on the brink. "You don't have to kneel. Just hold still."

I grabbed the hose and yanked, but he held on. "I'll do it myself."

Devil-girl grabbed onto the hose and pulled with Jesus, grunting, "That's. The. Point." It was a holy tug-of-war, with both good and evil against me.

Someone, somewhere, must have turned the faucet on, because the water sprayed me in the face all of a sudden. The hose twisted, and the water fountained into the air.

"You're not supposed to do it yourself!" the devil-girl yelled.

I let go of my end of the hose, and she fell back onto her butt in the now-soaked grass. Jesus stumbled back too, still gripping his end of the hose.

I launched myself at him to pry it from his hand, but his sandals slipped out from under him, and we both toppled together, the hose falling impotent to the ground. Jesus snatched it with his free hand, and I yanked it and twisted it in my direction, but only a light spray reached me—not nearly enough to get me clean.

Devil-girl stood up, her leotard dark where the water had saturated it. She stormed off, her face wet from the hose, or perhaps frustrated tears.

I let go of the hose. Jesus rolled away with it, his robe dragging across the ground.

I sat there, alone, no cleaner. I felt a hand grab my shoulder, and I knew it would be Pastor Kyle or Leader Jason or Counselor Dan come to drag me away.

But it was Matthew.

"Dude, what's your problem?"

The sun was too bright and hot, the grass too green and wet, the sky too blue. The kids skipped and frolicked away from the mud pit with their relay rewards. They danced and laughed at the feet of the Jesuses and their plastic green hoses.

"*This* is my problem." I waved my arms around at the circus scene. "I don't want some kid holding some hose over my head waiting for me to give him a blow job or whatever."

Matthew shook his head. "It's just a game."

"All these girls dressed up like she-devils with their boobs all over the place. Like, do you see the irony?"

"No, I see the metaphor."

Of course, I saw the metaphor too. The mud was our sin. We got dirty, we got stuck, yet we continued on to win the prize. In our case, food and Internet and money.

"Fuck this place!" I shouted.

And that's when *People* magazine's Sexiest Pastor Alive arrived. "Let's go," he said, grabbing my elbow, not even trying to be nice anymore.

He didn't call for the cross for me to carry. He didn't try to lay hands and pray. Even he could see I was too far gone for salvation and games.

I looked back to see Matthew heading over to kneel at the foot of a Jesus. Charles positioned himself at the top of a pyramid of still-muddy Disciplettes having their picture taken. The twins, Chris and Christina, were hugging out their forgiveness over the donkey inequality, I assumed.

I followed the pastor to the medical building, where he handed me a hose.

"They could've just let me have it," I said. "I get the Jesus washing sins away part."

He ran his hands through his hair. "Those counselors are just kids like you."

"I don't want to play these crazy games anymore. They're not real. It's not real," I said. "What happens in *real* life is real. What happened on those signs and on that screen, that's real."

"I think you take for granite—"

"Take for *granted*," I corrected.

The pastor just stared at me.

"It's granted, not granite. Do you know how many words you mess up? I have a list in my journal. You know that? I don't write down your scripture. I write down your misuse of the English language." I shook my head and turned off the hose.

The pastor didn't get mad, like I thought he would. Like I hoped he would, frankly. I wanted him to punch me. I needed him to punch me. I needed everyone to take their hardest shot at my face.

"It's your job to know words, but you mess them all up," I said, daring him.

He continued to look at me—not with fury, but with what I thought might be pity. Then he nodded and said, "I may mess them all up. But you're an asshole."

My mouth dropped open.

He raised his eyebrows at me. "Did I get *that* word right?"

I tried to muster indignation, but he was right. He had that one right.

Jack was no doubt somewhere nearby, offering another standing ovation.

PRAYERS AND CONFESSIONS

Matthew: Sarah wasn't tits and ass. She was—is—beautiful. Her voice when she sang. Her smile when she looked at me. I do miss her.

Dan: The next time I punched someone, it was my dad.

Pastor Kyle: It's the impact, that metal on metal, that jars me from sleep. It's thinking about Gabe in his car seat in the back that keeps me from falling asleep at all. A simple text and I could've killed my favorite little guy.

◆

Pastor Kyle led me back from the medical building, down the sidewalk to the sanctuary. He fiddled with the lock on a door, and I stole a glance into the custodian's office. Holly was inside, stacking toilet paper on a cart covered in canvas. She started when she heard the pastor's keys jingle. When she saw me, her face softened, and she dropped the sheet over the cart as she stepped toward the door.

"You missed the mud pit?" I asked, kind of hoping she hadn't witnessed the scene.

"Not the whole thing. Just had to get this for—"

"For Jesus."

"Let's go," the pastor said, tugging at my arm.

Holly smiled slightly. "I'm sorry about all this."

The pastor pulled me into a room I hadn't been in before. A dim light barely glowed from the ceiling; the walls were gray and rough.

"Is this a cave or something?"

"A tomb, yes." He waved toward the risers. "Have a seat."

I picked the ground-level bench in the center and wondered about the room's purpose.

Animal sacrifice, perhaps.

Pastor Kyle sat across from me and leaned forward, his elbows on his knees, his hands together. He looked into my eyes for a moment. "I'm sorry for calling you an asshole."

I shrugged. "I deserve it."

"Something is going on with you."

Well, it didn't take a behavioral expert. I had wrestled with Jesus in a puddle in the grass raging against a hose.

"Nothing is going to get better if you don't confide in someone." He sat up, held up his hands. "I know it doesn't seem that way, with what's going on at camp right now. And I'm not saying I'm that guy for you. Not at all. I believe grace comes through Jesus. But I also believe that we can be that for other people too. I know you reached out to your sister the other night on the phone, and obviously you didn't get what you were hoping for."

I shook my head. But I hadn't really been hoping for grace from her. I had wanted her to ask for mine, honestly. But like Jack said, maybe you couldn't ask that of people. You just had to say the thing and see what happened.

"Maybe when you get home, you can talk to your parents. I can help with that if you want."

There was no way I was talking to my parents. I'd gone months withholding what would only cause more hurt to them. But I said, "Yeah, sure," just to make the pastor happy.

He was dubious. He didn't know all his grammar, but I think he knew people.

"You know where we're sitting?" he asked.

"A tomb," I repeated. And then I got why he brought me to this creepy place.

"That's right. The tomb where Jesus lay for three days while the world waited for Him." He nodded, leaned back, and looked at me again. "We all need the dark times to recognize His light."

I didn't believe in what he believed. I didn't believe in Jesus as the son of God. I didn't believe in a God who thought we had to hurt just so we could heal. Who set us up to hurt for the benefit of healing us. That just sounded like codependency.

"We have to wrestle with our demons, we have to spend forty days in the desert, we have to carry our own cross. This is religious jargon to you, isn't it?"

"Yeah, I guess. No offense or anything."

Pastor Kyle smiled. "I believe it, though."

"I would hope so, given your job and everything."

"Yes. But that's not what I mean. Not as a man of God. I believe it as a human. I don't think you can *see* if you haven't been blind. I don't believe you can recognize grace if you haven't been stuck in a tomb."

"Wait." Panic cracked my voice. "You can't lock me in here."

"Is that what you think?" He laughed. "Now that's crazy, locking you in some jail cell."

My jaw dropped again. I wanted to point out the Donkey Lottery, the selfies with prostitutes, and Judas with his noose and coin purse. Rap turned into gospel. I had just been told to kneel before a teenager dressed like Jesus while some other hot teenager strutted around in a shiny red leotard.

Locking me in a tomb seemed par for the course.

He slapped his knees. "I *am* going to leave you in here now, but I'm not going to lock the door. You stay as long as you like. Or follow me out." He scratched his jaw. "Anyway, I don't think I need to lock you in a dark place. I suspect you're in one now. Quiet time is a gift, so take it if you want."

Quiet was torture. Boring at best, it invited memories and ghosts and guilt at worst.

But I guess that was his point. The being alone with yourself, the silence poking at you, beating you, torturing the truth out.

Pastor Kyle stood up and opened the door. He turned around one more time.

"My job is not about words, by the way. Preaching is not about all those words." He pulled out a small book from his back pocket. "It's about *the* Word. And I pray before I use it so that I get it right." He slipped the little Bible back into his jeans. "Grammar gods be damned!" At this, he laughed and pulled the door closed behind him. It clicked in place, and then everything was silent.

Really silent.

I couldn't hear the campers or counselors, birds or planes.

I wanted to stand up and leave, but I honestly had nowhere to go. I'd embarrassed myself out by the mud pit, and I was afraid to face Matthew. I owed the two counselors an apology, but I wasn't ready for that either.

I lay down on the bench, and I felt the silence and memories tear into me like bamboo under my fingernails.

♦

After my sister's wake, after everyone had left what remained of my family in our silent house, we sat at the kitchen table while my mom poured some wine for herself. My dad drank something dark with whiskey.

It's my fault hung like cigarette smoke over the whole house, heavy and thick.

My dad pulled something from his front pocket. He slid it across the table at me. At first I thought it was a coin, from the metallic drag it made across the wood, but then I recognized it as a key.

"What's this for?" I asked.

"Hide it," he said.

I looked at my mom, and then we both looked at my dad.

"Hide it anywhere in the bedroom."

"Honey, what're you doing?" my mom asked.

"I want to try something."

"How much whiskey have you had?" My mom asked. My parents didn't drink often, and when they did, they didn't drink a lot.

"What does it matter?" My dad was not the belligerent type, but he'd just been to the funeral for his daughter, who shot herself. "Nick, I said hide the key."

I picked up the key. "I don't really want to do this," I said.

"It's like hide-and-seek, Nick. You hide it. I seek it. How hard is it to find this key?"

My mom teared up, sank into a chair, but she didn't tell him to stop.

There was something else thick in the room, beyond the guilty haze. I was scared of it. It was a tension I'd never felt. My parents had stood united their whole marriage—through the chaotic kid-taxiing, my dad's layoff, selling the house, the Charlotte drama.

But the death of their child.

Diana's suicide.

Like a sharp blade ready to cut the fragile string that kept everything peacefully tethered.

I scooted my chair back, the legs scraping against the linoleum, and walked out of the room.

My dad watched me, dark-eyed, but eager for some sick game where he tried to find a small key hidden in a small room. My mom walked over to the kitchen sink and poured her wine out. They both followed me to the living room. She stood against the wall, arms crossed, and watched my dad sink into the couch. I continued down the hall to my parents' bedroom, where my dad had always hidden the key.

The shades were drawn, the lights still out, the air stale. I sat on their bed and looked around the room. I wasn't pondering a hiding spot. I was waiting for the requisite amount of time to make it *seem* like I was pondering a hiding spot, to make my dad think I was playing his game.

It was ordinary, this room. The closet door, open a bit. Dark dressers, a jewelry box, a photo album. It was an old album, filled with Diana's school pictures, the one my mom pored over regularly.

I counted thirty more seconds and then walked over to closet, pulled out the old Monopoly board game. I opened the box—the edges of the lid were broken—and set the key next to the metal dog and car game pieces, the little plastic hotels. I put the box back up on the shelf and walked out of the room.

That's where he always kept the key to the gun cabinet, and I knew he'd never look there.

♦

"I'm not one for Bible-thumping, but I dig what that cat's got to say."

I opened my eyes.

Jack.

"Nice demonstration out there, by the way," he said to me. "You really showed that hose."

"I'm really exhausted."

"You just napped."

"By you." I sat up. "I'm exhausted by you."

"Yes, yes, yes. Where's your catalyst friend, Natalie? She has great taste in literature."

I rolled my eyes. He'd clearly heard what she'd said about him up on the hill.

"What was that book she gave you?"

"It wasn't one of your books. You wouldn't call what she gave me 'literature.'"

"She's a fire under your ass, that's what she is."

"Don't say something perverted here."

"She burns bright, doesn't she? All firefly and firelight and sunglare."

"I guess, yeah."

"Like your sister. Matthew too, a little bit, though I'm not sure you like him the way you like Natalie." Jack winked at me. "Or maybe so. I do not judge."

And it was true he didn't. But on this point, he couldn't. Rumors flew all over about his romances, with women and men alike.

He stood up and walked around the room, running his hand against the wall.

"You know that poster in your room. The people who read that poster, who read that book—" he spit the last part out, his mouth curled in disdain.

"*On the Road*," I said for him.

He nodded. "They're thinking that was me, that I was mad and crazy and capricious and destructive and distrustful and irrevocably wild and wistful. Because I wrote the damn book, they think I was a Roman candle," he said.

I hadn't read the book. But yes, I believed that too. He was the author, after all. Of a book about freedom and living and lust and debauchery. And finding yourself within and without all of it. About liberty.

"I *was* and was *not* that. I was and was not a Roman candle." He continued, "I was quiet, I observed, I appreciated everything around me. I loved God, I missed my brother, I looked for angels, I was scared of God and ghosts and my mother."

He paced for a moment. "If it weren't for the mad ones, if it weren't for the Roman candles, I might never have taken to that road. You hear me?" He turned from the wall to make sure I had.

I nodded.

"I was as much the guy on that road as I was the man stuck in his bedroom, mute fingertips against the typewriter, digging around in my brain for the Great American Novel. I needed Neal, I needed Alan—you don't know who they are, but trust me on this point—or I don't hop in a car and go back and forth across the continent and down into Mexico.

"And I see that in you. That dichotomy. You've got the madness in you. I see it. Your sister saw it. But you need other people."

"Like my sister," I said.

"And like Natalie. They light you up, make you brighter. We're not all Roman candles, but we're all meant to burn bright."

"My sister burned herself out."

Jack looked at me warmly, offered a slight nod. "That she did. But you won't."

I wanted to believe him. I wanted to believe what my sister had told me when I was a boy, that I had ten lives and I just had to choose to live big. "But I don't do anything. You say it yourself. So how do you know I'm mad too?"

"You must be, or I wouldn't be here." He sauntered down the risers. "We're all mad here. You're mad. I'm mad." He was clearly reciting something.

"Did you write that?"

"The Cheshire Cat."

"Lewis Carroll?"

"The very one."

I hadn't read that classic either, but I'd seen the movie. A rabbit's hole, pills and libations making Alice bigger, then smaller, talking flowers, a caterpillar smoking an opium pipe. "He was pretty messed up," I said.

"The great ones always are. And they are vilified and adored for it." Jack was suddenly standing at the door. "So, how long are you going to hide in this dungeon?"

I shrugged. "I don't know what else to do."

"What do you want to do?"

"Find the box."

"Have you been listening and seeing?" he asked, dark brows raised.

"Uh, yeah, but it doesn't help."

"Then you're listening without ears." He opened the door. "And seeing without eyes." When he walked out, he left the door open.

♦

Listening without ears. Seeing without eyes.

I'd been able to investigate the custodian's office. Maybe I needed to check the barn. I'd been in one cabin; I could sneak into the others. I needed to keep at this. I needed to find Magic Jesus. After all, I was in too much trouble to get into more, and everyone already hated me.

There was liberty in being the outsider—like standing at the edge of a cliff. It kind of made nothing matter. I wouldn't let Dan tell me to stay and play games. I'd skip the pastor's evening message. I wouldn't show up for the Trust Circle or the pranks. Instead, I'd stay up all night, if that's what it took to find that robed savior-custodian.

But first, I had to change my clothes. Bits of mud still stuck to my legs. And I needed my shoes.

I walked down the sidewalk and was halfway through the grass when I stopped dead.

There was Magic Jesus. Just ahead of me, setting up his table. I walked toward him as he settled in the middle of the field next to the volleyball courts. His entourage hadn't spotted him yet. Perfect timing.

"Hey," I said.

"How's it goin'?" It was his Hillbilly Jesus voice.

The campers were done with the mud pit. Some were being rinsed off in an industrial setup like a car wash. Some had already done that and were heading into their rooms to change. Doors were slamming. Open, closed. No one was approaching us.

"I looked up that Bible verse," I said.

No one was at the pool. Everyone was going into the cabins. Coming out, running down stairs.

Jesus looked around him. Now he'd noticed the running. "There's a few of those."

"The one you told me about," I said.

No one was playing volleyball or buying ice cream. They were just running in and out, to their own and then other people's cabins. In and out.

What the hell?

Shouting, tears.

"Nick!" Matthew shouted. "Get up here."

"We'll talk later," Jesus said. He folded up his table and headed off across the green.

I ran up the stairs to our room. Charles was sitting cross-legged on the ground, crying.

"What's going on?"

"The confessions," he sobbed. There was red paint on his palms.

I heard voices in the bathroom and walked in, Matthew behind me. Payton and Chris stood looking into a stall.

Oh, gawd. Had Jack left another graphic illustration of the crucifixion?

I peeked in, over their shoulders.

No. It was words. Blood-red words painted on every stall wall.

Charles had paint all over his hands. "And he blamed me," I said. It was obvious from the get-go that he'd wanted me to get in trouble. But he'd been caught. Literally red-handed.

Chris said, "This is bad."

They were all staring at one painted confession:

Please forgive me for threatening the school. I wasn't really going to shoot the teachers. I want to go back to school.

Wait.

There was only one kid who wasn't in school, public or private.

Oh.

That's why Charles had been crying. He hadn't been caught painting. And that's why he'd been all fidgety lately. He'd had another confession in the box.

"Charles was the first one in here," Goth said.

"Trying to wipe it off."

And they kept talking. But I wasn't listening anymore.

The paint.

The custodian's office.

The paint was all on that shelf in his office. That's why Jesus had been just standing there. He'd been watching the chaos he'd created unfold. And then he'd fled the scene.

He had opportunity. He had motivation. And now I had the evidence. But before going to the pastor, I was going to go to that office and get my confession.

I headed toward the door, but Payton grabbed my shoulder. "Where were *you* when this was painted?" Payton asked.

"What?"

"You left the mud pit."

"I know. I was with the pastor."

"We saw the pastor come back." Matthew watched me.

"I know. He left me in that tomb place."

"By yourself?"

"Yeah."

"So you were alone?" Matthew continued.

"I didn't paint these," I said. "Why would I paint these?"

"Why would anyone paint them?"

"I told you. My confession's in that box, and I want it back just as bad as you."

"We haven't seen it," Matthew argued. "We haven't seen anything about your sister." Matthew was looking at me, just as I'd looked at him when the box disappeared. "That's gotta be what your confession is about. It's the thing you don't want to talk about."

And I glared at him as if my eyes could shoot bullets. He wasn't on my side anymore. "Everybody already knows my sister shot herself. It's not a secret."

"Yeah, and it's also not a secret you hate Charles. And it wouldn't be hard to figure out this was his confession," Payton said.

"Are you serious right now? Listen, I think I know who did it."

"Dude, are *you* serious right now? Are we supposed to believe you?"

Yes, Matthew *was* supposed to believe me. He and Natalie had been the only ones left who weren't throwing spitballs at me or kicking me or glaring. "Someone did see me in that tomb place," I continued.

"You just said the pastor left. You're lying. Or you're insane."

I was. I was insane. Jack had been the only one who saw me in that tomb.

But Holly had seen me go in.

"Okay, if you really think I did it, go tell on me. But I have to do something."

I ran out of the bathroom, past Charles sitting on sad road. I was now one of hundreds of kids running out of my cabin. But I wasn't off to read another gossipy confession. I wasn't seeking solace with my bestie. I wasn't praying to some god.

I ran past the other campers. Past the empty volleyball court, past the empty pool, past Magic Jesus or Hillbilly Jesus, or whatever role he wanted to play. I had him now. But I wanted my confession—and the evidence—in my hand before I turned him in.

He stood watching the melee, arms folded, no one seeking his miracles.

◆

The door was closed when I got to the custodian's office, but I let myself in. It was my third time entering without being asked.

The cart with the paint buckets wasn't there. But the laptop was.

I opened it up. And there it was.

Not child porn. The slideshow. It started out as rap, then contemporary lyrics. And then confession after confession. It had a hundred twenty slides.

So it *was* Jesus. Jesus by day, custodian by night, confession bandit behind the scenes. I scanned the shelves again for the PC Box. Maybe I had just missed it the night before. I spun around, looked up and down. No, it wasn't there. I opened the cupboard. The paint cans were gone, and there was no box.

I spotted the two buckets from the night of the garbage can pranks. They were stacked where I'd found the one behind the custodian's work apron. The apron thing wasn't there now, so it was easy to see them. And easy to see they weren't stacked properly.

When I lifted the one out of the other, I saw why. The bottom bucket was a foot deep with little scraps of paper.

I set the bucket down and knelt next to it. I dipped my hands in, and the papers shifted away like sand. Every confession.

I would turn them in, turn in Custodian Jesus. But I wanted mine out first. Surely, the pastor wouldn't let me dig through them later.

I dumped them all out on the floor. Then I read and read and read, discarding each into the bucket if it wasn't mine. Some of the prayers were ridiculous to me—bigger boobs, bigger penis, hotter girlfriend, any boyfriend. But some were devastating—cancer and Alzheimer's and abuse and poverty and meanness and guilt and loneliness.

So much loneliness. Like nobody understood one another. Like nobody loved each other.

And then I saw one that I recognized. Not the confession, but the handwriting.

I knew the handwriting.

I'd seen it in the book she'd given me, the handwritten inscription and sample margin notes.

I was holding Natalie's confession in my hands.

Please pre-forgive me for running away to find my meth-y brother. And then there was a sketch of Frankenstein's monster.

Or a zombie.

I put my head in my hands.

That was, in fact, the nickname of meth heads. Zombies. Heroin addicts were sleepwalkers. Meth heads were zombies. Zombie camp wasn't some drama thing. I hadn't really heard her.

There was another sentence on her confession. I read it. My stomach clenched. I read it again.

Forgive me for shooting up too.

My face flushed. I should not know this. I should not have seen this. I felt some kind of sick shame for her.

She hadn't lied about her confession. She would not be going to City School if this got out. It violated every contract any high schooler ever signed. It violated the law.

And she was running away.

I'd seen her on the hillside twice. I'd even found her on the hillside with her backpack on. Full of food and water. Had she been running away then? Or trying to?

I'd seen her just that morning. She'd given me that book, and she'd seemed weird for a second. Then she'd gone back to normal.

But I hadn't seen her the rest of the day. She wasn't at the mud pit. I'd seen Kim, but I hadn't seen Natalie.

I had to tell Pastor Kyle.

Right after I found my confession.

I set Natalie's on the desk, then sifted through another handful of papers and found mine—all caps and a lot shorter than what other people had written.

"What are you doing here?"

I turned around, hands up in surrender.

Not Dan this time, but not Jesus either.

It was Holly.

"Hey, I know this looks bad. But I found all the confessions," I said, sweeping my hands over the pile on the floor.

She stepped in the room. "I see that."

I stood up, my confession in hand.

"The custodian took them," I said. "I know everyone thinks it's me because I said weird things and I found one of the confessions, but it wasn't. It was that Jesus guy, which makes sense because he has access to them. You know, the guy with the master key always has the most power." I was rambling.

"Everyone had access to them," she said. "They were on the stage."

"Right, yeah, but I meant at night."

"The doors were all unlocked." She looked at me. "You would know, right?"

"Know what?"

"That, with the exception of the tomb room, all the doors are unlocked."

I stared at her. "Are you talking about the pranks?" She was not acting alarmed. "You know about the pranks?"

"You mean the night you snuck in here and accused Jimmy of being a pedophile because my laptop was open on his desk?"

"Who's Jimmy?"

"The custodian?" She sighed. "Jesus?"

Hillbilly Jesus's name was Jimmy. Dear gawd, the universe was so perfect sometimes.

"Dan said that, not me."

"Whatever, Nick. I saw you in here."

"Yeah, okay. So I'm going to go talk to Pastor Kyle."

"Nick, please don't do that," she moved to the center of the doorway, her hands out, stopping me from walking out.

"Wait . . . *your* laptop," I said. And that's when I saw the paint—a little on her palms, a little on her fingers. Red. And smeared. "You had opportunity . . ." I said, mostly to myself. She had access to this office. And she'd come out of the sanctuary last, later than anyone that night. She'd been so distracted. She'd been more Holly and less Red Lips Ho-Lo. She had the slideshow with all the confessions.

"Opportunity?" she asked.

I'd seen her with that computer bag. I'd seen her loading the cart with paints. She'd had a folder of papers in her cubby. Maybe more confessions, to tape to more signs and post all over camp again. "Yes," I said. "But motivation?" I looked from her hands to her face. "Why would you steal these confessions? Why would you put them all over?"

"Oh, my God." She pulled her hands through her hair. "You have no idea, do you?"

"What don't I know?"

"Do you know what it's like to be condemned, over and over and over again?"

That word. Condemned. What had Diana said once? *They condemn me for the love I have to give.*

"All. Year. Long. They just keep telling stories about me. Do you even know how many *true* stories there are to tell about me? Two, Nick. Two true stories. I've slept with two guys." She bit her lip. "And maybe that's a lot. Maybe that's a lot for a sixteen-year-old Christian girl. Or maybe it doesn't matter. Or maybe everyone is fucking everyone else too, but the goings-on in my vagina are of utmost interest."

Her face folded, like she was going to cry. I reached out for her and she shrugged me away.

"Do you want to know the worst part of all of it? Those aren't even the stories I really hear about myself. I don't hear the truth. Nobody talks about me and Payton. Nobody talks about the other guy, who also goes to our school." She laughed. "No, it's all just made-up stories. If I sigh, I'm breathing all hot and heavy. If I put my hand on someone's shoulder, I'm flirting. If I walk just so, I'm shaking my ass."

She put on a California-girl accent, "Oh, my God, did you see how much makeup she wore? Oh, my God, she's not wearing any makeup . . ." Back to her normal voice. "Yeah, 'cause even ugly me is scandalous." And then California Girl returned. "Oh, my God, she curled her hair today. Oh, my God, her hair's straight today. Who is Holly after next? Who's on Holly's 'play' list? Who's on her greatest 'hit' list?" She looked at me, "Oh, you haven't heard those? Get it?"

She squinted her eyes and put on a look of fake interest. "Have you heard about why Payton broke up with me? Let me tell you the boring truth. I *didn't* have sex with anyone. I got too drunk at a party one night. And, guess what? So did everyone else at my school. But that was too boring, so let's make up a new story—according to my classmates, I slept with like five guys that night. All of us! At one time! In the parents' bedroom or some shit!"

She raised her eyebrows at me. "Yeah, that's why Payton and I broke up. Because I"—air quotes—"cheated on him. I didn't fucking cheat on him! I went to a party and got drunk and probably batted my eyes at cute boys. But even Payton, who's supposed to *love* me, believed the stories instead of me."

My stomach twisted. I didn't want to hear this. I felt guilt, and shame. I had listened to the stories about Holly. I had laughed at the jokes. Even when I started to feel uncomfortable, I had never stood up for her. I never really asked her if she was okay.

My shame and her shame churned inside me.

I felt Charlotte's shame too. As much as I didn't want to, I felt it. She had been judged over and over. Everyone around her had insisted she could only be one thing, just like they tried to fit Holly into a tiny box. And she must've felt the same anger and desperation. The solution, for her, had been to choose something new. To grab on to God—no, to grab on to a list of rules that she got from her understanding of God.

That's not how everyone did it. But that's what Charlotte did. I didn't agree, but all of a sudden I saw, through Holly, why my sister grabbed on so tightly. Why she still hadn't let go.

"Holly . . ."

"You mean Ho-Lo, right? Yeah, I know what they call me."

She shook her head.

"Do you know what Matthew's confession is? Or do you know what it should be? Have you ever asked him? Ask him why his parents sent him to Valley Christian. Ask him about his pregnant girlfriend."

"I didn't know about that," I said.

"I know you didn't. People from school know, but we don't talk about it. It's *impolite*." Holly air-quoted. "But my business is open to everyone twenty-four seven. Do you know all the shit in that box? Well, you do now, because I put it out there."

"Holly—"

"You probably think I'm so, so, so evil. And maybe I am. But more than evil, I am tired. I am so fucking tired of being the story that everybody tells. Look around at what's going on in people's private lives. I am *not* the only one. And that's what I want them to see. I want them stop talking about *me*. Because everybody has a fucking story!"

Holly's face was splotchy, from tears and fury both.

She'd stolen every hope and every secret. She'd publicized them.

And they would crucify her for it. She would lose everything—certainly her work scholarship to camp. Her boyfriend, every friend, her private school.

"I won't tell."

She wiped snot from her nose. It was not hot. It was real. "What?"

"I promise. I won't tell anyone."

She laughed then. Like a crazy-witch laugh. "Yeah right. You have every reason to tell. You're the one serving the sentence for everything I've done. They made you drag a cross." She shook her head. "Like you'd steal anything."

She sounded like Jack.

"I won't tell. But you need to," I said.

"Oh, hell no."

"Not everyone. Just Pastor Kyle." Then I added, "John 1:9."

"Did you just quote the Bible to me? Like, actually?"

"I mean 1 John 1:9." I wouldn't make her think there was some light she couldn't see. Though, I guess that was true of all of us. We were constantly searching.

"Are you serious right now?"

"Listen, everybody knows this place isn't for me. But, Pastor Kyle, he's . . . I don't know . . . he's looking out for everyone." And I believed what I was saying. I had seen him working with the campers. I had seen them come to him in tears and in laughter. I had seen him stand up on that stage and speak. He trusted in the Word, and he believed his own words, and he wanted to share the beauty and truth he knew with everyone else. He was what this camp was really about. Not Charlotte, not people like her. The pastor—grammar abuse and all. "If you tell him, I won't tell anyone."

She considered. "Give me one more day, Nick."

I stared at her. My confession. Natalie's confession. I would need Charles to math out the chances that any one confession would be pulled out in a twenty-four-hour period. It was the Hunger Games all up in here. The odds may have been in our favor, but we had all seen what happened to Primrose Everdeen anyway. "Why would I give you one more day?"

"I'll make you a deal. Take your confession. I'll give you that. You give me another day."

And I could hardly believe myself, but . . . I wanted to give her something. Because we—all the campers—had taken and taken and taken. We told stories that stole her truth. We told jokes that stole her dignity. We talked about her like she was our story to tell. And maybe we owed her something: the chance to tell her truth. The *choice* to tell her story. What Holly was doing was wrong, but she still deserved what she'd wanted all along. The power to say what really happened.

"If I give you a day, will you tell Pastor Kyle?"

She sighed and looked down at the floor. "Yes."

I clenched my confession in my hand and thought of my parents. What these words would do to their barely-there connection. The way they argued, the way they turned sullen, the contempt that festered between them. The silence that had grown so large that it had pushed my dad out for a while. They'd told me he was traveling, but I wasn't stupid. And now he was back. I didn't know the chances of them getting a divorce, but if they knew what I'd done, they had to be exponential.

I hesitated. "I take one confession, you get a day, and you go talk to Pastor Kyle tomorrow?"

Holly nodded.

I picked up the slip of paper on the desk. I read it, and I read mine. Finally, I dropped my own confession back into the pile.

I stirred up the papers before I changed my mind. I was battling math. Fighting the probability that Holly would pull that confession.

"This is the one," I said.

My confession shouted at me as I ran out the door. It beseeched me to come back for it. But I didn't.

I held on to Natalie's.

Natalie's probability of having her confession pulled was the same as mine. But if it was pulled, the chances of her getting kicked out of her school were 100 percent. My parents divorcing . . . well, there was no way to know. And I couldn't tell people how to live their lives. I couldn't control their *afters*.

♦

Pastor Kyle was in Babyl On counseling a sobbing girl. I could see them through the window. The door was locked; I knocked on the glass.

He opened the door and leaned his head out. "Nick, give me a few minutes."

"I just have to talk to you about Natalie really fast." I figured he'd respond quicker to her name than to some heathen like me.

"Okay, buddy. I've got a situation. Make it fast."

"I'm worried about her."

"I'm worried about a lot of these kids, Nick. Look around. A lot of hurting people."

I wanted to tell him about Holly. But I couldn't.

But if I told the pastor about Natalie, he could help me save her. And it's not like he was going to post her secret for the campers to see.

"I think she ran away."

"What makes you say that?"

"Well, she wanted to see her brother."

"You know about her brother?"

"Kind of. He's a—"

"A methamphetamine addict, yes. At a clinic nearby." And then he patted my shoulder.

He already knew the truth about her. Imagine everything else he knew. I bet half those confessions weren't even surprises to him.

"But don't worry, Nick," the pastor said. "He checked out."

"Wait, what? He checked out?"

"Of rehab."

On the hillside the day before, she'd said he was there, at zombie camp.

And she was running away to go see him. Because she thought he was still there.

"Did you tell her he checked out?"

"Hold on a second, Nick. This is a longer conversation than I can do right now. Give me a few."

He slipped back inside and sat down across from the still-sobbing girl.

I stood there and waited.

Natalie was going to walk twenty miles to see her brother, only to find out he wasn't there. And she was going to be alone when she heard he was gone.

I waited.

Natalie was going to learn her brother was out on the street, probably doing drugs again. What would she do? Would she keep running, or walk back to camp alone?

Would she shoot up again? Did she have something on her?

I didn't know what she would do, but she shouldn't have to be alone when she heard this.

Pastor Kyle kept looking over at me through the window, flashing his hand, holding up fingers. Giving me a five-minute sign. A ten-minute sign. The minutes were definitely going the wrong way.
"How long will you walk down waiting road?" It was Jack.

"Someone's going to see you!" I grabbed at him to pull him toward the wall. But my hand slipped through his jacket.

"Nobody sees me but the madness in you."

"Other people might see ghosts!"

"Ghosts." He laughed.

"This isn't funny."

"You found the doer of wrongs. I told you so."

"You didn't tell me. I figured it out."

"I whispered through the dark swirl of the Ouija."

"Seriously? You gave us a list of Christmas songs."

"I saved it, best—and truth—for last."

I went through the list in my head. "The Holly and the Ivy." That's what he'd said last.

He smiled. "The end, Nicolas. Everything is settled in the end. The end is the *it* of it all."

He swayed. "Did I tell you who was at camp?"

"Yes, Muhamm—"

"Muhammad, Buddha, Jesu—"

"Are you drunk?"

"Whoop, look at that! Jesus *can* turn it all into wine."

"For God's sake, you are now."

"That ol' Indian—"

"It's Native Ameri— Can you just leave so the pastor doesn't catch you?"

"Catch *you*, you mean. Talking to the nothing-wind."

I glared at Jack, then looked through the office window at the pastor and the sobbing girl. "Just say a prayer and get on with it," I mumbled at the glass.

"Waiting road goes down a winding thing toward everywhere, which is nothing."

I was tired of his word-puzzling. "What am I supposed to do?" I snapped. "I just want him to help Natalie and he won't open the door!"

I expected Jack to snap back, to explode into his torrent of impatience. To call me the Great Editor and spin into nothing like he sometimes did. But his voice stayed calm. "You found the box, and the *doing's* not done." He sounded almost kind again. "I can't do the *doing* for you."

Oh.

He wouldn't say it outright—he was still waiting for me to hear it and see it without him ever saying it. And most of the time, I couldn't see or hear what I was supposed to. Not just with Jack. With people. With my family. With Diana. Most of the time, I felt surrounded by broken bridges. But I understood him then. I actually understood his word-bridge.

He wanted me to live a little.

He wanted me to go a little mad.

He wanted me to break the rules.

And so I did.

♦

I walked quickly back to my cabin to check the camp schedule. I needed to know how long I'd have before someone suspected me gone. There were several more hours till free time, then a service, then dinner. Nobody would be looking for me in particular at the service. We didn't have assigned seats or anything. They might wonder at dinner, but then they might assume I was still imprisoned for stealing the PC Box, since my cabinmates still thought I had. Only the pastor and Holly knew for sure I wasn't still being punished, but they were both preoccupied.

I looked through my cabinmates' cubbies and gathered any unopened snacks. Sour Patch Kids, two bags of chips, two cans of Monster. Now I was actually stealing something from them, and I didn't care. I filled my water bottle from the bathroom sink and then went over to Dan's bunk, knowing he'd have something slightly more sustaining. And he did—a half-filled, Costco-sized bag of trail mix.

I'd never walked twenty miles.

And that was just to get *to* zombie camp. There was also the twenty miles back. Forty miles.

Forty miles through the desert.

I stole three more water bottles from my fellow campers and filled them up too.

I tossed a sweatshirt and sweatpants into my backpack. I figured I'd be spending the night, and it was bound to be cold in the desert. Well, colder than the ninety degrees it was during the day. I couldn't take my blanket off my bed because that would be too obvious. I considered taking the pillow, but I doubted it would fit in my backpack.

And then, to cheer Natalie when I found her—because I assumed she'd need the cheering—I shoved *Sixty Scenes of Sexy* into the bag too.

I slipped my arms into the shoulder straps and opened the door.

And that is when I heard the voice of the Lord booming from the heavens.

Or rather, I heard the donkeys braying for their afternoon snack.

I'd never walked twenty, or forty, miles before. And I wasn't about to now, either.

♦

The donkey braying got louder as I approached the barn. I pulled an armful of hay off a bale and threw it into the shade of the barn's overhang. They ate, and I assessed. They all looked of the same build, the same motivation, the same intelligence—which is to say, not much of any of it. But then a brown one made eye contact.

He accidentally volunteered himself.

"You," I said to the brown donkey. "You're the one from the other night. You're coming with me."

The donkey shook his head and ducked down for more hay. Now, he might've been trying to rid his mane of flies, but that seemed like overt defiance of my command. Stubborn ass.

"It'll be an adventure."

The donkey chewed.

"As opposed to getting my ass chewed, my ass is doing the chewing. Get it?" The donkey did not laugh. "Fine, you eat. I'm looking for the bridle."

It was too much to hope for a bridle and a saddle. Did they even make that kind of stuff for donkeys, or were they assed out of the equestrian tack business?

I put a halter over Donkey's ears. "You look like a horse mated with a rabbit." And he did, all ears and teeth.

The hay was almost gone, and I was polite enough to wait for him to finish chewing his last bite. I attached the lead rope the counselors had used the first day for the Donkey Lottery, and then I walked him through the gate. It was unlocked. Apparently donkey theft wasn't an issue. Yet.

I looked at the hill behind the barn. It was steeper, but we had to go that route or we'd be spotted. We might still be spotted. A donkey is not exactly inconspicuous.

I prepped my travel companion. "We gotta haul ass."

My donkey was humorless. Maybe he'd been the butt of too many jokes in his lifetime.

"Actually," I said, and closed the gate behind me. "Ass has to haul me."

◆

Donkey and I made it up the hillside unnoticed. Maybe because he is a part-time ninja. But mostly because a lot of the trail runs through a crevasse where no one could see us.

I stumbled up over the ridge, my sure-footed companion by my side. I led him down the dip into the valley and walked over to the crosses, still out of breath from climbing so quickly. I took my first sip of water and stared at my donkey.

"Wait here, Ninja." He didn't argue about waiting, or about his new name. I figured there had to be some trademark issue with calling him Donkey, thanks to the creators of *Shrek*.

I wanted to take a peek at camp again. I lay on my stomach and crawled across the dusty ground till I could see it sprawled out before me.

Eden Springs was an oasis in this desert. A man-made paradise of lush grass and trees that revealed the glistening underside of the leaves when the breeze blew. The pool water was crystalline, the cabin and paths and outbuildings all perfectly situated and planned. Anywhere you stood in camp, you could see the whole property. You'd always know where everyone was and what they were doing. It took effort to disappear.

I scooted back down the decline and then stood up, looked in the direction Natalie had been headed when I'd caught her with her backpack. That's what I had to go on—straight toward the horizon in the direction she'd pointed the day before. It was barely noon, and it was already hot. And I didn't see a single tree. I knocked on the wood of the middle cross for good luck, then walked through the small strip of shade it offered.

I had about eighty ounces of water. That wasn't even enough for one full day of healthy hydration, but I knew it would be enough to survive twenty miles, which I'd cover by dark, if my calculations served me. If Charles didn't hate me, perhaps I could've had him double-check my formula. It was hot, and that's what worried me most. There was bound to be minimal shade. The land was all shrubs and sharp rock and dry earth, everything dusty yellow and sage. I knew there'd be rattlesnakes, and I anticipated maybe some coyotes, nothing too vicious.

Without a compass, I planned to find landmarks to keep my direction. The three crosses would be in my sight for a long time, and they always had to be to my back. If I got to a point where I couldn't see the crosses, and there was nothing else to track my location by, then I would abandon this mission and head back toward the crosses.

I led Ninja over to a rock.

"Don't move."

He didn't. Or if he did, I couldn't see it because, well, he's a ninja.

I swung my leg over his broad back. And slipped right off. I swung again, and slipped off again. The third time, I got enough leverage to hold on. After some grunting and shifting and pulling—Ninja just standing there all the while—I got myself onto his back.

I reconsidered naming him Job because, like the dude in the Bible who came down with the plague and his kids all died, the donkey had a shit-ton of patience.

Unfortunately, he just kept standing there. I didn't have a counselor to lead us.

"Go," I commanded.

He didn't.

I rocked back and forth. "You have to walk."

He did not walk. Perhaps because he's a silent assassin and *just walking* requires no stealth. Or perhaps because there were no shadows in this godforsaken desert. A ninja needs shadows.

"Please?"

A ninja need not have manners.

So I kicked my heels into his sides and hoped he'd seen enough cowboy movies to know this is how it was done. Clearly he was a fan of John Wayne, because off we went.

I considered renaming him The Duke.

◆

The sun beat down. After a while, I took my shirt off, but the heavy rays only got worse when they landed directly on my skin, so I put it back on.

I made sure to look back often to check my direction. Only once did I think we would have to go back, when I turned around and noticed I couldn't see the crosses, but then we came out of a dip and my landmark reappeared.

After about an hour, I clambered off Ninja to give him some water and a break. I saw a building, maybe an old barn, way off in the distance and felt good that I had another landmark to keep our path true.

I took hold of the lead rope, and we walked on.

The scraping of my feet, the clank of Ninja's hooves on shale-like rocks, and my breathing were all that I could hear. I stopped to sip water, the unzipping of my backpack a rip in the silence, my gulps intrusive.

Everything was beige and brittle for as far as I could see. Everything silent without the drag of feet and hooves across the dust. The crosses were specks on the horizon behind me, the barn to my left just as small. The air coughed up a breeze and a light rattle of leaves on the bushes. I'd never been so alone.

"No offense," I said to Ninja.

No one knew I was there. I decided I had better not think about that too long, lest I go insane.

And then I realized something.

What I was doing *was* insane. Stealing a donkey and then hiking out into the desert wilderness with little food and water, looking for a girl in a place I was not even certain was out here.

Zombie camp. Rehab.

I slipped my water bottle into my backpack again, and the pack back over my shoulders. I led Ninja to a rock, and it only took me two tries to get astride his back.

I *was* a mad one. At least on this day.

Diana would've been proud.

♦

The miles drifted away in the dust of Ninja's hooves. When my butt hurt, I walked. When my feet hurt, I got back on.

The sun was sharp in my eyes, hot on my face. My breath was louder in my head, and I was so hot. I couldn't see the crosses behind me anymore, but I caught sight of another outbuilding a ways off. I didn't know how far we'd walked, but it had been over three hours. I had missed lunch, which my stomach reminded me of just as much as the position of the sun did. But I wanted to keep walking.

I started seeing flashes of figures, small little people, bright and flickery, in the bushes. Desert trolls, I decided to call them. I'd been walking into the sun too long. I made an effort to look off to the left for a while, to give my eyes a break from the brightness.

Out of the corner of my eye, I saw two figures—two men—walking toward me.

I turned to get a good look, but then I couldn't see them anymore.

I wasn't dying. They weren't a death mirage, but maybe, like the desert trolls, they were shadows of my vision from the sun.

But then I saw them again. Two men. Maybe a man and woman, hard to tell. And what looked like a child. I stared straight ahead and realized there must be some hilly areas on the plateau up ahead. I kicked at Ninja's side, but he wouldn't go any faster, so I slipped off his back and jogged toward the figures. Maybe they knew how far I still had to go. Maybe they were from zombie camp.

"Hello?" I called.

Ninja's ears perked up, startled at the break in the silence.

I waited, but no one called back.

My eyes were playing tricks.

The sun was blinding me and fooling me.

The shimmering bush creatures reappeared again. I kept walking, Ninja grumpy behind me, until I knew I'd reached where I'd seen the two people and the child, but they were nowhere.

What was I doing here? Here in this hot desert, but more so, here at this camp, this camp for people who loved a God I could not believe in.

I couldn't believe in some old guy sitting in the clouds.

I *could* believe in some guy in a white robe living two thousand years ago and being killed for being politically insane. But I couldn't believe God sent him down, that he was God in a man's body.

There had been men before Jesus who had claimed to be the Messiah. They were similarly killed on a cross.

How did Jesus get to be so famous?

"You're just the son of man," I said out loud. "Just like me. I'm the son of man too, but I'm stuck in the desert, not hanging out in the air-conditioned sky eating grapes fed to me by virgins and angels."

I heard the sharp cry of a bird. *Kree*, it whistled, fast and hard and lonely across the sky. Like a bullet.

And Muhammad. I'd read once that Jesus told people of the coming of a great prophet. They had been in cahoots.

I walked a bit faster, breathing hard now. It wasn't dark, but the loneliness of it all was eerie.

And what about Joseph Smith? Now there was a weird dude. Finding magic plates and reading prophecy with magic rocks. In Upstate New York!

And the Jews. Still waiting for something. Someone. Something holy.

The bird called again. Sharp, like the wail of a saxophone.

I stopped, looked around. Where was that stupid thing? I couldn't see it.

A rattling in the bushes behind me.

"If the bush lights on fire, I'll believe in You," I said to all the holy men in the sky.

Nothing. Just the heat of the sun.

I was losing my mind in broad daylight.

Ninja, on the other hand, being a donkey and a trained killer, was unfazed by questions of morality and mortality.

I led him to a tree up ahead that promised a bit of shade. The tree was huge, its trunk thick, splitting at one point and breaking off into large branches and then smaller ones, pewter-green leaves flickering in the sunlight.

I sat against the trunk and opened my pack for some water. I poured some water in the bottle cap and held it up to Ninja's muzzle. I offered him some Sour Patch Kids, but he demurred, probably watching his figure. I popped a few in my mouth while I fished out the bag of Tim's Cascade potato chips. Salt. I grabbed a Monster too. Perhaps it would clear my head of the voices and visions.

I leaned back and kept my eye out for the people I'd seen earlier, and the desert trolls. I remembered the bird and looked up into the branches. It wasn't there.

Chewing the plasticky candy, I remembered this news story about two old people who'd gone out in Utah to hike the Wave, a protected area where they only allowed twenty people to hike each day. Ten permits were reserved in advance, and the other ten were issued in a daily lottery. On a day in July, this sweet old married couple had been two of the ten people to win permits to hike the Wave. It'd been over a hundred degrees and they were in their seventies, a point in life when the body didn't regulate itself properly. But it was a once-in-a-lifetime thing, and they'd won the lottery. The authorities—under heavy scrutiny—had let them go. Nobody had known what happened exactly, but they'd pieced together a sad story of a dying woman and her chivalrous husband. They'd found the man a few hundred feet away from the woman. It appeared as if he'd started off to find help after she succumbed to the heat. He'd left her in the shade of an anomalous tree, and that's where a hiking party had found her. Still leaning up against the trunk, the shadow of the tree protecting her body, still and silent and just as dead as her husband lying on the desert ground not far away.

How does shit like that happen?

"Like this," I said. "Being a stupid ass."

Ninja took no offense. He was clearly of the mind that ignorance was bliss.

♦

The bird's cry woke me. I looked at my watch; not even an hour had passed, but I grabbed my backpack, threw it over my shoulders.

Ninja stood in the exact same spot. I led him beneath a tree branch, where he stood as I climbed up the branch and onto his back. On the first try.

We walked on, and I was thankful for the tree as a new landmark.

Now that I'd rested, now that I'd cleared my head, I noticed that it had cooled. The sun was closing in on the horizon, and I was getting worried I wouldn't make it anywhere before dark. But I had to. It couldn't be much farther. It wasn't like I was literally in the middle of a desert, in the middle of nowhere. We'd passed buildings on our way into camp. We'd driven through dusty towns with houses decked with peeling paint and trailer homes.

But I didn't see any then.

Kree, the bird called, and I wondered if he was following me, waiting for me to die like the old woman under the tree. Or now like the old man.

The thing about the Wave, the thing that killed the man and his wife and others who had gone before and after them, was not just the heat or the perilous cliffs you can fall over if you're not paying attention, or if it gets dark. It's that people get lost. It all looks the same. There's no clear way to go. There are no landmarks. There are no guides pointing you in the right direction. There is no clear path.

You do not know *the Way*.

It's the price you pay for wanting to go where man has not gone.

It's a little dangerous, it's a little scary. You might not make it.

Your senses must be keen. You have to pack well and pack smart and listen to your instincts.

You have to be willing to take the risk.

I saw a flash of something on the horizon, but I couldn't discern it because the sun was right there about to touch down. It had to be someone or something. It wasn't one of the imps behind the bushes; it was still a bit too far off. But I knew I was going the right way. I knew that was zombie camp up ahead, and I was going to make it in time for dinner.

Surely a rehab facility would take pity on me.

Ninja walked on, his hooves kicking up more dust, scraping hard on the sharp stones. I watched for that flash, and it didn't take long before it came from different points. The sun was catching on a whole line of metal. It was a chain-link fence with three lines of barbed wire at the top.

I hopped off Ninja. "Follow me."

I walked the perimeter, knowing it would lead to the entrance. If I didn't find Natalie in one of those buildings, I still needed water, or to call my parents, or to get a ride back to Eden Springs. I needed a horse trailer.

Now that I'd found this place, I knew I wasn't going to have to spend the night alone in the desert, likely being eaten alive by yet-to-be-discovered desert carnivores. Not that I didn't trust Ninja to kill everything that approached, but . . .

We didn't get very far along the fence before I saw a swatch of color on the ground up ahead. A big piece of plastic, like a tarp, or a coat.

Or a backpack. It was Natalie's backpack. I walked quicker, worried that she'd dropped it, worried what that meant.

"Natalie?" I called out.

And then I saw legs, and I saw her shorts, and I saw her lying there. With earbuds in. Her eyes were closed, her head rocking back and forth. I'd thought she was dead or seriously hurt, and here she lay on the desert floor, jamming to a song that I could actually hear through the buds.

I shook her shoulders, called her name again, and her eyes popped open.

"What—" she practically yelled, sitting up quickly and yanking out the earbuds. "Holy crap, Nick. You scared me." Her eyes were swollen, her cheeks red. She'd clearly been crying.

"Are you okay?"

"I'm fine," she snapped. Which meant she wasn't. Those were the only words I really understood, because that was my standard answer to everything.

"What the hell is that?"

"A donkey."

"I see that."

"His name's Ninja."

"What are you talking about?" Natalie tossed her iPod down on top of her backpack and stood up. "What are you doing here?"

"You're mad?"

"What the hell are you doing here?" Her eyes blazed anger.

"I found the box. I know who did it."

"That has nothing to do with me."

"It has to do with all of us," I said.

"How'd you even know I'd be here?"

I handed her her confession.

"You *read* our *confessions*?"

"Well, no, not really. I was looking for mine and—"

"But you read them." Her eyes were daggers. "You read them."

"I didn't want to know that stuff. I just wanted to get mine. And then I saw yours and—"

"I don't care. You read it!"

"And then I took it out so that no one else could!" I shouted back. "I could've taken mine. I can explain the whole thing, but listen. I got yours out to save you."

She scoffed. "To *save* me?"

"Well, yeah. I mean—"

"Have you *met* yourself?"

"Not *save* you, but save you from—" Shame. Everyone's shame—mine, Diana's, Charlotte's, Matthew's, my parents', Holly's. Natalie's.

"If I were you, I'd worry about saving yourself."

"What's that supposed to mean?"

"How about calling your sister a bitch? Let's start there."

"How do you even know about that?"

"Everybody knows everything about everybody!" She threw her hands up in the air.

"People didn't know that stuff in that box. I didn't know about your brother. I didn't know you were planning to run away. I didn't know—"

"You weren't supposed to!"

"I know I wasn't supposed to!" I shouted. "I just didn't want you to lose the chance to go to your school. My confession is still in that box. I left mine in to save yours!"

"Look, Nick." Her voice was steady and cold. "This may surprise you, but not all of us feel so dismal and hopeless and melancholy or whatever it is. We have hope. We have something you don't want to believe in. You might think we're fools, but we're doing okay. We're not all wallowing in self-pity."

"Self-pity?" Rage flared in the marrow of my bones. "You think what I feel is *self-pity*? You think I'm *wallowing*? My sister killed herself, Natalie. She shot herself in the head." I ran my hands through my hair. "You wanna know where she got the gun? Me. I gave her the gun." I was breathing hard. "Yep, that's what happened. I handed her the gun and the bullets, and she shot herself. That's my confession: I KILLED MY SISTER."

Natalie's eyes widened, and her mouth moved as if to speak.

"And you think I feel '*self-pity*'? No. I fucking wish that's what I felt. I feel *self-loathing*. I *hate* myself. And when my parents find out—they're not going to survive. So I can chalk up their impending divorce to me too. And your God and this camp can screw off with your crosses and your mud pits and your Magic Hillbilly Jesus and your she-devils and rap songs and family dinners served by second-class citizens. I'm done!"

I threw my hands up and whipped around, walking quickly away, back into the darkening desert from which I'd come.

From which *we* had come. Me and Ninja. Who I left behind because I was mad, and let's face it, he doesn't walk very fast.

♦

The rage roared through my skull, loud and thick and pulsing, and I hated that I'd walked twenty miles to—what? Save her? And I'd just told her. Gawddamn it, I'd just told her the thing that I swore I'd never tell. And I'd shouted it at her. I'd thrown it at her, every word bludgeoning and true and sharp. And now it was out there, and she knew. And the trees knew, and the earth knew, and the whole gawd-damn world knew!

"Ahhhhhhhhhhhh!" I shouted. And the rage kept coming. From the pit of me, from my stomach, from my bowels, from my chest, from my throat. It was everywhere, and it was pouring out.

And then the bird came again. *Kree*, it screamed with me.

"Go away!" I shouted at the bird. I picked up rocks, chucked them into the darkening space. I threw them at the bird I couldn't see, that wasn't there.

Something stirred behind me—a footfall, the kick of a rock. Like it had that afternoon. I looked over my shoulder, but there was nothing there. At least nothing I could see in the dusk.

"Go away!" I shouted. "Leave me alone!"

Why was I here? How did I get here?

I tripped on a large piece of shale, caught my balance.

"Ugh," I growled.

I was hearing things, but I couldn't see a gawddamn thing. Not even the stones in front of me.

Echoes of rocks kicking up behind me. I spun around. It was too dark. I could see, but not enough. I walked on, the drag and scrape of the rocks, my breath, the bird, my words, something in the bushes—all the sounds tumbling around like a crazy chant of craziness.

You're going mad. I heard these words, but not my words. Not my voice, but in my head.

"I *am* mad!" I was pissed. I was incensed. I was furious.

Madman road, I heard.

I stopped moving. Listened. Listened inside my head. Nothing. Outside my head. No sound. No bird. No voice.

"What do you want?" I shouted.

We're all mad here, the voice said. And this time, I knew who it was. I missed that voice, but it couldn't be real. Diana was dead. I don't even know if her dead body had a mouth and a tongue left after the bullets ripped through her face.

"Leave me alone," I said. "Leave me alone, leave me alone, leave me alone," I chanted.

The bird cried, *Kree.*

"Just go," I said, to the bird, to the voice, to the footsteps behind me. "You left me." The words tumbled out, a mumble, half in my head, half out of my mouth. "You left me here, and now you want to call me mad, sending some bush-rattling creature or some bird. Whispering in my head." I rattled on.

You're talking to yourself, her voice said.

"I'm talking to *you*!"

But I'm not there. Nobody's there. Just you.

And you made it that way! How could you leave me?

I left myself.

Yourself? You're so selfish.

You're mad at me?

Of course I'm mad at you! "Yes, I'm mad at you," I said out loud at the nobody in my head, at the trees, at the earth, at the sky. "I'm fucking mad at you!" Then I shouted into the sky. "I'm mad at you both!"

"I'm mad at you," I pointed in front of me, like she was there, like the Diana in my head had a space on this earth by my side.

"And I'm mad at You," I pointed up at the sky. "You want people to believe in You, stop being such an unfair asshole."

You're seeing it wrong, Diana said.

The bird cried, and I hoped I was near the tree.

I'm going to die out here, and I'm not going to see you in heaven.

Is that what you're afraid of? Because I was gay? Because I died by suicide? Like Charlotte said. You think God makes a heaven only just big enough?

I'm not going to see you in heaven because I can't look you in the face.

Because of what happened with Leah? So, you kissed her. So, you loved her. How could you not?

No, I loved *you*!

So, it's not shame?

No, it's your face! I can't look you in the face. Your literal face!

Because of the gun.

Yes, the gun I gave you! Why did you *let* me give it to you?

How many bullet holes are in your head anyway? How many shots did you fire into your skull? Did you miss? Where's your face? Where's the top of your head? Where's your jaw?

"Why were there two bullet holes in the car?" I shouted.

Silence.

"Did you do a practice round?"

Silence.

"Did you mess up the first time?"

Silence.

"Did you put the gun in your mouth?"

Silence.

"Did you put it to your temple?"

"To your forehead?"

"Under your chin?"

"Did you hear the sound of it when it went off? Did it hurt your ears? Did you feel the bullet go in before your brain exploded?"

I was crying. I could feel the tears pouring down my face.

Did you think for one second about buying your own gun? Did you think about what you were doing when you walked into our house? Did you even think of me for one second?

I stopped. I looked up at the sky. "Why are You punishing me?" And I knew I was yelling at Diana. But I was also yelling at God.

I didn't do anything to You! Is it because I don't believe in You? Is this Your jealous revenge? The dark night of the soul?

Kree. The bird's bullet-cry was close. The tree was visible.

I was sweating. The anger in my head beat inside my skull. The yelling hurt.

I didn't want to talk in my head anymore.

It's called prayer.

And that's the last thing my sister said to me inside my head.

◆

I reached the tree, slid down the trunk. The bark lifting my shirt and scratching the skin off my back. I was out of breath, exhausted, bitter, bitterly exhausted. I leaned my head back.

"Man, oh, man, she's a mad one."

Jack.

He sat up in a branch, his back to the trunk.

"Get away from me."

Jack rolled onto his stomach, slipped down from the branch, and hung there for a moment. Then he dropped to the ground and walked behind the tree.

"Did you hear that bird?" He came around the trunk with a bottle in his hand. "That, my friend, is an instrument of heaven. That sound, so pure, so sharp."

"Seriously, I can't do any more madness."

"You seem undone."

"Really? I seem undone to you? I'm in the freaking desert in the dark with a man who's been dead for half a century while my dead sister talks in my head!"

"But you did it."

"Went mad like all the great ones before me? Yeah, I did."

"Yes, yes. And no. You said it all out. You told the truth. You told it out."

"So? It doesn't make it go away."

Jack set down a bottle between us. "Have some wine."

"I don't want wine." I unzipped my backpack and reached in for my sweatshirt and sweats. "I'm not getting drunk with you." I pulled on the extra clothes.

"The wine is for forgiveness." Jack reached into his pocket for his pack of smokes. "And it'll warm you up."

I sighed, reached for the bottle, put it to my lips. It was lukewarm, like the beer had been, but it seemed okay. It tasted like my grandpa's barn, all wood shavings and damp earth. It wasn't bad. It was rich and warm.

"I thought you might want a sip," he said.

I returned the bottle to an even spot on the ground.

Jack crossed his legs. "It's time to put your cross down now, Nicolas."

I shook my head.

"This isn't about Jesus. Or it is, if you want it to be. It doesn't rightly matter. But, you're a boy, you're not meant to carry anything. You got some guilt, some shame, some thing you did in this world that's got you believing you're some heavy sinking stone, not worth the freedom of lightness, weightlessness. That's some bull. Put your damned cross down."

"I can't," I muttered.

Jack softened his voice. "Your role in whatever goes down on this earth's already dead. You carrying on like you own a bit of any of that is indulgent and, frankly, selfish. You can't do anything more than what's already been done for you, so drop your tiny bitch-ass cross."

"Bitch-ass cross? Seriously? From beatnik to gangsta?"

He blew his cigarette smoke in my face. "Don't change the subject."

I put the heels of my hands to my face. "Did you see Natalie's face when I told her?"

"Yes. Shocked."

"Disgusted," I said through my hands.

"That was hurt. Hurt for you. Horrified for the story."

"It'll kill them."

"Kill who?"

"Whom."

"The Great Editor avoids the question."

"My parents. Leah. Anyone who knows me."

"No, the truth never kills anything. The truth only grows things. It connects things. It is your bridge."

He took a sip of the wine, wiped his mouth, and handed the bottle to me. "Now take one more sip of that liquid forgiveness."

I could use forgiveness of any kind. So I did as Jack said. I had a few more sips than I should've.

I lamented leaving Ninja behind. Jack made jokes about being a smart-ass.

And then Jack and I talked a good long time about my sisters, his brother, my parents, his parents. His wives, his daughter, his friends. We talked about religion and regret, forgiveness and friendships.

When we got tired of the serious, I took out *Sixty Scenes of Sexy*.

What happened to the Great American Novel, he wanted to know. Did anyone aspire to that anymore?

We squinted in the moonlight so we could read parts aloud to each other. We mostly laughed, though he did get morose a couple times, indignant that this was what the American reader craved. But then we'd find a sentence, a paragraph, read it aloud in accents of varying sophistication, and we'd fall into a fit of giggles. The laugh-till-you-cry kind. The kind that stole our breath. The kind that threatened to kill us with the absurdity of it all. The kind that left us spent and determined to sleep.

THURSDAY

◆

Something velvety, cool in my face. Then a prickle and a snuff of hot air. I opened my eyes, the sun too bright, my back stiff from the ground, from not shifting during the night. Hooves scuffed on rocks near my head, and dust blew into my eyes.

"Ninja."

I sat up and spotted an alien-long shadow coming around from behind the tree.

Natalie walked past me, nudging something with her toe. A bottle clanked across the ground, and I panicked that Jack had left the empty wine bottle behind. But it was just a metal water bottle. She stood over me, studied me.

She handed me a protein bar.

I unwrapped it, took a bite. "Thanks."

"Welcome," she said, and we both ate our bars in silence.

My eyes felt swollen. I had a headache. From the sadness as much as from the wine I drank.

"I can't believe you stole a donkey," she said.

"His name's Ninja."

"I can totally see why."

I stuffed the wrapper into my backpack and pulled my sweats from over my shorts. It wouldn't be too long before I got hot. I kept my sweatshirt on.

"Did you bring an extra toothbrush?" I tried, hoping to break the tension.

"Look," she said. "I'm sorry about yesterday."

"No. *I'm* sorry. I didn't even listen to you. I came to be a friend, and then I made it all about me."

"I'm sorry about your sister."

"I'm sorry about your brother."

"I'm sorry you walked twenty miles for a tongue-lashing."

"I didn't walk the whole twenty miles. Give Ninja some credit."

"We stopped for grass, by the way."

"There's grass?"

Natalie nodded.

"Where? I didn't see any—"

"Never mind about the donkey," Natalie said. "I need to explain my confession."

I held up both hands. "No, it's private. You don't have to explain."

"Nick, please."

I had been selfish the night before, so consumed with my own burning fury. I'd been so caught up in the *idea* of helping Natalie that I hadn't even done the bare minimum. I hadn't even listened to her.

She was looking straight into my eyes. "I did heroin one time. But I did do it."

I nodded. "So, then, can I ask why?"

"Gah, it's just so gross." She sighed. "I swore I would never tell a soul."

"I won't tell anyone."

"I know. But, you know, it's even hearing my own words." Her face pinched. "This isn't the first time my brother's disappeared from rehab. He's been in and out." She looked off into the distance, seeing something in her own mind. "So, one time, I went looking for him. I knew where he stayed sometimes, when he was using. Murder Block."

"What?"

"I'm not even joking."

"And you went there?"

"Sh. It's my story." She smiled briefly. "It was Fourth of July. And I knew where my brother stayed sometimes, in this camper a couple blocks up from the highway. So, on this particular day, I went to go find him. But he wasn't there. One of the guys I'd met before was around, though. Big Rev." She raised her eyebrows. "As in 'reverend,' yeah. He said I could wait for a while. I was really nervous, like sweaty and jumpy. Kids up the street kept lighting off fireworks, but they sounded like gunshots. All these people kept coming to the camper.

Everyone was really nice. Asking me questions about school. Telling me stories. Except these two older woman shouted stuff about the 'little white girl' hiding out. But then Big Rev dismissed them and told me not to worry, they were just drunk. There was an older guy everyone was taking care of. He was in a wheelchair. This lady with marks all over her face kept getting in and out of cars. It was fascinating and horrifying. I was there for hours." She looked away. "I didn't go there to do drugs. I went there to find my brother."

She stopped talking.

"It's okay."

"None of it is okay. I couldn't save my brother. I can't save him. But, that day, I thought I could maybe understand him better." She bit at her lip. "I didn't shoot up myself. Big Rev did it for me."

I wanted to throw up, imagining this teenage girl putting out her arm.

"I kind of slept or passed out or whatever. I never found my brother. I got sick and threw up and then went home. It was the stupidest thing I've ever done."

"Do you understand him better?"

She shook her head. I had no idea what to say, so I didn't say anything. I put my hand over hers and held on.

We both analyzed the dirt for awhile.

"Do you believe in signs?" she finally asked, her voice a little lighter.

I shrugged.

"I do," she said.

"This does not surprise me about you."

She smiled, taking it as a compliment, which is how I had intended it. "I'd written the confession, but I didn't know if I should really run away. I mean, here I was going to look for my brother again, after what happened last time, right? But when the box was stolen, I knew it meant I had to go. Remember when you found me on the hillside?"

"You were running away then."

"I was. But then you appeared over the hill and I thought, this is a sign too. I wasn't supposed to go. There was something I was supposed to wait for. I even thought you might have some wisdom from God to tell me. Because that's how I hear Him, mostly. In the words of others. And you and I'd been talking and really connecting, or so I thought."

She'd thought right. I thought we had too. The words between Natalie and me flowed, made sense, were easy. They actually felt like a bridge.

She fake-glared at me. "Don't laugh. I'm not even done yet. And I'm not crazy."

"I'm not laughing, I swear." I was way crazier than reading signs. I was hearing the voices of people who weren't even on earth anymore. I was hanging out with the dead. I was talking to stolen barn animals.

"So, I stayed. But the confessions kept coming. And I knew I had to go. That was a sign. Or, that was a counter-sign. The universe redirecting me back up that hill to my brother."

"A bad sign."

"There aren't bad signs, just signs."

She kind of sounded like Jack on that point. No right or wrong. No good or bad. Things just were what they were.

"Anyway, you showed up last night after everything, and I realized I'd misread everything. I didn't understand any of what I was supposed to do and not do."

"After everything what?"

She sighed. "My brother wasn't there."

"I know. That's why I came." I told her about first going to Pastor Kyle, and how he knew her brother had checked out of rehab.

She nodded, sat thinking for a moment. Then she said, "I don't see him often, ever since he was sent to this place. You know, it's far away and my great-aunt won't drive me down here. She's old, you know?"

"I was under the impression you lived with your parents, who owned yachts and mansions, so no, I don't know."

"Right. Pastor Kyle is the only one who knows the deal. Both my parents are actually meth heads."

"Are your parents in rehab?"

"Doubt it. Sometimes they show up at my aunt's and ask for money. Sometimes they're in jail. I don't know." She took a deep breath. "My brother really tried. He's been in and out of rehab for like three years, and we write and stuff. But his letters got shorter and just *off*. So I suspected he'd left again. And then, yeah, he wasn't there. But don't worry, I won't be going to search for him on Murder Block."

"How can you just leave rehab?"

She teared up. "You just can. Because it's a choice."

"But how did Pastor Kyle know he left if you didn't?"

"I have no idea, but I intend to find out."

"Maybe he's friends with the Big Rev." I squeezed her hand. "Men of God and all that."

"Ha, yeah, right," Natalie said. "So, do you think less of me now that you know about my sorry-ass life?"

"She didn't mean that, Ninja!" I called over my shoulder. To Natalie, I said, "You are as cool as an Obama/Uncle Sam mash-up with a Rosie the Riveter attitude. There's really nothing sorry about that."

She laughed and nudged my shoulder. "Do you remember when I told you that when I was a little girl, I was scared and self-conscious all the time? I was the girl who didn't even stand against the wall at dances?"

"You peeked through the wall from the other side."

"I meant that literally. One time, I spent Christmas in an attic in some crack house, because everyone was freaking out that the police were coming, so they hid us up there. My brother and I just lay there on the floor, peeking through this little hole in the ceiling, waiting for Santa to come because we knew he'd sneak us out in his sack of toys."

We both laughed softly, a sad-funny laugh.

"I *am* Obama/Uncle Sam/Rosie the Riveter strong and interesting and cool—if I do say so myself." She winked at me. "But, I am also scared and nervous."

"At the same time."

"Simultaneously, two opposite humans."

Like Jack, who was and was not a Roman candle. "I get that."

"Which brings me to what I want to say. When you showed up last night, and I freaked out on you like a crazy person and you freaked out on me like a crazy person? That was a counter-countersign. The sign I was meant to see."

"I'm afraid to be implicated in this."

"I recognized your crazy. When you were standing there, yelling at me, but really yelling at the universe, I knew that feeling. I knew maybe you'd understand why I would ever put a needle to my vein. What I did, it was pure stupid crazy, based on my own guilt. I survived, my brother didn't, right? You survived, your sister didn't. And all that grossed-outness and self-loathing. I get it."

She was right. It drove me mad. It did.

Diana hadn't had it that bad. She'd had food and clothing. She'd had two parents, and they loved her. Sure, she'd struggled with her identity—or rather, the world struggled with her identity. And yeah, she'd had some emotional things going on. But she'd been surrounded by people who loved her.

Natalie's brother was born to drug addicts, grew up in a meth house, bounced around from crack house to crack house. He never had a Santa, or anyone else who could save him. Obviously worse off than my sister.

But then, Diana was ostracized and judged by half the planet. She could never be her full self, full-time. She was told the love she had for others was dark and deviant, that she was not entitled to inalienable rights. She'd been hiding in an attic too.

It wasn't even fair to compare two people's hurts. To say this was worse than that. It just *was*.

"You know how you said you talk to your brother sometimes, like a prayer?" I asked.

"Yeah."

"I heard my sister last night, like a prayer." I swallowed. "Like a reverse prayer."

Natalie didn't say anything, just reached out and took my hand. I held her hand in my lap, looked at her thin fingers, felt the warmth of her palm against mine.

She'd reached out. And I reached back.

I told her the story that no one had heard. Not my parents or my grandpa or Leah. I told her to be even. To find grace. To share my crazy.

♦

The day before Diana came over, the day before she died, Leah stopped by the house. She'd come to talk to me, not my parents, she explained. She stood in the doorway in her skinny jeans, high boots, long sweater. Her hair was back, wisps in her face. But her face was wrong—it was tight and dark, not like normal. Still beautiful, but not eager to laugh, to joke, to say something self-deprecating that put people at ease, made you feel like you fit in and mattered.

I was so relieved to see her. I hoped it meant she and my sister were getting back together. And not even for Diana. For myself. She was—and maybe is—the person I hold everyone up to.

I loved Diana, but she was way far out there on the crazy spectrum. Leah was a willing participant with a whimsical streak and an ability to balance that with a college degree and a job.

I wanted her around, and she hadn't been around. I ached for her to come back into our lives. And here she was, and she needed my help.

"Your sister's being really weird," she said.

"My sister is always weird."

"Ha, right, yeah, but . . . weirder. She wants to drive across the country. 'Go East, Young Man,' she keeps saying. I don't even know what she's talking about."

She'd been asking Leah to get back together, and every day she called or texted with some new, far-fetched plan. Cool ideas, but erratic.

Leah continued, "She wants to take me fishing or golfing or scuba diving in Hawaii. Hunting, go-carts, horseback. Like adventure stuff."

"That's normal," I said.

"It is, yeah, but quitting our jobs and crossing the country? That's weird."

"She used to want to join the circus. Weird is relative."

"Nick, she put half her life on Craigslist. She's really going. She really thinks I'm going too. And I'm not."

She asked me if Diana was drinking—which she was; she'd always drunk heavily—or on drugs. I wouldn't know that part.

"Just talk to her, will you? I know you're her baby brother"—and that part stung—"but she respects the hell out of you."

I would have done anything for Leah. I loved her, despite the near-decade between us. I promised her I'd talk to Diana, I'd text her when I did.

The day my sister shot herself, I had woken up late. I was playing video games. Diana interrupted me, and I was tired.

I'd been irritated with her for months. She'd been distracted every time we hung out. She'd stopped taking me cool places in favor of darting off with people I didn't know. Leah had broken up with her, and it was her fault.

And the last time I'd seen her she'd been drunk. Breathing heavily in my face, telling me she loved me. *Don't worry, you're fine.* Like she always said.

And I hadn't seen her since.

The day my sister died, we stood in the kitchen, and she was talkative, but not being funny. Just rushed, not wanting to hang out.

"What's up with you driving across the country?" I'd asked.

"Oh, you know."

"Not really. Leah just told me about it."

She shrugged. "I'm not going to follow it anymore."

"Follow what?"

"Kerouac's path." She held up her phone. "Have you seen the app?"

I had no idea who Kerouac was, what path or what app.

She pulled *On the Road* out from her purse and handed it to me. "There's an app. You can do his whole trip."

"Huh. But you don't want to do that anymore?"

"No."

"Because Leah said you were trying to get her to go. And selling your stuff."

"No, I'm not going." She leaned back in her chair and crossed her arms.

"Okay. So everything's okay? I tried to hand the book back."

"You keep it." She waved her hand at me. "I don't want it. You can do it someday. Hit the road."

"Okay."

And it was. Because we did do a summer road trip thing every year. So what she'd said, that made sense.

I'd talked to her, like Leah had asked. And it was okay.

And because it was okay, I wanted go back to my game.

"I'm going to the gun range," she'd said. "Leah and I are going."

And I believed her.

I believed her because it matched Leah's story, about the cool but erratic ideas she was having.

I believed her because I wanted it to be true, to have Leah back.

I believed her because I was tired and impatient. I was relieved she wasn't asking me to go. Because I was also tired and impatient with her.

"I couldn't get ahold of Dad."

"Dad won't care."

"I know, but I need to borrow his gun," she'd said.

"They're in the case."

"Yeah, but he moves the key."

I scoffed. "No, he doesn't."

"You know where it is?"

Of course I knew where it was. My dad trusted me. He'd taught me to use the guns. I'd grown up hunting. He'd taken me to the range. Taken me to the woods. Diana had gone with us. If I'd been listening—if I hadn't been tired and impatient and hopeful and lazy—I would've noticed this question was odd. I would've noticed.

I was being emotionally lazy. I wasn't hearing the full truth. The truth means you have to do something, and I didn't want to do something for her that day. I wanted to do the easy thing.

I walked back into my parents' bedroom, and she didn't follow me. Why didn't she follow me? I went to the closet, slid open the door, and pulled out the Monopoly game. I lifted the lid, found the key amid the game pieces, and unlocked the case.

"Which one do you want?" I called out.

There were several guns. A shotgun, a .22, an antique handgun, a .38.

She didn't answer.

Maybe she didn't hear me. That's what I want to believe. I want to believe she didn't hear me ask that question. Because if she did, and she paused for those seconds, what filled that time?

Maybe she was reassessing. Maybe she was reconsidering. Maybe she wouldn't have done it if I hadn't unlocked the cabinet and pulled out the .38. If I hadn't grabbed the box of bullets.

I walked out of the bedroom. I had a gun in one hand and bullets in another, and I held them out to her.

And what was that look that passed over her face? Because there was a look.

Maybe it was disappointment that I didn't see what she was going to do.

Maybe it was realization that now she had to do it. She had to take the gun, because it matched the story she'd just told me. And since she had the gun, she had to follow through.

Or, maybe it was resolve. I like to tell myself it was resolve. That nothing I did mattered in the end.

But it all mattered.

You can do that some day. Hit the road. She should've said *we*. And I should've noticed.

But I didn't.

I went into the room. I unlocked the cabinet, chose the gun, and put in her hands.

It was my fault.

It was my fault.

It was my fault.

♦

"When my mom told me—because the police called them, or the hospital—I don't even know, she told me in the kitchen. She said, 'Diana shot herself.' My dad was at the hospital with my grandpa. And, I thought—I reasoned—it occurred to me—she shot her toes. My dad and grandpa were there to visit because she shot her toes. Because the gun accidentally went off.

"That's what I remember. Standing in the kitchen, looking at my own toes."

The tears fell as I told Natalie this.

"She was in the hospital because they were keeping her alive. To save the organs. She was a donor. There was no Diana to visit.

"I don't remember when I understood that she shot herself in the head." I swallowed. "I imagine it all the time. Where she put the gun. If her hands were shaking. The only thing that makes me feel better is that the doctors could use her eyes. She still had her eyes. Something of her was still there."

I wiped the tears off my cheeks.

"Someone has her eyes," I said. "Someone sees the world how she saw it. She saw it so big."

I leaned my head against the tree trunk.

"She wanted to see it all, do it all, have it all. And she couldn't. She couldn't even have half of it. That thing she said to Leah—'Go East, Young Man.' I looked it up. I thought it would reveal something, something to make it better. It was just a play on a famous quote 'Go West, Young Man.' Horace Greeley. He was all about Manifest Destiny. My sister was too, in a way."

After a while, Natalie said, "Your parents will figure this out for themselves. They're adults."

And she was right. But at the same time, I'd wanted them to be adults and protect Diana. To hold Charlotte accountable, to stop feeding the arsenic idea that *we should consider the perspective* of intolerance. They let their other daughter's hatred exist, let it eat away at Diana. They didn't protect her, and I was afraid they couldn't protect me.

Maybe I should hate them. But I didn't. I *needed* them. And I needed them to stay with me.

"They're going to hate me," I said, which wasn't exactly what I meant, but I just couldn't explain it all.

"They are not going to hate you."

"Look what I did to their daughter. Don't you hate your parents? What they did to your brother?"

I noticed then that she was crying too. She'd been crying for me, and now some of those tears were almost certainly about herself. "I don't hate them. They didn't do that to him. He had a choice. We all have a choice. Look at me. I'm not a meth addict. Or a heroin addict."

"You got lucky."

"I didn't get lucky. I made a choice. To survive. To survive whatever happened."

This conversation sounded so much like the one I'd had with Charlotte, about all the little things in our lives being choices. But Charlotte's conviction about our sister's choices was judgment. Natalie's was not.

But what about my sister?

"My sister goes to hell," I argued, "because the Bible says. That's what people say."

"Why don't you let God do His thing? Quit worrying about what it all says, what it all means? It is what it is. She was a homosexual. She died by suicide. That doesn't mean she's going to hell. You don't know her heart, and God is too big for our comprehension. You'll drive yourself crazy trying to do His job."

I sighed. "You want to know the worst part?"

The look on her face suggested nothing could be worse than my complicity in suicide.

"When Diana died, I kept wishing it was Charlotte. I prayed I would wake up and it would be swapped. I told God I'd do anything to bring her back. I'd trade anything." I put my hands to my eyes. "And I still wish it would've been Charlotte. If I have to hand someone a gun—" I broke off and pressed my hands into my forehead.

Natalie put her hand on my back until I had no more tears.

"He doesn't bargain," she said quietly.

"He doesn't understand," I said.

She didn't correct me.

We sat for a long time against that tree, and the bird shot song bullets through the sky.

"Forty miles, not forty days, but . . . crazy things happen in the wilderness," she said after a while. "Satan tempts you, Gabriel tells you to read scrolls, you reach Nirvana."

She was talking about Jesus, Muhammad, and Buddha. I wanted to tell her about Jack. How he said they were all here. Plus some Native American god and Ereshkigal and who knows who else.

"We could try it out, under this tree," Natalie said. "I mean, I don't think this is a banyan tree, but maybe enlightenment doesn't require particular flora."

This girl. This mad, crazy girl on pretty road.

"Why are you looking at me like that?" she asked.

"Because you never say a commonplace thing." A line from the poster on my bedroom wall.

She nudged me. "That might be the nicest thing anyone has ever said to me, Nick." Then she stood up, dusted off her shorts, and tugged my arm. It was time to leave.

Ninja, as always, didn't argue.

◆

As we walked side by side, Ninja lumbering behind, a lead rope completely unnecessary at this point. We seemed to be walking slower on the way back than I did on the way there, like neither of us really wanted to return. But, then, what awaited but a frustrated pastor with rockin' abs (I'd seen him in the pool) and an unknown punishment?

"What are you going to do about your brother?"

"What's to be done?"

"Go find him?"

She laughed drily. "He's in a city somewhere with stringy hair."

I didn't know what to say to that. "What about Eden Springs? Will you come back? Even though he's gone?"

"Yeah. I mean, I have a scholarship. I kind of have to come back."

"Well, you don't *have* to." I thought of Holly. "So, you're on work crew too?"

"No. I'm indebted to some mysterious philanthropist."

"How did you get out of sweeping stray pubic hairs off the bathroom floor?"

"I just got a call from the camp office one time. I was in sixth grade or something."

That seemed really weird. "That's not really how it works for normal people," I started to explain.

"I think we've established that things don't work normally for me."

"Maybe by next year he'll come back to zombie camp."

Our shoes scraped across the rocks, and that was the only sound. I noticed we were walking toward the sun again and worried I'd see the shimmering faces in the bushes. The desert trolls. But I felt safer with her there, like I wasn't going to lose my mind.

"So, will you be coming back to Eden Springs next year?" she asked.

"Ha. I don't think so."

Natalie smiled. "You seem kind of judgmental about it all."

"I think they're crazy, that's what I think. I feel like I'm stuck in some Salvador Dali painting half the time."

"They are crazy. That's the best part."

"If you like that kind of crazy, I guess."

"You of all people should understand. You're the one who likes Jack Kerouac."

I shook my head. "No, I do not like Jack Kerouac. I've already said that. My sister likes him."

"Okay, but you like the quote about the mad ones."

I nodded. "I'll concede that."

"Then concede this. Those people down there. Those people who operate Eden Springs and the people who go—Charles, Kim,

Matthew, Dan, Jason. Me. They're just Mad Ones. They're mad to live, mad to be saved, desirous of everything."

"But it's all wrapped up in religion," I argued.

"Yes, it's about Jesus for them. They're mad for Him. Mad to be saved by him. So, you're not. That doesn't make their madness less cool just because you don't share in it."

"What about those guys who blow up abortion clinics in the name of religion?"

"Not okay. Right-wing terrorism," she said and kind of laughed. "But, Nick, who cares what other people are mad about if they're not infringing upon the rights of others? Why do you let them bother you so much?"

I knew why it bothered me. Or, at least, I knew part of the reason, but it was so much, a garbage bag of things to explain.

"I don't understand how they can all be happy," I said.

"Are you jealous?"

"Ignorance is bliss and all that."

"But they aren't ignorant. Jeez, Nick, listen to yourself. What is the difference between you hating the conservative Bible-thumpers and them hating you because you don't believe? And those people, down at Eden Springs? They don't hate anybody. They love everybody. They just want people to come to their little oasis and party for a week in the name of Jesus. Don't you get that?"

"It's stupid, Natalie. They're stupid. The guy was a guy. Jesus Christ, the real one, not the hillbilly dude at camp, was a guy. That's it."

"Yeah, the maddest guy of them all." She looked at me like she felt a little sorry for me. "Whether you believe in him as a religious figure or as a historical one, he's mad as hell."

"Well, that makes two mad Jesuses."

Finally, she said, "Nick, don't let man's rules and religion get in the way of the divine mysteries of the universe."

PRAYERS AND CONFESSIONS

Holly: Please give me the strength to be who I am. All of me. Even the parts other people can't accept.

Dan: I didn't say sorry. My dad did, over and over. I pray he really is, Lord. Please help him get sober.

Monica: Thank you, thank you, thank you, thank you, thank you, thank you, thank you, thank you, thank you, thank you, thank you, thank you, thank you, thank you, thank you, thank you, thank you, thank you, thank you . . .

♦

The three crosses stood tall and expectant on the horizon. I was relieved to have the forty-mile journey in the wilderness over. But I was also disappointed to part with Natalie.

Not long after first seeing the crosses, I saw the silhouettes on the horizon. Two men waiting for us.

"Are they going to send us home?" I mean, we'd both run away.

"Maybe you. Not me." She wasn't joking. I was just the new kid. And I'd actually stolen camp property. Ninja didn't like to be objectified like that, but he didn't understand the human legal system.

We kept walking. The men headed toward us.

"Two more things before they nab us," Natalie said.

We hadn't been talking much the last hour. I raised an eyebrow at her.

"You need to believe in something."

"Me? Or everyone?" I asked.

"You *and* everyone." Natalie tugged at my sleeve to stop walking. "In a way, we're all at zombie camp."

"We're meth heads?"

"Don't be stupid. I think we're all a little like zombies. Walking around a little dead inside, looking for something to fill us up."

"Drugs or . . . Jesus . . . or . . ." I held my hands up in a shrug.

"Horses . . ."

"Horse people are really weird." We both laughed.

"Cats . . ." Natalie suggested.

"Old lady cat lovers!"

"Video games."

I narrowed my eyes. "Child porn."

"Ew." Her face curled in disgust. "Anyway, believe in something, Nick."

"Anything?"

"Okay, not child porn. Too far."

We laughed and kept walking.

"Okay, so?" I asked.

"So . . . ?"

"You said there were two things."

"Oh, yeah." Natalie blushed. "Do you like Holly?"

"I mean, I like her, but . . ." I couldn't finish that statement.

"You're not into her?" She looked at her feet. "I mean, a lot of guys like her and she seems kinda into you."

It was flattering that Natalie thought for even a second that a beautiful girl like Holly would sincerely be interested in me.

"She's actually really smart," Natalie added. "Like STEM-nerd smart. Like MIT smart. Her IQ happens to be triple her bra size."

I knew she was smart, and I wished I could tell Natalie the whole truth about the confessions, but I'd made a promise. So I told her a different truth. "She might be smart, and she might also be the girl that everyone thinks is hot. But I like your theory."

"My theory?"

"About the horizon," I said, blushing. "About watching people walk away." That maybe the way you can tell if you love someone is when you keep looking for them, keep seeing them, even when they're not there anymore. I looked at her. "I don't just like your theory. I believe it."

She moved closer. Her arm bumped mine.

"So, there you go. I believe in something."

We walked in silence the rest of the way.

♦

We soon heard Pastor Kyle and Jason, the quiet deep rumbles of their conversation rolling toward us.

Then it was the four of us, standing there awkwardly. They breathed hard; we barely breathed. Their lips were tight with disappointment; our lips hung open in anticipation of the smackdown.

"Why don't you walk with me, Natalie," Pastor Kyle finally said, and they stepped out of the square and headed off toward camp, Ninja on a rope behind them.

Jason watched me watch them go. I didn't want to look at him.

"I'm sorry," I said, probably for the trillionth time in four days. My list of sins against Jason and his zealous love for all things Jesus and Eden Springs exceeded my lifetime list of all other sins combined.

"Let's go," was all he said, and we started walking toward camp. He didn't say anything for a long time. I just watched Natalie, Pastor Kyle, and Ninja disappear and reappear over small hills and valleys, their silhouettes becoming smaller. They seemed to be walking a lot faster than the two of us.

When we reached the ridge above the three crosses, Jason stopped. He looked over the camp. "We contacted your parents yesterday."

My face burned. They would be freaking out, thinking I was dead, imagining me being eaten eyeball by eyeball by something awful. "Were they freaking out?"

"We assured them you were safe."

"That's good."

"And they're here," he added.

"They're *here*?"

"We asked them to come."

"To pick me up?"

"To talk. And then, likely, to take you home, yes."

It made sense. The sending me home. Running away from camp was a major no-no.

"Does Natalie have to go home?"

Jason sucked in his lips. Finally, "No."

"Because she's on scholarship?" That kind of kid always got second chances.

"It's complicated."

Jason didn't take us down the steep decline, the way I'd come up to the crosses both times I'd followed Natalie. Rather, he led me down the wide path that snaked slowly into the camp.

Nobody noticed us, at first, as we crossed the green manicured lawn. But as we got closer to the pool, more faces turned in our direction. I swore I heard whispers, though that couldn't have been true, considering the bass that quaked from the speakers.

Just the day before, I'd felt a part of the camp experience, though still separate because I didn't believe what they believed. But just then, coming out of the desert, after the visions and the voices, after confessing that I'd handed my sister the gun that she used to blow her brains out . . . now I felt kept behind a glass window. Like camp was a fishbowl, and I could only look in.

The campers weren't smaller, by any means. I didn't feel superior in a fish-owner kind of way. I just felt far away, behind a cloud.

I caught sight of Natalie walking through the door to Babyl On, Pastor Kyle ushering her in, probably for a round of counseling and prayer. She didn't have a cross over her shoulders.

And Jason didn't drag one over to me. He led me in the direction of the cabins. I didn't know if my parents were in there, or if I was supposed to pack first.

Then Matthew was running toward me from the sanctuary. I could see him coming across the field. He was pointing at the fresh confessions painted on the sides of cabin doors.

"So you know I didn't do it now, right?" I said to Matthew when he reached me. "I wasn't even on campus."

"Not literally, right?"

"What? Literally, what?"

Matthew pointed to the door of our cabin. And there it was. On the door, my confession was painted in scarlet letters.

I killed my sister.

I looked at Jason. Swallowed hard. "Where are my mom and dad?"

It was time to find the right words. To cross the bridge between me and them.

♦

I told my parents. Told them everything they didn't know already. They already knew about Leah coming over. They already knew about my conversation with Diana. They knew about the mistaken pronoun. They knew that she'd planned on going to the gun range. All of these things we'd talked about in the days and weeks after she shot herself. But they didn't know the part about the key. That I went in for the key, that I unlocked the cabinet, that I chose the gun, that I selected the bullets. That I put them in her hand.

My parents didn't cry at first. Their mouths hung open, their eyes wide, their heads shook slightly. I knew they wanted me to stop, that they didn't want to hear the end of the story. But the real end, they already knew. Diana dies in the end. She always dies in the end. She was always going to die in the end. That was her after.

My after is this.

I confess. The sour words, the sour truth.

My after is also this.

My parents sob and reach for me and draw me in and surround me. Because there are both of us to mourn for. There always was. Me and Diana. Me without Diana. Them without Diana. And somewhere, there is Charlotte. There and not there, in all of it.

I don't have to tell them about the arsenic, about the slow poison. I don't have to explain to them how their support of Charlotte seemed like taking sides, that it ate away at Diana's spirit. They already know. We're all very good at taking blame after a tragedy. *If only, if only.*

They knock from my hands the bags of sadness and guilt and regret. Later, after they tell me it's okay, that they don't blame me, that there is no one to blame, that it's not my fault, that she would've found a way, they will pick up those bags and add them to their own burlap sacks of sadness and guilt and regret.

Because they're my parents.

Because that's what humans do. We step out onto broken dilapidated untrustworthy scary-as-shit this-bitch-is-gonna-break bridges, and we reach out. We say, give me that thing you're carrying. Let me carry that thing for you. Let me do this kindness for you.

That's humanity. That's compassion. That's grace.

And that's my *after*.

♦

There are two things I don't tell my parents, though.

I don't tell them about Jack. About the wise madness.

And I don't tell them about kissing Leah. About how holding on to her was just my way of holding on to Diana.

There are some things that weigh heavily, but simply are not burdens.

♦

When it was all over, Pastor Kyle handed me a slip of paper.

Holly had done as she promised. She'd confessed. She'd put the truth of what she'd done into the otherwise empty PC Box and handed it over to the pastor. She'd also told the pastor that I'd encouraged her to do it. Pastor Kyle hugged me. Hugging is not my cup of tea, but I let him do it.

Pastor Kyle and Jason, and my mom and dad, decided it would be good for me to stay the last night of camp. It was late; we'd cried till our eyes were mere slits. My parents would stay in the counselor housing, and I would stay that last night with my cabinmates.

On the quiet walk through the dark to the cabin, I wondered about Holly. About her *after*. I hadn't seen Payton all day, and I wondered if she'd told him too.

"Psst."

I turned around. The campus was empty, everyone in their cabins. Lights out was in a few minutes.

Something came flying at me from behind a bush. It landed at my feet. *Twilight*. Or rather, *Sixty Scenes of Sexy*.

"Where are you?" I whispered.

"Get me the second one."

"The second what?"

"You said it was a trilogy."

"Seriously?"

"I'm as serious as handcuffs."

I picked up the book, flipped through the pages. Jack had not only read it, but he'd finished marginalizing the whole thing. He'd done a remarkable job of making his handwriting look like mine.

I tucked the book into the back of my jeans and headed up the stairs to my cabin. When I opened the door to my cabin, all the guys burst with welcome and praise and the words teenage boys offer as apologies for their false accusations.

"Giant balls, dude," Matthew said, an expression of awe as he sat on my bunk. "I cannot believe you ran after Natalie."

I didn't know what I could say and what I couldn't, what I should say and what I shouldn't. I wanted to protect Natalie's privacy. And I didn't want them to know I hadn't really gotten in trouble. I felt like keeping that to myself was protecting Jason.

So, I told them about my walk, how I caught up to her. I didn't talk about the fence or the zombies. I didn't talk about the voices I heard in the desert. I didn't tell them Natalie's brother was gone, or why my sister was gone.

"You took a donkey? What, to like, go faster?" Everyone turned to look at Dan, standing outside the circle, leaning his muscle-swollen shoulders and arms against the opposite bunk. "You're an idiot."

I held my breath for the next part, the insulting part, the part that would make me shrivel, like Dan had been aiming to do this whole week. But Dan said nothing more, and everyone just kind of chuckled and moved away from me to get ready for bed.

"It's cool you went after her, Nick," Dan said. "I still think you're an idiot, and I don't want you in my cabin next year, so don't bother requesting it. But it's cool you didn't let her go out there alone. Seriously, life's pretty much crapped all over her."

"So you know about Natalie's family?" I whispered to him.

"We're friends." He shrugged. "I'm not a dick to everyone." Then Dan looked at me for a beat more, like he wanted to say something else, but he shoved off and headed toward the bathroom.

When he came back carrying a briefcase, I realized that the guys hadn't been getting ready for bed. They were dressed head-to-toe in black, ready for the final prank.

Dan flipped latches on the briefcase and revealed ten gallon-sized Ziploc bags with large bumper magnets inside. He handed one to each of us.

I opened minc and pulled one out one of the magnets. I Brake for Cute Sheep, it said.

Matthew held one up, "'My Other Ride's a Dildo'! I'm gonna piss myself. Where did you get these?"

Dan didn't answer. As usual, he was acting like he had nothing to do with any of us.

"'Fifty Shades of Gay'! That's awesome!"

Charles shook his head and crawled up into his bunk.

"You still out on this?" I asked Charlie as I read the next bumper magnet: Spank a Veteran.

"Nick, God is out on this."

"What if we find some that aren't so offensive?" I dug around in my Ziploc. "'Trump Supporter'? Wait, someone might actually get shot for this one," I said to no one in particular as I shoved it back in the Ziploc and pulled out another. "What about 'Ribbed for Her Pleasure'?"

Charles rolled his eyes and lay down.

"It's about condoms, Charlie," I reasoned.

"Don't call me that."

"Because it refers to the Viet Cong?" I laughed.

"No, because it's not my name."

"Okay, Charles. But the magnet is just about condoms."

"I know what it's about," he said.

"Sex is natural. And condoms are an environmentally responsible way of limiting offspring."

"Shut up, Nick."

Matthew laughed and pulled me toward the door. "Come on, let's go."

"I just feel bad that he's left out," I said.

"He's fine. He participates by never telling the authorities."

"Wait," I held up my last bumper magnet. "I don't get this one."

Everyone stared at the magnet, then at me, like I was an idiot.

"You're an idiot," Dan murmured.

"All it says is 'PRO-CHOICE,'" I insisted.

My cabinmates shook their heads and a chorus of mumbling circled the room:

"That might be crossing the line."

"I can't seriously put that on someone's car."

"Have you seen those abortion posters on the hill by the hospital?"

I shrugged. The hypocrisy among my fellow campers was widespread, but it was what it was. I was not going to be angry about it anymore.

Then I had an idea. I grabbed a pen and altered my magnet to my liking. I marginalized it.

After waiting the requisite hour to ensure all the campers—or, more importantly, all the counselors—dreamed of sugarplums, we finally slipped into the dark and walked silently to the employee housing. By the time everyone had emptied their Ziploc bags, every car had at least two magnets on their bumpers.

Dan even told us to put magnets on his car so it wouldn't be obvious.

I gladly offered to do that job. For Dan's car, I had saved my marginalized bumper magnet, which now read IF ONLY YOUR MOM WAS PRO-CHOICE. Then, for good measure, I slapped on the one that had a picture of Mount Rainier. I had revised it to say I SUMMITED YOUR MOM.

On our way back to the cabin, we weren't all that silent, despite Dan's admonition. We giggled like girls, then fell into the cabin, wondering how far down the highway the camp directors and pastors and counselors would get before somebody shouted at or propositioned them through a car window.

PRAYERS AND CONFESSIONS

Pastor Kyle: Thank You for Your mercy, Jesus. Thank You for keeping me safe, for keeping Gabe safe, for keeping the family in the other car safe.

Payton: Yeah, I really do want to be with Holly.

Holly: I *am* sorry for what I did with the confessions. Please forgive me, Lord. Thank you for Payton and Pastor Kyle, and even for Nick.

Matthew: I will never see the baby that Sarah and I had. I know I'm not half of who I need to be to be a dad. But thank you for the family who took him.

FRIDAY

◆

We were going to walk on water, Pastor Kyle announced at the morning sermon.

The pastor had invited my parents, but they had declined, opting for the camper-less pool area. I was relieved. I wanted to have more time with Natalie. I'd have the whole car ride home with my mom and dad. And I did want to talk to them. I wanted to talk to them about Charlotte, about how maybe I understood something about her now. Listening to Holly, bearing witness to how we'd all hurt her, it all had made me think about my older sister. How she'd treated Diana was inexcusable, and I couldn't forgive her for that, but maybe there was something left of the fabric of us. I didn't know what. But, maybe.

In the meantime, I was determined to make the last day of camp "Christastic!"

The counselors serenaded us out the door in the style of Rick James:

He's all right, he's all right.
The Son's all right with me . . .
Super Jeez, Super Jeez, He's Super Jesus!

Kids were supposed to demonstrate their trust in the Lord. We would go out in the boat and "walk on water." We didn't have to if we didn't want to, and I was dubious. I could see them out there, getting out of the boat, from my vantage point definitely appearing to walk on water, but then something would happen and they would fall in.

Sometimes they made it, though. They didn't fall in. And many of those kids got into the boat with their leaders and said a special prayer and accepted Jesus as their personal Savior.

I already knew I wouldn't do that, but fist pumps for Christ anyway.

Matthew and Charles and I swam and pushed and shoved our way through the lake. There was a water trampoline to jump on, a slide off the dock, and a diving board. I liked it more than the water park at camp, honestly. I liked the smell of real water when it dried on my skin. The way it collected sunshine. The way it smelled a little of dirt and a little of grass.

When Charles ran over to jump around with the Disciplettes and I lost Matthew to Kim's flirtations, I walked out of the lake to sit on my towel on the beach. The sun was perfect on my shoulders, and I closed my eyes for a moment.

"'What's your road, man?'" I heard from behind me, and my eyes opened as Natalie sank down onto my towel next to me. "'—holyboy road, madman road, rainbow road, guppy road, any road.'"

"Hey," I said to the girl on pretty road.

"Hold on, I'm not done." Natalie smiled. She was reciting *On the Road*. "'It's an anywhere road for anybody anyhow.'"

Her eyes were bright, as bright as brown could be. Her eyes were like gold flecks some forty-niner scooped up out of a creek.

"I'm done," she said, nudging me with her shoulder.

"Hey," I repeated, nudging her back.

"Hey." She smiled, blushed a bit, and looked out toward the lake.

"Probably madman road," I answered. "That's the road." And it was true, though I'd never tell her about the Jack Kerouac visions.

"Not guppy road?"

"Possibly. I like guppies."

"I think kitten road for me. They're so cute."

I laughed.

We both sat looking out at the lake, at all the kids screaming and splashing and dunking.

"I thought maybe they sent you home."

"Nope," she said.

"You didn't get in trouble?"

"Did you?" Her eyes widened.

I shook my head.

"I heard about your confession."

"Yeah. It sucked, but my parents are here."

"And so are you, so that's good."

"Happy endings and all that," I said. The end of it is the *it* thing? Is that what Jack had said? "But where've you been? What happened?"

She pursed her lips. "I found out about my scholarship. Where it comes from."

"Really?"

"They weren't supposed to tell me till I graduated or something. I don't really know, there was some contract. But my brother left zombie camp, so they don't owe him anything."

"Wait . . . what?"

"The King of Zombie Camp is my benefactor."

I thought I got it.

"My brother."

"Seriously?"

"Yep, the whole time." She shrugged. "Until he left, and then the money wasn't there."

"Which is how Pastor Kyle knew?"

"Yeah. He called the rehab place, and he was gone."

"So then, how'd you get to come if there wasn't any money?"

"Pastor Kyle paid for it."

Because despite our differences, he was a good man.

"Why didn't your brother just tell you?" I asked.

"I don't know. I kind of like that mystery."

"Does your aunt know that he's behind the scholarship?"

"No. Apparently she knows he's sending her money—he sends her what's left of the money he earns there, after the scholarship—but she never told me that part either."

"Wow. Are you glad you know?"

"He picked this camp because it was close to him." She smiled.

"So, yeah, I'm glad to know. And I'm glad you were here." She leaned her head on my shoulder, and I looked around for Dan, Jason, Kyle, someone who might yank me away and beat me with cat-o'-nine-tails like a Roman soldier.

When no one came for me, I leaned my head down. Her hair smelled of the sun and something floral.

"There's a billboard on madman road," I said, my stomach a heavy nervous thing.

She kept her eyes closed when she replied, "Read it to me."

"It says, 'I really want to kiss you.'" It wasn't outright kissing her, like Jack wanted me to. But I was living a little bigger, like my sister had encouraged. I was *doing* something. Something that I wasn't going to have to carry a cross for.

She smiled and nodded slightly against my shoulder, under my chin. "You will."

I wanted to kiss her right then, my stomach all lit up with the idea. "So you think kitten road intersects madman road?"

"If it doesn't, I'll just have to take the exit and meet you under that billboard."

I noticed Matthew and Kim heading toward us, and Natalie must've too, because she lifted her head off my shoulder. I immediately missed her. Then she stood up and walked toward the water, meeting Kim halfway. They both started laughing, and Matthew threw his arms up, fed up with something.

Then he shouted over to me, "Get in the boat with us."

I shook my head.

"Come walk on water," he insisted. "It's fun."

So I did.

PRAYERS AND CONFESSIONS

Jason: Holy Father, it's because of You that I have the patience and strength to be a rock for these kids. And because of my minor in geology. Double ha! Praise Jesus!

Author of *Sixty Scenes of Sexy:* I am aware of the disdain readers feel for me and my success. It's not like I won the Nobel Prize for Literature, though, so could we all calm down? The entertainment industry is burgeoning with art *and* fun alike.

Charles: I want to be a cheerleader in college like Jason. I have a lot of respect for him as a man of God. And, I admit, I like the feeling of polyester on my legs.

Pastor Kyle: I believe love and service are modes of worship. But lettering in volunteerism? As in a letterman's jacket? Varsity Volunteer? . . . Huh . . . That actually has a nice ring to it. T-shirt idea? Never too soon to start thinking about next year.

Ninja: Is it me, or are the kids just getting fatter and fatter? I cannot do this lottery shit one more year. And I sure as hell am not carrying some asshole through the desert ever again.

SATURDAY

◆

The day after I returned from camp, I walked out to the car, the green Volvo. I stood some feet away from it, analyzing the rusting bumper, the dull paint.

I walked to the other side of the car, slipped my hands into the handle of the passenger side. When I opened the door, the must of the thing leaped out of the car.

Jack sat in the back, leaned against the side, his feet propped on the window. He had a bottle of something between his legs, but he'd passed out. He looked older than usual. Unshaven, the wrinkles above his eyes deeper. He blinked at me, then rolled to a sitting position and crawled out of the car, leaving the bottle behind.

He had a notepad and a pencil in the pocket of his button-down.

"The passenger side, eh?" He looked me up and down. "Lettin' go. Just remembering now. Not searching." He nodded. "That's good. That's really good."

"Yeah." I looked over at his profile, strong jaw, clear eyes. "I read your book."

"I'm sorry," he said.

I chuckled. "It's actually good. I mean, it is a bit rambly, true. But . . . I liked it."

He sighed.

"I don't understand why you have such a problem with it."

"The book." Jack contemplated. "It's about awe. It's about looking out at the ever-unpredictable mountains and vast plains and mad people and unbelievable stories."

"Yeah, exactly, I liked that."

"You know how I keep telling you, there is no right or wrong, there's just the *after*?"

"Uh-huh."

"It's not the book. It's the *after* of that book. I couldn't handle the *after*."

"But you'd made it. You were famous. After so many years of rejection."

"That's right. And that's good, isn't it?"

"Well, yes, that's good. You finally wrote the Great American Novel. I mean, you've got cult fans."

Jack stared out the windshield. "And after that book, I drank and I rambled and I fell down in alleys and shit myself and challenged my friends to suicide plots." He exhaled, his lips a thin line. "That's not an *after* one aspires to."

He reached over and rested his hand on my shoulder. It was the first time he had touched me, and it was as real as anything.

He looked at me a long time.

I reached up and touched his hand, expecting liquid-chill. Or nothing. But there was something. Something warm and real.

He nodded. "You're good to go, kiddo."

I was surprised by the reality of his skin, by the tears that sprang to my eyes. "You can't just stop haunting me."

"I can." He opened the car door and stepped out.

I got out too, and walked around to head him off. "But—I'm troubled—or whatever you said. I'm smug and judgmental."

"You're fine," he said.

"No, I'm not. I'm doomed to a publishing house someday, you said it yourself."

He chuckled. "The Great Editor lets the truth bleed through that masquerade of words."

"I don't want you to go."

"I'm just a speck, Nick. I'm not the real thing."

I wiped the tears off my cheek.

"I'm going to walk that way." Jack pointed past the house, toward the trees. "And you can watch me till I disappear. But I am going to ask you to stop watching the horizon when you can't see me anymore."

Then he stepped forward and hugged me, which was not at all like the Jack I'd known. "Don't worry," he said. His body was real and warm, the fabric of his shirt rough on my chin. I just breathed in the smell of it, which wasn't vanilla or rose. It was just her. It was Diana. "You're fine."

And then he let go, patted my shoulder, and walked away.

"'Lean forward to the next crazy venture beneath the skies,'" was the last thing he said to me. And it was the only time he'd ever quoted himself.

He never turned around. He never waved. And his khakis disappeared into his button-down and were soon a shadow and a fleck that bounced and then steadied and then vanished. And I knew I couldn't see him. He wasn't there. It was just me, here, by the side of the Volvo.

I went around to the driver's side of the car, slipped into the seat, and looked up at the ceiling, at the holes where the rain seeped in. I put my fingers in those holes, those two holes where the bullets had pierced the roof of the car. From the gun I put in her hand. From the bullets I put in her hand.

I pulled my fingers away and looked up through the holes into the sky, dark and black. And small. Something so massive, made so small by two tiny holes in the roof of a car.

The stars were there. The moon was there. But I'd been trying to see the whole sky, the universe—the grand, inexplicable, magic universe—through my damage. Through tiny, man-made holes.

I stepped out of the car, looked up at the billions of bright stars that lit and dimmed in the summer night. That moon, giant and whole and golden, a sentinel in the twilight.

All the magic in the universe. Planets and beauty, comets and humanity, black holes and love.

The finite and the infinite.

It was all a divine mystery.

Author's Note

This book was inspired by my Aunt Dea, who died by suicide when I was fourteen. She never knew how "big" she made me. Even in her death, she continues to influence me.

Tragically, while I was editing this book, a young man very dear to my heart, Brooks Rolfness, also died by suicide. The loss shattered our very close-knit community. He is deeply loved and desperately missed.

Any one of us who knew these two precious people would have done everything in our power to help them and get them the support they needed. If you are struggling emotionally, reach out to the people around you, be it family, friends, or strangers. *Please* reach out so that we can reach back.

If you or a friend are in crisis, please call the National Suicide Prevention Lifeline at 1-800-273-8255. The National Suicide Prevention Lifeline is a national network of crisis centers around the United States that provides free and confidential emotional support to people in suicidal crisis or emotional distress twenty-four hours a day, seven days a week. For more information, visit SuicidePreventionLifeline.org.

Acknowledgments

I am just so grateful. I will never be able to convey all my thanks, but here are a few thank-yous . . .

The best writing advice I ever got was from my friend Mark Teppo. He said, "Sit your ass down in a chair and write." He's an author and a publisher, so I believed him. And, lookie here! A book.

The best publishing advice I ever got was from my mom. She said, "Don't give up after a hundred rejections. Not even two hundred." She is my mother, so I believed her. Her love of reading (she always had a book in one hand, and a cigarette in the other), and my dad's love of crossword puzzles, meant I grew up surrounded by beautiful words. It is my deepest heartbreak that my mom will not read this book. She is why I read, and she is why I write.

I am the luckiest person in the world to be surrounded by people who have loved me and supported me, whether it's with great advice or the space to write or the willing ears to listen to my rants. My family, my friends, and my community make a tribe of creativity cheerleaders. Andrew Sage built me an office and shooed the kids out of it so that I could write. He provided a special place and priceless time. Christy Johnson, Michele Goode, Melissa Murschall, Sarah Olson, and Aaron Richards listened, read, and answered my questions. More importantly, they asked *me* the questions. My aunts, uncles, cousins, grandparents, in-laws, nephew, niece, mom, dad, and brother believe in me, no matter what crazy idea I have, including writing a book. And all my students—past and present—offer me the joy and inspiration to tell stories.

A huge thanks to Karen Johnson, Jessica Lewis, Leif Peterson, and Lindsey Keaton for reading the first draft and saying *yes* to my ideas, then feeding me their better ones. Thanks to Amber Walker for fostering the love of literature among my students. Her book club members became my beta readers, and nothing motivates me more than a group of teenage girls (and food!). Thank you to the

Book Worm girls: Analise Walker, Abi Baker, Liz Racine, Carleigh DeLapp, Jessica Reitan, Salena Scoccolo, and Alison Barry. And thank you to the Yak, Snack & Read girls: Sophie Walker, Haley Yandt, Makena Miles, Elly Mark, Mya Wagner, Hailey Wagner, Samantha Lucier, Olivia Levchak, Petria Russell, Tara Hale, and Gaeby Wilson. Thank you, Knowledge Bowl, especially Emily Paris, for asking and asking about covers and titles and how it was going. All of you are the best kind of readers.

Katie Reed and Elizabeth Staple held my hand when I took my first steps in this publishing world. Melanie Jacobsen, Nikki Urang, Kimberly Derting, and Patrick Swenson gave great advice at every turn.

Sky Pony Press is full of rock stars! Rachel Stark is a lifesaver and a world changer, and I am *#blessed* to have her as my editor. My life had been in turmoil throughout 2016, but on Election Day of that year, she gave me hope. She offered to take my weird little book and put it out into the world. She has worked tirelessly to make this story the best book it can be. And then she gave me the greatest team of creatives. Emma Dubin believed in this book, and she has been its cheerleader and my wise counselor. Kate Gartner, Pete Ryan, and Joshua Barnaby designed a book that—inside and out—is more perfect and clever than I ever could have imagined. Seriously. Thank you, Sky Pony Press.

Natalie Lakosil took a chance on this absurd tale, and she took a chance on me. She is a supreme navigator, and I would be lost and stepping all over my own feet without her. Thank you, Bradford Literary Agency.

And best for last . . . McKay and Cole, you are the reason I do any of it. My favorite stories have all been for you, starting with the nightly installments of "Dream Boy"! All I ever want is to bring you as much joy and delight as you bring me. And maybe not embarrass you too much along the way. I hope you always have a lot of wisdom and a little madness.